RIPTIDE

KATHRYN NOLAN

That's What She Said Publishing, Inc.

Editing by Faith N. Erline
Cover by Kari March

ISBN: 978-1-945631-63-4 (ebook)
ISBN: 978-1-945631-64-1 (paperback)

090821

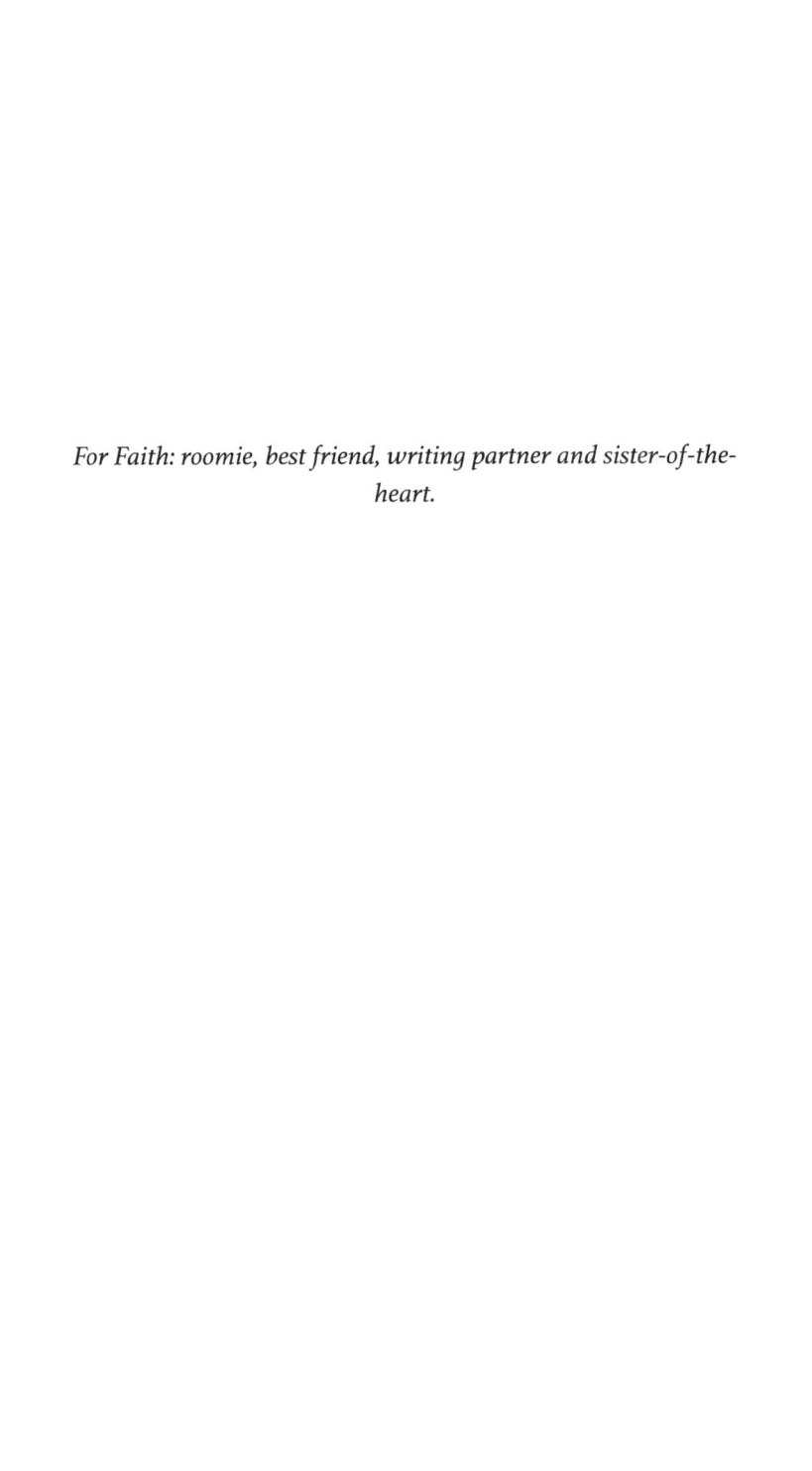

For Faith: roomie, best friend, writing partner and sister-of-the-heart.

1

AVERY

*M*y insomnia had led me to Playa Vieja.

The strip of beach extended for more than a mile, but at the farthest corner was a rock outcropping that rarely attracted anyone except me.

I was huddled against the wind as it whipped across the ocean, my fingers wrapped around a thermos of hot coffee. My back ached from perching on the rocks, and my toes were freezing in the wet sand.

But it was all worth it for the view. Not the ocean view, which I was currently spending my entire career thinking about how to monetize.

No, I had stumbled upon my favorite view on this whole damn beach.

The Surfer.

I'd seen him a dozen times already. He also favored this far corner at the edge, and even though San Diego was home to thousands of surfers, this spot was always empty, at least in the very early morning.

The sun had lifted itself beyond the horizon but not by much. Everything was cast in a dream-like glow.

The Surfer was already out here when I arrived, which meant he was one hell of a morning person. And today he was joined by a friend. The waves were rough—a continual roar—and my stomach clenched as he and his friend were knocked off their boards.

But The Surfer sprang up like a dolphin every time, shaking water out of his hair and climbing back on. Tenacious.

He had an easy grace in the water. Over the crash of the waves, I could hear him laughing with his friend. Joyful and free.

The Surfer was swimming for a bit when a larger wave came cresting up to his right. He paddled quickly, popped up onto his feet, and caught it, running his fingers through the swell. He rode for a full minute before it died out and he dove, head first, into the foam.

I found myself grinning, then stopped.

He was paddling and swimming *constantly*. My arms ached just to look at him. As he stroked through the water, I wondered what his arms looked like. They'd be muscular, with strong shoulders and defined edges.

That must have been the insomnia talking.

I took a sip of too-hot coffee and burned my tongue. A suitable punishment for the distraction. I was about to achieve a career milestone I'd been working toward for two years, and in that time I'd denied myself men. Relationships were too messy. Too many distractions.

It was definitely not a time to fantasize about arms.

He caught another wave, and my heart leapt, just a little. Bad news, but I was exhausted and stressed out and dreading going to work, career milestone or not.

Three more months. I'd chanted this like a mantra these

past few days. In the shower. As I walked to work. Here on Playa Vieja with my toes in the cold sand.

Three more months on the largest hotel project I'd ever been given—one of the largest hotel projects the Bella View had attempted in the past *decade*—and I wouldn't be able to sneak down here and spy on a surfer at sunrise. Because in its place would be a 300-room luxury hotel. Golf course, tennis courts, five-star restaurant. A lazy river water park that gave guests a perfect 360-degree view of this gorgeous beach.

The Surfer was resting between sets, straddling his board. He and his friend bobbed up and down in the water like sailboats. No place to be. No rush. Just the steady push-pull of the waves against his legs. I closed my eyes, remembering. I used to love that feeling.

These past two years had been a whirlwind of heartbreak and achievement. Hotel development was like that, I'd learned. Every piece of the building—the bricks, the mortar, the tiny, pale starfish painted on the bathroom tiles—became a living, breathing entity. It wasn't *mine,* but over time, that's what it felt like. The first time a hotel I'd worked on broke ground, I felt that shovel strike deep in my bones. A calming sense of satisfaction—of plywood and nails and screws slowly growing upwards. A permanent mark on the land.

But in my most stressful moments, I thought of The Surfer. I thought of him like this, resting. I thought of him riding the waves. His laughter. The total-body high you could just *tell* he was experiencing. It was soothing—like hot tea on a rainy day.

My toes snagged on something sharp. Wincing, I picked up the conch shell, peach-colored in the tepid morning light. On instinct, I held it up to my ear, listening. A memory slid in, of digging up shells with my brother on the beach back home. My mother must have been nearby, cautioning us over and over again to put them back. But every conch shell I found went right to my ear, simulating wave sounds drifting in.

"It's the ocean!" I kept exclaiming until my oldest brother pinched my elbow and said, "No way. Shells can't make sounds." I'd looked at my mother for confirmation, but she'd been staring at the sunset dreamily, her curly hair turning a pale orange. I ran ahead of my family, still holding the shell, listening. My arms ached—I must have pulled weeds for hours that morning.

I had imagined another girl, continents away, grasping a similar shell between her ear and her shoulder. Straining to hear the sounds of waves—not the ones in front of her but faintly, miraculously, the waves of a foreign, beautiful place. I imagined that girl living a normal childhood. Indoors. Her arms aching from jumping rope or curling her hair or any number of things I imagined little girls doing.

I threw the shell down the beach, shifting myself back into the present moment. Although now I was remembering I hadn't gotten a letter from my parents in a few months. I made a mental note to give them an update on the hotel, knowing they wouldn't care. Or, worse, my mother's handwriting would come back stark with her disappointment.

The Surfer was paddling again, a larger wave cresting like a bolt of lightning behind him. He caught it and dropped down the face of the wave. I couldn't see, not really, but I knew he was smiling. Had to be.

I looked at my watch, the office beckoning.

Three more months.

∾

THE OFFICES for Bella View Hotels were in downtown San Diego with a million-dollar view of the beach. It was an international chain of luxury hotels, catering to the kind of rich and famous clientele that cared about things like thread counts and fair-trade caviar.

The Bella View Hotel proposed for Playa Vieja would be the very definition of a luxury hotel. The golf course would be first-class—I drooled, daily, at the mock-ups I had of rich, rolling green set against a Playa Vieja sunset. The five-star restaurant would embody the Southern California that Americans dreamed about—palm trees threaded with twinkle lights, open fire pits, glamorous people sipping high-end liquor overlooking a beach so beautiful it looked fake... only it wasn't, simply untouched. The Playa Vieja community was *old* and traditional and grouchy when it came to tourism. But it meant their beach was a sparkling paradise just waiting to be mined for hotel gold.

Until the city council vote, there wasn't much more I needed to do except maintain the progress I'd already made these past two years. The design and architecture were done. I'd gotten it completely financed. I'd prepped the marketing, secured an environmental analysis, finished every single type of revenue and expense projection there was. If (really, *when*) San Diego's city council voted to approve the building permits, all I had to do was click "send" on a flurry of emails and my job would be done.

Sal had all but assured me the permits would go through, although it hadn't stopped my nights of incessant, heart-pounding insomnia. Something about being the sole person in charge—not a project assistant—made the weight of their decision rest heavy on my shoulders. Sal had been my boss for the past four years, ever since I got my MBA and was snatched up by Bella View just a few weeks later. He'd taken a liking to me almost immediately and was the person who spoke out most strongly in favor of me taking the lead on the Playa Vieja project.

"You're the hardest worker I've ever met," he'd said to me two years ago. "And I believe in you. Plus, this city council will never say 'no' to the ridiculous amount of money this hotel is going to make for them."

That was the second half of the mantra I'd been repeating to myself recently. *Three more months. The city council loves money.*

I couldn't wait until this damn thing was over. Although in a lot of ways, insomnia and stress were the two constants of my life ever since I'd arrived in San Diego a week after my high school graduation. I'd put myself through college and then grad school—attending classes during the day, working as a waitress at night—and I couldn't remember a time when I wasn't stressed, exhausted or both.

Watching The Surfer helped. But I was worried about growing too attached to the mystery man in the wet suit. The surf culture here was rampant. It wasn't hard to deny myself romance the past two years. What few men I'd dated in college had been hard to find since surfers had never been my type. I hated their mellow highs, sunburned noses, and rippling laughter. They'd doze on the green between classes, worn out from early mornings on their boards. Meanwhile, except for the five or six hours I struggled to sleep, I was working, moving, hustling. In constant motion. Forward.

I parked my car and walked toward the office doors, running through a mental checklist of what I needed to do today. I was looking down at the ground, lost in thought. Distracted.

I almost walked right past him. The protester.

I stopped, did a double take.

Yep.

He was a *protester*. He was standing in front of me with a large sign that read, "*Bella View Hotels: Destroying Our Environment Since 1966.*" He was surfer-shaggy with a scruffy beard and wild, unmanaged hair still a little wet from the ocean (presumably). Around his neck was a shark-tooth necklace. He was barefoot and reeked of sunscreen.

I walked right up to him, neck straining. He was at least eight or nine inches taller than I was. He arched an eyebrow at me, silent and disapproving.

My eyes narrowed. "Who the hell are *you*?"

2

FINN

A half-ton of water was currently holding me under the waves.

Usually, my thoughts were centered on *not drowning*. Feeling for, and focusing on, the crescent of light I knew would lead me to the air I desperately needed to breathe.

But sometimes, before the discomfort and the mild panic set in, I relaxed under the waves. The absolute quiet. The force of the ocean could leave you in complete awe if you let it. A living, breathing, wild world we almost never saw.

A dangerous one, for a surfer.

My head popped out, the sudden rush of oxygen making me feel faint. Rico's hand reached for mine, dragging me onto his board.

"Fuck, that was nasty," he said as I caught my breath. I could feel my board's leash tugging on my ankle.

"Yeah," was all I could cough out. I hadn't taken a hit like that in a long time, not since training to surf Titans of Mavericks. And the wave that had just slapped me out of the air was *minuscule* compared to the waves I preferred. Big waves. Giant waves.

Tsunami-sized.

The set calmed down, and I found my board, pulling myself onto it.

"How much longer are you going to stay out?" I asked. Ever since I was nine years old and my dad gave me my first surfboard, I'd surfed, by myself, in the early hours of the morning. Every day. But Rico—my oldest friend—merited an exception. He had short black hair, light brown skin and tattoos covering his arms. We'd met when we were thirteen and Rico had just moved here from Mexico.

"Wish it could be all day," he said wistfully, gazing at the shore. I knew the feeling. Unlike other beaches in San Diego, this beach was for locals only: surfers and families, dogs and joggers. San Diego was no longer the groovy paradise it had been in the sixties and seventies. This beach was all we had left.

"Same," I replied, and we sat in companionable silence for a moment, enjoying the untouched paradise in front of us.

"You think you'll surf at Pipeline in the winter?" he asked, turning over his shoulder to glance at the set of waves coming our way. They looked small, and through a kind of shared, silent, communication we decided to let them play out. We were big wave surfers by nature. We needed a wave that stunned.

"Definitely," I said. "The day after Mavericks, they called to invite me. Plus Billabong wants to do a shoot in Hawaii during that same week, so it works out perfectly."

Pipeline Masters attracted some of the most elite big wave surfers in the world, all vying to drop down the face of forty-foot waves.

Rico rolled his eyes—hard—in my direction. "How many bikini-clad models will you be surrounded with this time?"

"Dozens," I said, grinning. "Maybe hundreds."

"Good," he said. "Keep them in mind while I share some bad news with you."

I turned toward him, concerned. "What?" I asked. "What happened? Are you okay?"

"*I'm* fine," he said, hand on his chest. But then he nodded at the beach. "This place though? Not so sure."

I tilted my head at him, and he sighed, paddling closer. "Look, when I was home this morning, my parents told me they saw a posting in the local paper about community feedback for a new building in Playa Vieja." He paused. "A hotel. A luxury hotel. Built right on the beach."

"Fuck *me*," I said, then immediately regretted it. I wanted to say something inspirational. Or at least witty. "Are you serious?"

"As a heart attack," he said. "Which means this place is done for."

"Wait, let me get this straight. A hotel company—"

"—a hotel *chain*—"

"—is planning on building on *Playa Vieja*? But we... we don't *have* hotels on this beach. It would ruin everything." Not to mention bring the kind of smoggy, noisy infrastructure San Diego was now known for. And the beach wasn't huge. A luxury hotel would dominate every square inch.

"I think it would have a golf course too. A tennis court. Some kind of restaurant. You know the kind."

"*Jesus.*"

Rico's expression looked pained. He knew how much I

loved this place. He knew how much our neighbors loved this place.

"I've been dreading telling you all morning." He paused. "Are you still thinking about those bikini-clad models?"

"I'm... I'm, I don't know, dude, I'm... *angry*?" Rico had known me since I was a kid. I didn't *do* anger. In fact, there wasn't much that even irritated me.

"First time for everything," he said, staring again at the shore. "I'm pretty fucking pissed too."

"What can we do?" I asked, suddenly feeling nostalgic. I'd witnessed this conversation before, hundreds of times. My parents, feverishly discussing some societal issue, the relentless sound of my dad's feet, pacing back and forth. The *click-click* of spray cans as my mom painted protest signs in our hallway.

"Finn," he said. "You think there's something we can do? You know the deal. Been this way since we were kids. Rich people spot a paradise they can't have. A year later, a big ugly hotel is there." He shrugged. "I'm not saying it's not wrong. I just don't think there's much we can do against the machine, man."

"No," I said, shaking my head. "No, no. I can't accept that."

"You sound like your dad," he said, smiling back at me. "Or, actually, my dad too."

"You think they'd get involved?" I asked, feeling the gears of my mind whirring into action. Something else, not anger but close, was fluttering in my chest.

Rico laughed. "Wait, you'd really do something?"

"Why did you tell me if we're not going to do anything about it?" I asked.

"I want you to seriously think about what you're saying," he said. His parents and my parents had been activists our entire lives. We'd marched together plenty of times. I wasn't sure why it seemed so bizarre to him.

"Tell me the name of the hotel again?" I asked, my mind snagging on something.

"Bella View. They have that huge one in La Jolla." I hated that hotel. Once it had been built, La Jolla had flipped from a sleepy, seaside town to a paradise for millionaires. But it was something else entirely that had me hung up.

"Wait," I said, snapping my fingers. "Do you remember that dinky little surf competition we did in Cabo San Lucas when we were seventeen?" He and I had been new on the international scene, although we'd been competing in San Diego for a couple years at that point.

"Yeaaah," he said, with a lopsided grin. That smile had convinced me to do *a lot* of dangerous things in the past. "I remember riding a perfect wave to third place. Beating you, my friend."

"Not that part," I said. "Which is a lie, by the way. We all know I won." Rico flashed me his middle finger. "Do you remember the party we had afterwards in that little town, just outside of Cabo? We went to that bonfire on their beach, and there was this huge construction going on."

I remembered so clearly—a handful of surfers huddled around a campfire, flush with underage drinking, exhausted but happy. The beach had been beautiful, empty except for us. And the giant pit of bulldozers and forklifts. In the moonlight, the skeleton of the hotel rose from the sand. A behemoth, completely out of place. And a sign, whimsical and happy, reading: *Welcome to The Bella View Hotel. Paradise Has Arrived.*

The fucking Bella View.

Rico cocked his head. "A little. I remember the guy we were with talking about how much everyone hated it."

"More than hated it," I said, the memory rushing back now. "Everything was more polluted. The air was getting worse. Trash in the ocean. It didn't feel like their home anymore. It felt like someone else's. I remember sitting there with you, thinking about Playa Vieja."

"Because we'd always say, 'Not here.'"

"Never here," I echoed Rico and the sentiments of countless community meetings we'd attended over the years. Playa Vieja was special. Different.

"Can you imagine that happening here?" I asked as I spotted the most beautiful wave in the distance. He saw it too—felt it with a surfer's sixth sense. Under our feet, the roar started.

"I mean, no... but also, when I saw that ad in the paper, I just remember feeling completely hopeless. It all gets taken, dude, in the end," he said, even as he was positioning himself. It was hard to deny our true nature.

"Take the wave," I said, laughing now. "You want it."

"I don't want to come home to find my parents are riled up. They don't need that in their old age."

"I can't—" I started to say, but the wave was suddenly on us, and I watched my oldest friend glide under the swell. This was our home. *My* home. And while I wasn't the type to get that angry, I also hadn't been raised to be complacent. To let the machine of capitalism and consumerism run me over.

No. I had been raised to fight back.

*B*ongo drummers were outside my office.

It was Monday. One week after the tie-dyed, barefoot protester had shown up in our courtyard. Since then, each day their numbers had grown, just a little.

It was alarming. Just a little.

My boss, Sal, had sent out an email a few days ago strongly encouraging us to "just ignore it." To many of my coworkers, they were a joke—a merry band of Grateful Dead fans who'd wear themselves out before any actual damage was done.

I wasn't so sure. And now they had bongos. I had grown up on the sound of bongos. And hated it.

"And you are?" I asked warily, stepping over the legs of the elderly drummers. One was an older white woman with long, gray hair wearing a purple dress. The other was an older white man wearing a straw hat and a shirt from a Phish concert.

They would have been cute if they hadn't been playing the bongos incessantly for the past hour.

"Jack and Marla," the man said, extending his hand to

me. I shook it, still unsure. "I'm guessing you're not here for the protest of the Bella View Hotel on Playa Vieja."

"No," I said, "I'm not. In fact, I'm the person in *charge* of the project."

"Ah," Marla said, nodding at me. "So you're the enemy. It's nice to meet you."

"Um..." I said, fighting back a deluge of curse words. In times like these, my sailor's mouth worsened. "Let me guess. You'll be out here, bongo-ing away, for the next three months or so?"

"Of course," Jack said cheerfully, pulling Marla into a half-hug. "This is our favorite thing to do."

"Great," I said, with as much sarcasm as I could muster. Which was a lot. "And just so you know, I'll be calling the cops on you every day."

"Wonderful. We haven't been arrested in a while," Marla said.

Sweet Jesus. I turned from them to bump smack into the shaggy surfer. The Protester. I stepped back quickly, embarrassed. I didn't know how to feel about him—the Patient Zero of this daily chaos. I'd seen him every day for the past six days, and our interactions had been minimal but heated. I didn't even know his name. But I did know I wanted a dart board of his face.

Now, he grabbed me by the shoulders in apology. "Sorry, Ms. Dacosta. Couldn't see you over my righteous indignation. And good morning."

"Literally. What the fuck?" I bit back. "Why are you here again?"

"I'm guessing that during the night you *didn't* decide to halt progress on the Bella View Hotel and pull the permits?" He was wearing what I now thought of as his uniform— tank top, board shorts, sunscreen, and a shit-eating grin. He was white, about my age, with dark blue eyes and a deep tan.

"Never going to happen," I replied, moving past him to my office. Another twenty people had shown up since yesterday, holding various signs. Chanting. Some jam band playing softly in the background, now accented by Marla and Jack's bongos. A memory threatened to push its way in, but I shook it off.

"I'll see you tomorrow!" he called after me, and I threw up the middle finger in response. Not my most mature move, but the last week had worn on my nerves like a mosquito bite I couldn't scratch.

Also, the two giant windows of my office looked out into the courtyard. Meaning the blond, shaggy head of the protester was in my direct line of sight, all damn day. I watched him greeting the new people. Whoever he was, he seemed to be well-liked. Constantly smiling. Every other minute he'd crack a joke, putting people at ease. The sun glinted off his shoulders.

I just didn't get it.

When I sat down at my desk, there were a few pieces of paper out of alignment. I straightened them, wiping away a speck of dust. I liked my desk to look like my life—clean. On the wall hung my diploma and MBA, both from UC San Diego. A daily reminder of what I was capable of. A daily reminder of all that I'd given up.

I turned on my computer and a hundred emails tumbled into my inbox. I sighed, leaning back, my ears picking up the sound of protesters outside.

Sal knocked on the door, and I nearly jumped out of my skin. He came in, crashed himself into a chair. He habitually had this "terrifying Santa" look to him, huge grin and wild white hair. He was a white man in his early fifties, boisterous with a loud laugh. And his face was always red with a weird combination of stress and happiness.

He hooked his thumb at my windows. "Freaks, huh?" he said, laughing. I laughed too, albeit weakly.

"Something like that," I finally said in response, one eye on the action outside. "And I hate to even ask this, but should I be worried about these guys? Or doing something about it?"

Sal snorted. "Please. I've been in property development my entire life. I'm telling you. You're doing something *good* if the hippies are protesting you. Playa Vieja has always been like that. Want to keep that beach to themselves. But that's not the business you and I are in, Avery." He rapped his knuckles on the table. "We're in the business of making rich people happy."

I nodded. *And creating things*, I wanted to say, which was the real reason why I loved this job. But I also understood the other side of it. Was pretty comfortable with it, actually, except this protest was making me uneasy.

"They almost always flame out in a couple weeks," he said.

"*Almost* always?"

"Avery. It's a bunch of surfers. They'll get distracted by something soon. Stop worrying about it."

"Okay... well, good. I mean, I'm not going to say it's keeping me up at night"—*except it was*—"but I know how important this is, and I'd do anything not to fuck it up."

"You won't. The Bella View Hotel chain has the city council eating out of its hand. By the time the vote comes up, the members will be begging for you to start building. And these guys—" He pointed outside. "—will be sunburned and defeated."

I glanced at a framed picture on my desk of my parents

and me on my graduation day from college. My dad was wearing head-to-toe tie-dye. My mother wore a long dress made of hemp. They were both holding their index and middle fingers in a 'V,' the universal sign for peace. I looked embarrassed and unhappy—even seven years later I remembered how I felt that day. That was the first—and only—time my parents had visited me here.

"I'm happy I'm not the only one who doesn't take them seriously," I said firmly. "Anything else you need for today?"

"Only some good news, if you want to hear it." His cell phone rang, and he pulled it from his pocket, glancing at the name on the screen. He groaned, then tossed it over his shoulder onto the floor of my office.

"Um, do you need to get that?"

"It's just the wife," he said, grin on his face. "I've been staying at work too late. Wants me home more." In the four years I'd worked here, this was a long-running joke. Sal thought *I* was a hard worker, but I was pretty sure he had missed every one of his kids' birthdays.

"And anyway, last night I had a long conversation with some of the higher-ups in the company." The Bella View was an international hotel chain, and quarterly the head developers checked in. "And you came up."

"Me? Why?" I asked, hopeful.

"Because you're doing a bang-up job, Avery. I know you're young, and usually we don't give projects like this to people unless they've had a lot more experience, but they see something in you, like I did. I think if this city council vote goes well..." He stopped, laughed again. "Aw, who am I kidding? What I mean is *after* the city council approves the permits, let's talk about your future here."

"Yes, that would be... well, that would be great."

"And when I say future, to be clear, I mean a promotion.

Moving up. Potentially to our East Coast offices in New York," he said.

Butterflies exploded in my stomach, and I fought a smile. *Play it cool.*

One time, selling produce in town as a teenager, I'd found a magazine that had pictures of New York City in it, and I'd dreamed of living there ever since. I wanted suits and briefcases and martinis and crisp, fall weather. I wanted a bunch of Type A lawyers to flirt with me at a mahogany bar.

"New York City would be a wonderful place to live," I said, cool as ice.

If my ambition could live somewhere, anywhere, in the world, I *knew* a city like that would be the place for me.

Or, let's be honest, any city that *wasn't* San Diego.

"Good. Let's talk more about it later, but for now, keep it up. We've been very impressed so far. I can see how eager you are to climb that ladder."

I nodded but hopefully not *too* eagerly. "I'd like to be in more of a leadership position," I shared. "And to do more for the company."

He stood, clapping me on the back forcefully. I almost fell out of my chair. "That's what I like to hear from my employees. At a certain point, Avery, you will live and breathe this company. Become one with it. Like me. And then you can have a beautiful family you never see just like me." He laughed, throwing his head back, before giving me one more pat.

"Thanks for the pep talk, Sal," I said, an interesting mix of anxiety and excitement thrumming through my veins. He walked out of my office, leaving me with my thoughts. I looked at my hanging diplomas. My parents and their tie-dye. I thought about that career ladder, how the rungs would feel under my fingers. The accomplishment. The triumph.

Outside, the shaggy protester was laughing uproariously, a baby perched on his hip. A baby that was delighted by him. A baby that was wearing a tiny onesie that read, "Stop the Bella View Hotel. Save the Earth."

"Goddammit," I said, before stalking over and yanking the blinds closed.

4

FINN

*W*hen you spend three entire weeks of your life protesting a woman's workplace every day, you feel like you get to know her a little bit.

This is what I knew about Avery Dacosta.

She showed up to work at exactly 7:45 a.m., on the dot, Monday through Friday. On Saturdays, she came in at 9:00. Sunday was her day of rest, although I suspected she worked from home.

Avery was white with dark eyes and dark brown hair always pulled back into a tight bun. She favored business suits that covered up every inch of her skin. She carried a leather briefcase like a weapon. She was poised. Smart. Take-no-prisoners. She had the mouth of a sailor and wasn't afraid to use it (even in front of children).

The bongos were my idea, although Marla and Jack would have done it eventually. And I had just called my mom and invited her commune members out to our radical resistance—clothing optional, of course. I wanted to push Avery.

The other thing I knew about Avery was that she pissed

me the fuck off. Which took a lot, considering that in my almost thirty years on this earth I'd very rarely gotten angry. Stoned? Yes. Sunburned? All the time. Slapped around by a giant wave? Of course.

Angry? The kind that made you want to stand up and fight for what you believe in? Well, that honor went to her and her only.

This morning she'd stalked through the protesters like a cheetah across the plains of Africa. I'd come to expect this, these past twenty-one days. No matter where I was in the crowd, no matter what I was doing... she found me. And I wasn't even sure she knew my name.

Every morning, I *tried* to start our interactions off friendly.

"Mornin', Ms. Dacosta," I said, as I always did. I was holding two handmade signs, and my shoulders were starting to ache. I'd been so caught up in my thoughts this morning I'd ended up swimming and paddling in the ocean for longer than usual.

"*You're* still here?" she asked, rolling her eyes. This. This was why we always started in on each other: Avery's incessant irritation at our very existence.

"Every. Fucking. Day," I said with the biggest smile I could muster. "Until you halt construction on the hotel that will destroy our community."

She narrowed her eyes at me. They were brown and seemed to grow darker every time we spoke. "Can I ask kind of a silly question?"

"Sure." I shrugged. "I'm an open book."

She waved her hands around, indicating the audience. "*None* of you have jobs, correct? You just spend your days fucking up other people's jobs and attempting to stop vital economic development? Wasting away on the beach, getting high on sunscreen? Or..." She looked around. "Probably other things as well." She crossed her arms in front of her, so prim and proper I wanted to shake her. Crack her open. See what was behind the curtain.

"No," I said quietly. She leaned in a little to hear me. I caught her scent—some kind of lavender. "You're wrong, and you know that. Every person here has a full-time job. Children. Family to care for. Lives to lead. They choose, *every day*, to come here because Playa Vieja is our *home*. They're selfless."

She opened her mouth to reply, but I cut her off. "And just to be clear, Ms. Dacosta, their jobs might not look like yours, but they still have value. They might not be corporate robots whose only motivation is greed, but that doesn't mean they're any less hard-working than you are."

Avery stepped even closer to me, dark eyes flashing. "Selfless?" She tipped her head over to a couple of my friends smoking a joint and kicking a hacky sack around. "I'm not sure what kind of sacrifice your community is making. Every day out here is basically a Phish concert on steroids. Plus, you use up all of our free parking. And *secondly,* I resent the idea that my only motivation is greed. You don't know a damn thing about me."

Her hands were on her hips, haughty. A wisp of hair from the tight bun on top her head broke free. She snagged it, tucking it behind her ear.

The door of the office opened, and a large, terrifying-looking man popped his head out. "Avery? Our meeting?" She turned, smiled at him, and nodded. She hauled her giant briefcase onto her shoulder—for the first time, I noticed how packed it was. Did she really bring that much work home every night?

"Seems we're in a bit of a standoff again," I said, grabbing a joint that Rico passed my way. I took a long, hard pull on it, then exhaled the smoke through my nostrils. She almost looked impressed. "Guess I'll just get back to my Phish concert and meaningless existence."

"And I guess I'll get to work with my corporate-robot colleagues, destroying this beautiful planet."

I almost smiled at her in return before I realized who I was talking to.

"Fine," I said instead.

"Fine," she said back before huffing past me for the front door. I watched her walk away, the smoke from the weed burning in my chest.

"That woman drives me up the goddamn wall," I said to Rico, handing him the joint. He only looked at me, a small, secretive smile on his face. "What?" I said.

"Nothin', man," he replied. "Oh, I came up with some new chants last night. You ready to get this thing started?"

"Always," I replied, lifting the bullhorn to my mouth.

I stood in front of a hundred people, crammed into the surf shop my dad and I co-owned. Only a few blocks from my house, it sat right on the beach. A giant wall of windows and a patio faced the ocean. Old pictures of our favorite surfers donned the walls. A poster-sized picture of me, riding a wave at Titans of Mavericks, hung near the surf wax whose company I modeled for.

Back in the day, Beyond the Breakers was *the* place to go if you were any kind of surfer, from here to Ventura. I'd sit in the corner, one hand on my child-sized board, and try to memorize every single thing the surfers would say. Laugh at the jokes I couldn't get. Agree with opinions I couldn't begin to understand. To me, the cadence of their voices, the soft pulse of their laughter, the smell of sweat mixed with salt water... it was home.

Now, staring in the faces of my community, standing in the place I loved the most, my heart threatened to burst.

"Thank you all for being here this evening," I said. "It's been almost a month since the protest started, and I watched my parents enough growing up to know a little organization of these things can go a long way." My parents were in the corner—vibrant and healthy-looking, even in their sixties.

"We have eight weeks until the city council votes on the building permits. I've been speaking with our representative, Councilmember McAffee, who is one hundred percent *against* building this hotel for the very reasons we are against it. Which is good. But there are seven members, and she holds a minority opinion. I'm looking for a handful of volunteers to schedule meetings with the other members. And we need to take the fight to those districts—flyering, attending their neighborhood meetings. It'll be a lot of work, but we might be able to sway them to our side."

"We *will* sway them to our side," a resident called out, and everybody clapped.

"Now, I think we need to start getting the press out to the protest. I was contacted yesterday by a local newspaper. Nothing big, but every little bit helps. I think—I *know*—they won't be the only news outlet looking to get our side of the story. Every day our numbers grow bigger. Every day we grow louder. We're getting noticed. We're being seen," I continued.

I handed out half-sheets of paper with bullet points on them. "In case any of you get grabbed for an interview, I've been working on talking points—key elements to our argument." I looked at the list. I'd stayed up half the night working on this and was pretty proud of it.

"Jack and Marla were nice enough to write up fuller briefs on each of these points—" I nodded toward a giant stack of paper next to the cash register. "—so please look over so you can expand on your argument if you need to. But for now, our arguments for halting construction of the Bella View are as follows." I cleared my throat.

"One. Loss of affordable housing. Playa Vieja is one of the only communities left in San Diego where most residents have been born and raised there. Luxury hotels—and the development that will follow—will increase property values. Which will increase our rents and taxes. Families and community members who have lived here for generations will be forced out, unable to afford the homes they've lived in for decades."

"Two," I said, holding up two fingers. "The environment. The Bella View Hotel corporation has a terrible reputation when it comes to the environment. That luxury hotel they built in La Jolla? Environmental law firms have sued them three times now. In Cabo San Lucas, the town fought against a Bella View Hotel being built in a small beach town like ours. Fought and lost, unfortunately. Since the construction and tourism, their drinking water has tested positive for harmful chemicals. Air pollution has gotten worse. Overfishing is rampant. Tourists leave trash all over the beach."

I swallowed against a wave of emotion. After I'd put two and two together, I'd researched that hotel I remembered from when Rico and I were teenagers. That small beach in Mexico had *not* thrived, as I'd secretly hoped. Their present was Playa Vieja's future.

"And finally, number three—the hardest point to talk about. We want to keep Playa Vieja to ourselves—or, that's how the Bella View will frame it. But Playa Vieja has always been an insular community. And we've always pushed back against well-intentioned outsiders. We don't *need* Playa Vieja to look like every other commercialized beach town in California. Not that we don't welcome people—that we specifically have never welcomed *tourism* development just for development's sake. All of us here have watched as San Diego has been eaten up by the tourist industry. Smog, traffic, pollution, overcrowding... the once beautiful beaches we grew up on are now filled with tourists. Hotels. Bars and clubs. I know that, economically, tourism is a smart idea. But I also know that, at a certain point, it has to *stop*. Some part of Mother Nature has to be left alone."

My parents beamed at me, their unconditional love as pure as the day I was born. I'd never thought much about politics myself—always focused on catching the better, bigger wave. Having fun. Being happy. I'd always participated when my parents asked—and I did care about the issues they cared about—but this was different. This felt like *mine*.

"I know how tired everyone is, and we still have two months to go. Just... just know how fucking *proud* I am of all of you. Of us. You have very busy lives, but you've made this your priority. That makes me proud to be a member of this community."

"And we've got a good leader," Marla called out. Everyone clapped. I waved it off. I didn't mind the praise when it came to surfing—was used to, in fact, fans and crowds and signing autographs. But this wasn't about me. This was about our *future*.

"Well, thank you all for trusting me," I said sincerely. "And let's keep giving 'em hell."

5

AVERY

*I*t was important to know if the person leading the protest against your hotel was a beloved local celebrity.

It was a Friday night, a little over a month since the shaggy, obnoxious, infuriating protester had shown up at my office doors. I had refused to learn his name, or really anything about him, even though every day our interactions made me so angry I couldn't see straight.

And every day, their numbers grew. Sal's smile was strained now, and he'd sent me an email demanding a meeting tomorrow morning. It didn't say why, but I wasn't stupid. It was about the protest. Had to be.

I took a deep breath in the grocery check-out line, steadying my nerves. I thought of The Surfer, drifting in the ocean. Inhale. Exhale. In front of me, a trio of young women was clearly buying things for a party. They were shiny-haired and confident and couldn't seem to stop laughing. I found myself leaning near their warmth and light. Even in college I rarely went to parties, too tired from the endless cycle of classes and homework and diner shifts. And I didn't think I'd been to one since.

As a child, our parties had been epic—bonfires and bongos and the entire ocean to ourselves.

I hefted the tub of ice cream against my side. Instead, I was spending my Friday night prepping for a work meeting and planning to eat every ounce of this ice cream.

My eyes drifted over the magazine covers, snagging on the middle of one. Or, notably, on the hard ridges of the cover model's abs. I paused, my fingertips to my mouth. Being celibate these past two years hadn't been terribly hard. Other sexual partners I'd had before had never really rocked my world. Sex had seemed like a chore to them, and I chalked the lack of passion up to some issue with me. Sex and relationships, because of my upbringing, were... tricky. Not easily navigated. So the past two years hadn't felt like a huge loss.

Except recently. I was masturbating more, swept up in sudden waves of arousal that threatened to knock me over. *After the vote,* I'd keep repeating to myself. The vote was less than two months away now. Eight weekends. Eight more Friday nights, like this one, and then I could go to some bar, grab the first hot guy I saw (*non*-surfer, preferred), and fuck his brains out.

This cover model though... board shorts were slung around his lean waist, slightly untied. Careless. Like they'd come off at the tug of a finger. I wondered what his tan skin would taste like. If I dragged my tongue over every single inch of his stomach, what would he do? Would he groan, threading his fingers in my hair?

A steady pulse beat between my thighs. His chest was even better, lean but broad. Because his shoulders, well, they were another story altogether.

"Miss? *Miss?*" The check-out clerk's voice stampeded through my thoughts.

"Hello," I said back, dreamily. Was it possible he wasn't wearing underwear under those shorts?

"Would... uh, would you like to check out now? There's quite a line behind you," she said.

I reluctantly tore my eyes away from the paradise of the cover model's nipples and slid forward.

"Just, um, just this tub of ice cream please," I said, suddenly aware of the sad, lonely stereotype I made. Ice cream on a Friday night. No six-packed, sweaty lover awaiting my arrival at home.

"It's okay," the clerk whispered, leaning over. "I stare at that magazine cover all the time. He's a total stud."

I laughed despite myself. "Which one is it? I didn't even see the name."

"*Surf's Up.*"

"Oh," I said, digging through my purse for my wallet. "It's a surfer magazine? I don't usually go for guys like that." Another sign that I was losing it. Surfing made me think of the protester, which made my blood boil.

"He comes in all the time, you know," she said, handing me the ice cream.

I looked up, head tilted. "Wait," I said, turning back to the magazine and grabbing it. When I saw the model's face, I had to bite back a yelp.

"*This* guy? Comes in here? Who is he?"

"Finn Travis," she said, like it was totally obvious. She grabbed the magazine from me and fanned her face with it. "I actually went to high school with him, out in Playa Vieja. You know he's leading that big protest?"

"Um... um," was all I could say because she was absolutely right. The scruffy, smiling, shaggy-hair-in-his-eyes cover model was the protester. Finn Travis. I rolled the name around on my tongue, grimacing. I'd gone from low-level turned on to pissed in a matter of seconds.

"Is he... um, is he some kind of big deal?" I asked, dreading the answer.

The clerk had an amused expression on her face. "Kind of. For San Diego, I mean. You could say he's a local celebrity. Wait," she said, reaching forward and grabbing my wrist. "You've never seen him before?"

I shook my head no, completely dazed. This... this was not good. "Could you ring that up too, please?"

She smirked, typing quickly on her screen. "Sure, hun. Wouldn't be the first woman to come in here and buy this magazine just to drool at the cover."

I sighed, suddenly anxious all over again. I had a very long night ahead of me.

IT WAS 9:00 am and time for my mini-battle with Finn. I'd barely slept the night before, watching videos of Finn. Reading articles on Finn. Scanning through his Facebook fan page, which had more than 100,000 followers.

The meeting with Sal was not going to go well. But at least I had some ammo to shove in Finn's face.

He wasn't in his usual spot today. Instead, he was sprawled on a lawn chair, chatting with a couple of people. It was so obvious now that he was more than just a friendly guy with charismatic leadership qualities. People *respected* him. And they flocked around him, every morning, like moths to a bright, smiling flame. In that moment, a small part of me saw past the anger and the hurt and recognized that Finn really, truly cared about people.

Which made him especially dangerous.

About two hundred people were here, and in the background Marla and Jack's bongos beat a steady rhythm. Someone was strumming a guitar and softly singing. The smell of frying tortillas clung to the air.

He caught my eye as I made my way through the crowd, and I held his gaze, smug.

"Well, well, well," I said, staring down at him in his chair. I liked this vantage point, felt extra powerful. Finn was all long arms and legs. His tank top clung to his hips, and I remembered what they'd looked like. What my tongue wanted to do to every inch of his hard, lean stomach.

He must have noticed my change in expression because he smiled, tantalizing and slow. "What are you thinking about?" he asked.

"Oh... just that, from one fellow corporate robot to another, I wanted to say *well done.*" I held the magazine up, nodding my head at his image.

He shrugged with an easy laugh. "Sometimes I'm a cover model. Like what you see?"

"Surfers aren't my type," I said sweetly, hoping it sounded like the truth. It essentially was. I'd only (briefly) been attracted to his body. And ambitious, type A lawyers could *also* have bodies like that. "How do you feel about perpetuating an unhealthy body image to sell surf products for a giant, faceless corporation? And what are the environmental practices of that corporation?"

He shook his head. "Excuse me, but selling surf products cannot be equated with what *you're* doing. And I'm not selling an unhealthy body image. That's what I *look* like because I've been swimming every day of my life since I was four years old."

I rolled my eyes. "You know they wouldn't have chosen

someone who wasn't conventionally attractive to sell their products or be on the cover of their magazine. You're just a pawn in the big capitalist machine."

Point for Avery.

Finn stood, suddenly towering over me. I really needed to invest in some eight-inch heels.

"How can you possibly think this *magazine*—" He snatched it from my hands. "—has the same impact as what you do?"

"And that is, exactly?"

"Get paid to destroy the environment and force good people from their homes," he said. He looked at me, *really* looked at me. His eyes were the deep, dark blue of the ocean right before a storm.

I opened my mouth to respond. Closed it. This conversation was not going how I'd fantasized.

"You're a jackass," I finally said, turning on my heel and heading toward the door.

I heard Finn snort behind me, and when I looked back, he was rubbing his hand along his jawline, shaking his head.

"What?" I said, one hand on my hip. Some part of me wanted him to lash out more, to push me further.

"Nothing," he responded, his gaze making me flustered. "Just... good morning, I guess."

THIS WAS what I'd learned last night.

Finn's father, Mark, was *huge* in the San Diego surf scene in the sixties and seventies, winning local competitions, which in this town basically made you a hero. Finn's trajectory had been similar, but at this point his fame had far eclipsed his father's.

Finn was a big wave surfer, a discipline of surfing that was extremely dangerous. The waves he surfed—*chose* to surf—routinely swelled over thirty feet and often much higher. I watched a video of Finn last night riding a wave he'd had to be towed to... because the waves breaking near the shore were too deadly. He'd won surf competitions around the world, gaining a fair amount of notoriety. He even had a few sponsors, and *Surf's Up* wasn't the only magazine he'd modeled for. Calendars, ads. Finn was becoming the face of big wave surfing.

But then last year he'd won Titans of Mavericks, the biggest (and most deadly) surf competition in the entire world. Every year, if the waves were right, a small set of surfers rode freezing-cold, sixty-foot swells in Northern California that broke upon miles of sharp reefs. A handful of surfers had even died over the years.

And Finn won.

In San Diego, this, apparently, essentially made you the mayor. Not that you'd know it by looking at him.

My archnemesis was a beloved, charismatic icon. And the protest was *not* going away. It was only growing bigger. Day after day. Because the truth of the matter was, even with my late-night anxieties, I hadn't really thought Finn and the hippies would stay around. I knew his type, had *known* his type, my entire life growing up. They posed no threat.

Or so I thought.

Thus, the meeting with Sal I was dreading with every fiber of my being.

"Avery." I looked up from my computer. Speaking of.

"Sal. Good morning," I said, indicating he should come in. "You wanted to see me?"

"I did." He was uncharacteristically somber. This wasn't good. Sal was almost never serious.

"It's getting out of control," he said, and he didn't have to say what. "But you know that."

"I agree," I said, choosing my words carefully. "But you told me not to worry."

"I was wrong," he said quickly. "*We* were wrong." I bristled a bit at the *we,* since I'd been worried since the beginning, but everyone else had just laughed and laughed.

"True," I said, knowing this was as close to an apology as Sal would ever give me. "What would you like me to do about it? I don't want this to reflect poorly on the project."

He sighed. "It already is, unfortunately. Not that we haven't had this happen before, but at a certain point, we became proactive, not reactive. We're on the reactive side now." He paused. "You're young, and this is your first big project. It's a mistake all of us have made."

I tried—and failed—to bite my tongue. "I resent the implication, Sal. My age and experience have nothing to do with it. I'm not sure we could have seen this coming."

"Did you do your research on the protesters? Did you know who we were up against?"

"No," I said, defensive now. "Because *we* had decided not to worry about it." That day, in my office, he'd dismissed all of my concerns. But Sal was a company man through and through. He wasn't going to take the fall for this. His underling—me—would.

"Well. That's where you fucked up, Avery," he said. "And the president of the company is getting involved now."

I closed my eyes for a second. "I'm sorry to hear that. I'd hate to involve her time." It was embarrassing, like having a parent tell you how disappointed they were in you.

"It's for your benefit. She can make a statement and nip

it in the bud. Plus, she wants to get you in front of the cameras, talking about why this is the compassionate, smart, economically savvy thing to do. She'll make a statement at four today. Then it's all you."

"The media is that interested?"

"Now they are. Now that we have two hundred and fifty people outside of our offices every day, they are." He couldn't keep the gruffness out of his voice, and it stung. I'd witnessed this eat-or-be-eaten side of development before. But it hurt more when I was the one taking the fall.

"What else can I do?" I asked. I was torn between being completely pissed at Sal's behavior and wanting desperately to cling to the opportunity I'd been given. And now I worried my promotion might hang in the balance.

"Work harder," he said, the most Sal advice ever. It was his style. Problems at work? Simply work harder. Sleep? Don't worry about it. Eat? Go hungry. More and more I was mimicking his actions, my insomnia worsening with time. Stress levels out of control.

"Okay," I said, wanting to slide beneath my desk. "I can do that."

He stood up. "And get ready to be on camera. Constantly."

IT HAD BEEN two days since the president of the company had made a statement. And the media wouldn't stop coming.

Which was why I'd spent extra time each morning putting on the most bad-ass pantsuits I owned. Show no weakness, especially not to a bunch of hippies. And Finn.

I'd gone to see The Surfer that morning, who'd ridden

wave after wave. His enthusiasm was contagious. I smiled at the memory.

As I turned the corner, I saw Marla and her husband Jack drumming away.

"Good morning, Avery!" they said cheerfully. Their sign this morning read, "A Vote for the Bella View is a Vote for Destruction."

"You do remember I'm the enemy, correct?" I asked, shifting my briefcase to my left hand.

Jack smiled and kept up a steady rhythm. "That's a real black-and-white view of the world, Ms. Dacosta."

"You'll stop in a bit though, right?" I asked. The sound was a constant irritant. Even though, deep, deep down, I still thought the two of them were kind of cute together. Not that I'd *ever* admit that to anyone.

Marla nodded and nudged Jack with her elbow. "We will, we promise. We know how it bothers you."

"Thank you," I said through gritted teeth. The nicer the protesters were to me, the angrier I seemed to get.

When I turned the corner, the courtyard was absolutely filled with people, more than I expected on a Monday. Four news stations were planted at the entrance. Our PR company had given me plenty of media training the past few days, and after doing a handful of interviews, I felt more than comfortable. I liked it, in fact. Liked knowing *I* was the chosen expert on this issue, the voice of reason. The face of progress.

Reporters were currently interviewing Finn, who, of course, looked like he was born to be in front of cameras.

"Here's the thing," he said, looking briefly over at me. I narrowed my eyes at him. "People can write us off all they want. But we're not just going to roll over for a massive hotel chain. Especially one with as horrific an environmental track record as the Bella View. Ms. Dacosta can talk about how 'green' they are all she wants. *We* know the truth. Bella View Hotels don't care about the environment one bit. And we do."

I felt my hands forming fists down by my sides. Everything he said was just plain *wrong*.

I straightened my shoulders and stalked loudly across the courtyard. The camera guys noticed and rushed over, leaving Finn in the dust. He glanced at me in surprise, and I arched an eyebrow.

"Ms. Dacosta," one started, mic in my face. "What is the current timeline for development of the Bella View Hotel in Playa Vieja? And what do you have to say in response to the accusations of the protesters?"

I shook my head. "Bella View Hotels is still planning on beginning eighteen months of construction on Playa Vieja as soon as our permits are approved at the city council meeting in eight weeks." I paused, staring right through them and at Finn. I held his gaze. "We've had many initial conversations with the city council, and they are in favor of this *absolutely vital* development. With regards to the accusations, well... all I can say is, we still don't see these protesters as a threat. And their accusations, to me, won't hold any weight until cold, hard facts are there to back them up." Finn crossed his arms in front of his broad chest. Even from here, I could see the anger simmering above his skin like asphalt on a hot summer day. "Now, if you'll please excuse me, I have to get to work," I said as sweetly as I could manage.

I brushed past them, heading to the office door. That is, until Finn's big body blocked me.

"Please *move*," I said, trying to push past him. He was *so* tall, and I hated looking up at him, hated the feeling of vulnerability it gave me.

"No threat?" He said, voice dangerously low. For the first time since I'd met him, he wasn't smiling. No. He looked *pissed*.

"You heard what I said."

Finn made an exasperated sound. "I've read about a dozen reports from San Diego's environmental commission about *your* hotel in La Jolla. And they *very factually* enumerate the ways your company doesn't give a *shit* about the environment. Or the people who made that beach home before you came along."

"You don't think environmental commissions have a bias? Please," I said, stepping around him. "I call bullshit."

"*Avery*," I heard him say, the first time he'd ever called me by my first name. Usually it was "Ms. Dacosta" or "corporate greed robot." I wasn't sure I liked how it sounded coming out of his mouth. There was anger there and something else. Passion.

I slipped through the office door and stood behind it, my heart pounding. It didn't matter that we'd been doing this for over a month now. Every day I grew angrier, more sure that I was right. Shocked that anyone could be on the other side. I knew why locals despised hotels and the tourists they brought. I understood. Sort of.

But Finn claimed over and over again that Playa Vieja was his home... that he loved it.

Didn't he want it to prosper?

6

FINN

*T*he news anchor wouldn't stop flirting with me.

"Now you, handsome... you sit here." She squeezed my shoulders, depositing me on a medium-sized green couch. And not without flashing me a fair amount of her cleavage. She was older, with severely dyed blonde hair. "We'll be live in about ten minutes, so until then, just make yourselves comfortable." She winked at me before leaving us alone.

I could *feel* Avery rolling her eyes next to me.

"Do you have something to say?" I asked her, adjusting the mic clipped onto the collar of my shirt.

"Just that, if the two of you want to fuck so badly, I can leave."

I snorted, looking over at her. She was smiling, just a little.

"Is that Avery Dacosta... *smiling*? Wow. I must be a lucky guy."

"*Please* don't flatter yourself," she said, crossing and uncrossing her legs. She was nervous. She was also sitting about as far away from me on the couch as she could. "I was just laughing at the idea that any woman would want to have sex with you."

I turned to look at her. Even with her closed-off body language, we were still closer to each other than we'd ever been. Which was strange, considering we'd spent the last six weeks getting into bite-sized arguments.

"The attacks are getting personal now," I said. "What's next? Making fun of my hair?" I grinned at her.

She shifted a little on the couch, her knee accidentally brushing mine. Our eyes met. She looked away quickly.

"Sorry," she said. "I'm just..."

"Nervous?" I asked. "Me too. And no need to apologize." After about a week of heavy media, San Diego's *Nightly News* had asked Avery and me to do an in-studio interview. It was a big deal. "My parents are taping this right now so they can send it out to all of my family. They might make a mural of one of the images, hang it in the yurt they're living in."

"God help me," she said dryly. "Your parents seem ridiculous."

"Ridiculously *supportive*," I corrected. "Who's watching you tonight? Your parents?"

Avery looked down and away from me. "Oh... oh, I don't know. I don't even think they know about it." She bit her lip. "Don't you do this stuff all the time?" she asked, changing the subject. Quickly. "Like for your... surfing?"

I laughed. "You say the word *surfing* like it involves sacrificing kittens on a daily basis."

She tilted her nose up. "It's never really been my thing."

I gritted my teeth. She was too much. "Well, yes, I do a lot of media for my *surfing*. But this, I don't know. This feels different."

"Why?" she asked. I couldn't believe we were kind of, sort of, having a conversation.

I thought for a second. "My parents raised me to be politically active. And I am when I want to be. But it was always on the sidelines or something I did to make my parents happy. They gave me kind of the perfect childhood, so anything they asked of me, I'd rush to do."

An odd expression flashed over her face, so quick I almost didn't catch it. "On Playa Vieja, right?"

"Yeah. My parents basically raised me on a beach, which is a pretty unique experience." I shifted a little, turning to her. "And beautiful. But they never let me forget—*they* never forget—that things are much, much worse for the majority of people in the world. Which is why they were also so ready to raise their voices for justice. I never thought... well, I don't know."

"What?"

I shrugged, smiling at her. She smiled back—a very, very small one. "Surfing is my entire life. The media and the attention are... I don't know. I don't mind it, and it's fun, sometimes. But it's not why I surf. Not at all. And I always thought that, since I didn't use my *very* small circle of influence for evil, I was helping the world in some way. By being happy. By being a good son and a good friend. By being a good community member."

"And now?"

I found myself moving closer to Avery, almost imperceptibly. "I realized my very small circle of influence is a privilege. A gift. And if I don't use it for *good*, I'm just another part of the problem. I know that compared to other injustices in the world, saving Playa Vieja seems small. But just standing by and assuming that surely 'someone else' would step up and fight, well... it didn't feel like an option."

Avery was quiet for a moment. I caught her scent again —some kind of lavender. Her shirt was a crisp, bright white, and it shone against her skin. "I have a lot riding on this project. The success of this project. I've never..." She paused, cleared her throat. "I've never had this much responsibility before. My boss took this big chance on me, two years ago. And everything was going so well..." She trailed off.

I felt a small twinge in my chest. "Are you trying to make me feel guilty for the protest?"

She held my gaze again. Up close, her eyes were a rich, dark brown. "Not really. I think I was just... sharing." She looked a little embarrassed.

"This might sound odd, but you're doing a great job," I said. "I don't know what it's like to build hotels, but it can't be easy. I mean, technically, I hate them and everything they stand for but—"

She blushed, just a little. "Why is it odd to say that?"

"Because you're the enemy? I don't think we're supposed to compliment each other."

She fiddled with her earrings. "Oh, okay. Well, in that case, you're—"

"*All righty,* you two!" The newscaster, Cheryl, came storming back over. "We're going on in two minutes. Did the producer tell you what to expect?"

"Kind of..." I started to say.

"*Great,*" she said, squeezing my shoulder again. Avery coughed into her fist. "So we'll just be having a conversation, except about two million people will be watching." I heard Avery's intake of breath. I fought the urge to reach over and squeeze her hand.

"We'll be okay," I said quickly. "Avery and I are basically experts at this point." I looked over, giving Avery the tiniest of smiles. She met my gaze, nodded. Cheryl looked between the two of us.

"Excellent. You know, we've had a lot of viewers request this. This 'David and Goliath' thing is very *in* right now."

"Am *I* the David?" I asked, pointing at myself.

She laughed. "Oh, honey, probably not where it counts."

I heard Avery's soft *"For the love of..."* and then we were rolling, Cheryl sitting in the chair next to the couch. The studio was quiet, just a handful of camera guys and Cheryl's aggressively friendly smile. Her teeth looked bleached.

Just us, Cheryl, and two million people.

"Thank you for joining us this evening," Cheryl started, speaking directly into the camera. I was suddenly aware of everything—my hands on my knees, the set of my shoulders. Next to me, I watched Avery straighten her spine. Less than a foot of space separated us.

"Hotel development. Tourism. Environmental impacts. A community coming together. Some hot topics for you tonight, ladies and gentlemen. And let me start by introducing our guests." The red light of the camera blinked a strange Morse code in our direction. "Avery Dacosta. Finn Travis. Thank you for being here this evening."

It was now officially awkward.

The interview had been fast. They told us it was a ten-minute segment, which should have felt like a long time for two million people to be staring at you. But when your interviewer talked for most of it, it sure did fly by.

It had also gotten heated. Which always seemed to happen when Avery and I were next to each other—she'd say something I was outrageously offended by, and I'd give it right back. The vicious cycle continued. Except this time, as the camera guys unclipped our microphones and Avery and I stood—stiff as two teenagers on prom night—Cheryl had asked me out. In front of everyone.

I begged off as smoothly as I could. And now Avery and I were in the elevator heading back down to the parking lot, and instead of her lobbing dozens of barbs my way, she was silent.

"So... um," I started to say, leaning against the wall. The quick drop of the elevator was making me feel light-headed. That and the fact that Cheryl hitting on me had made me feel embarrassed in front of Avery. For reasons I wasn't quite sure of.

"You're not going to stop, are you?" Avery asked quietly. In the interview, she had been poised and sharp. Smart—smarter than Cheryl. Definitely smarter than me.

"What? The protest?" I asked.

She nodded. "It's going to get bigger. And you're not going to stop. And you're going to continue making my life a living goddamn hell."

"Avery—" I started, but when she turned to look at me, her eyes were blazing with anger. I felt my temper amp up in response.

"Why are you pissed at me right now?" The small space made our interactions feel more intimate. Close. She was no longer just that woman I argued with every morning for five minutes. She was... well, something else entirely. I couldn't put my finger on it.

"I'm pissed at you right now," she said, huffing through the opening elevator doors. "Because the development I'm proposing will help Playa Vieja thrive economically. You know your city hasn't bounced back from the recession, right?"

We were in the parking lot, heading to our separate cars. I stopped, crossing my arms over my chest.

"You don't need to tell me about Playa Vieja. I live there. I *know* there. And we're doing just fine."

She looked at me like I'd grown two heads. "You're ignoring it. You're too close. Playa Vieja needs *help*."

"And it's *your* kind of 'help' in particular."

"Finn, God, yes. Development. It's a tale as old as time. You need tax breaks and restaurants and redevelopment funding and karaoke bars and *people*. People who will spend money."

"I'm tired of that argument, Avery," I said, stepping closer to her. She moved back, putting distance between us.

"Well, it's true."

I shook my head. "Were you responsible for the hotel in San Marcos? That small town near Cabo San Lucas?"

Her brow furrowed at the quick change in subject. "Wait... what? The Bella View in Cabo?" She thought for a second. "I wasn't working there then. If my memory serves, that was built, like, ten years ago. I was in high school."

"Your company was involved though."

"Sure..." she said slowly, unsure of my angle.

"I saw the construction. I was there for a surf competition the year before I went to college. The community *hated* it. With every fiber of their beings."

"I don't deal in feelings, Finn. I deal in money."

My stomach clenched. "The reason why they hated it was because of the incredibly negative impact the hotel had on the environment. On their way of life. On their home. When I talk about environmental impacts, Avery, I'm not just pulling things out of my ass. It's real. It's documented. And it's going to happen to Playa Vieja."

She stepped closer now, her big, brown eyes staring into

mine. For the first time, I noticed the small cluster of freckles on her left cheekbone. "It was a surf competition, you said?"

"Yeah."

She nodded. "And what kind of impact do you think that competition had on their beach? Did a bunch of people come to watch it? Was there food?"

"Yes. And yes. What are you getting at?"

"Only that the hundreds of people who attended left a footprint on that beach, Finn. They drove there, increasing smog and pollution. Using up precious fossil fuels to fill their gas tanks. They ate food with trash associated with it. Which probably went onto the beach. Which goes into the water. Which, somewhere, a continent away, ends up choking some poor pelican."

I gritted my teeth. "I'd like the record to show I disagree with everything you're saying."

She smiled. "My point is, your existence on this earth leaves a footprint. In everything that you do. You can't fling that shit back at me without getting a little bit on yourself."

And with that, she turned and stalked away, leaving me furious and frustrated. As usual.

I WAS THREE BEERS IN, sitting on the sand in front of my house. Playa Vieja glittered in the moonlight.

I couldn't stop thinking about Avery. My slightly beer-hazy brain kept replaying, over and over again, what she'd said. Because Avery didn't know the rest of the story. A part I tried to forget as often as I could, even though the experience led me in a direction I'd never dreamed of.

The night Rico and I drank with those surfers from

Cabo, we'd fallen asleep on the beach. I'd woken up, sandy and disoriented, rolling over to see that damn hotel. In the daylight, it had looked even worse.

I'd stood up, desperate for water. In the early morning light, I'd seen shapes moving along the sand: people. With orange vests and trash bags. The competition yesterday hadn't been huge, but there had still been about three hundred people crowding in on the beach. In their wake, they'd left beer bottles and sandwich wrappers. Plastic bags floated down the beach like tumbleweeds. People were picking up the trash, their faces drawn and tired.

I'd walked up to one of them, a kid not much older than me. "What are you doing?" I asked in Spanish.

"Cleaning up," he said, shrugging. "Every time these surfers come through, they leave all this shit afterward." I looked around, saw the tiny tornado we had unleashed. The beach looked wrecked.

I apologized, asking if I could help. I felt terrible, asleep and hungover on a beach while local residents cleaned up around me.

He said no, waving me off. He re-joined his group, and I heard them laughing. In the middle of rapid Spanish, I caught the word "tourist" —*turista*—his mocking glance directed my way. The group laughed, then went back to their work.

I'd gone back and shaken Rico awake. We'd left, bodies tired and aching from the waves and the alcohol. He hadn't given a second glance to the way the beach looked, even though for days after I couldn't seem to stop thinking about it.

My parents were huge environmentalists. Of all the causes they fought for, their environmentalism affected me the most. When I flew home to Playa Vieja and stood, taking in the big, beautiful ocean I loved more than anything in my life, I knew why. Surfing was my life. Which meant the ocean was my life. And suddenly, thinking of those volunteers, cleaning up the mess *I* had made, I felt naive. Stupid. I assumed being a surfer automatically made me an environmentalist.

But I wasn't doing shit for the environment. In fact, I was a part of the problem.

When I started college that fall, I majored in Biology. And when I graduated, I immediately enrolled in a master's program for Ecology, the study of organisms and the environment. I focused on coastal communities: erosion, water pollution, overfishing, coral reef extinction. I began to see Playa Vieja, where I surfed every morning, as an exception to this rule, a place where overpopulation and development would never creep in.

I'd graduated with my master's degree four years ago and, after I got my diploma, threw myself back into surfing and competitions. Running my dad's shop. Having fun with laid-back surfer chicks who wanted to fuck and get high.

It all felt a million miles away... until. Until Avery Dacosta decided she wanted to destroy everything.

I shifted in the sand, draining the last of my beer. I felt that silken sadness that comes from drinking alone. Suddenly, the exhaustion of the past month truly hit me. Of fighting with Avery every damn day. And now, her words were stuck in my brain.

Because she was right. For the first time since I'd met her, I'd wanted to reach forward, grab her hand, and say, "I know. And I agree with you."

7
———

AVERY

I didn't sleep that night. Which meant I was back on the beach the next morning. With The Surfer. I sipped coffee from my thermos, thoughts jumbled with Finn. I'd taped our live interview and watched it as soon as I made it home. It was hard to see yourself on camera, to hear your own voice. I thought I looked tired and washed out while Finn glowed with good health and charm. And it was *so* clear during the interview that Cheryl had a crush on him.

"It's obvious, Cheryl," I'd said at the end of the interview. "The Bella View Hotel is the smart, efficient, economically savvy thing to do for Playa Vieja. Contrary to Mr. Travis's objections, we have a long history of conservation and working with local communities. And we are not about to back down just because of a little protest."

That had made Finn *furious*. It was odd, sitting next to him on that couch. Feeling the heat radiating from his body. Before the interview, we were almost *friendly*. Comfortable with each other, which made a certain kind of sense. You couldn't spend that many weeks arguing without developing an odd closeness. Although I didn't like it. Didn't like him or the type of people he represented.

His smile, though... Up close, that crooked, sly grin was almost too much. He'd flashed it at me a dozen times during our daily battles. But sitting a foot apart, shirt clinging to his broad shoulders, his woodsy scent everywhere...

I shivered, focusing back on The Surfer. Tried to lull myself into a sense of peace, watching him rise and fall on the water. And remembered the dream I'd had that morning, when I'd slipped asleep for an hour before jolting awake at 4:00 am.

Because The Surfer had started appearing in my dreams. Whenever I managed to fall asleep, he was there. And the dreams were *deeply* sexual. Which was weird, since I didn't know what he looked like. I knew he was tall, and I think his hair was blond. Other than that, it was all wet suit and surfboard.

It must have been his determination. The few boyfriends I'd had weren't keen to bring me pleasure. In fact, they barely paid attention to me. I could have been sitting next to them on the couch, up in flames, and they wouldn't have noticed.

The Surfer, though, had to focus. He had to understand the swell of the waves, the pulse of the sand beneath his feet, the tug and release of currents. The rough feel of the board under his hands. Water sliding down his body, over and over again. The dreams I'd been having were fractured: fingertips in the water, on my body. A wet suit against my skin. The endless pounding of waves, curling. Arching. I'd keep almost seeing his face, but then it would stop, and I'd wake up, a sharp ache between my legs.

I wondered if my dreams about The Surfer were tied to my new, constant need to masturbate. Or the fact that arousal would wash over me, hot and hungry, in the middle of sending an email. Sitting in traffic. Driving home from work, so intense I was tempted to pull over to the side of the road and get myself off.

I must have been reaching some kind of hormonal limit.

Seven more weeks. I bit my lip, thinking about sex. The dream I'd had this morning—those fingertips trailing up my thighs.

I watched The Surfer for so long that he started to paddle back to the shore. I got a better view of his face and something pulled at my memory, but I shook it off. I didn't know men like him.

He got to shore, stood up fully. He was *tall*. Taller than my brothers, who were both over six feet. He shook his wet hair out like a dog, droplets flying around his head. I smiled. Briefly, I considered moving since I didn't want him to know he had an audience. But then he turned away from me, facing the rising sun, and began peeling off his wet suit.

I'd had boyfriends who took great pride in their bodies, gym rats who lifted big, heavy weights. But their backs had nothing on a surfer whose muscles had clearly developed over a lifetime of swimming.

And, for *fuck's sake,* his shoulders were broad. I watched the muscles play under his skin as he peeled the wet suit off his right arm, then his left. And then down, down his body, stopping just where his ass began.

His waist was tiny compared to his shoulders, and two little dimples rested right above his hips. His biceps bulged as he lifted his arms over his head, stretching, rolling his neck from side to side, warming himself in the sun. The ocean must have been frigid.

And then The Surfer turned and began walking right toward me.

My eyes narrowed as his face came into focus. Shaggy hair, a bit of scruff. Full lips tilting up into... that smile.

"No," I said, hands to my mouth. I kept them on his face, trying desperately to ignore the rippling of his abs or his gorgeous chest.

"No, no, no," I said again, standing and grabbing my blanket and thermos. He could not realize I was watching him. Because The Surfer, the man I'd been watching for months, the man I'd just been casually fantasizing about, the man who was appearing in my dreams, was Finn *fucking* Travis—archnemesis.

He was close enough now to see me, and it was obvious that he had. His head tilted, all that blond hair in his eyes. My fingers itched to brush it away.

Finn called out to me, and I ignored it, rushing up the beach to the stairs that would take me to the Playa Vieja parking lot.

"Avery?" His voice again, louder this time.

I tripped a little in the sand. I ran up the stairs like my life depended on it, which, in my sleep-addled, sex-deprived mind, I'd convinced myself it did. Or, if not my life, at least my pride.

I reached my car and glanced back at the beach, praying he wasn't looking.

He was. Of *course* he was. I was too far away to read his expression, but it burned right through me anyway. I shivered again, and not from the wind.

This was *not* good.

I just barely made it home to shower and change. And then embarked on the long, drawn-out punishment of my drive to work. Every red-light mocked me. Every stop forced me to contemplate why, why, *why* I'd been secretly spying on Finn this entire time. And now dreaming about him.

53

My slight obsession with The Surfer hadn't really both-ered me, although I'd been a little worried it would lead me down the rabbit hole of my past. Ever since I left *everything* behind to come to San Diego when I was eighteen, any interaction with the types of people that reminded me of home (and that definitely included surfers) left a bad taste in my mouth, like old, copper pennies.

But it was so relaxing to watch him—and the past two years had been so fucking *stressful*—that any moment of peace, no matter how small, was something I clung to tightly.

I turned into the office parking lot, the chants of the protesters already seeping into the car. I parked, thinking. I was dreading going to work *and* seeing Finn. A tiny part of myself had looked forward to our daily interactions—he was a tangible way of letting my frustrations out, and I always felt better talking to him. *After* talking to him. Not during.

Not for the first time, I longed for another person to share everything with. I'd been too busy working in college to develop a close circle of friends. And once the Bella View hired me, I was devoted to my job, desperate to impress Sal with my work ethic. When he stayed late (which was every night), I tried to as well—it was one of the reasons, I'm sure, that he'd chosen me for this huge project. One of the ways I could rise above the other employees and prove that I was worthy of a promotion. Worthy of moving across the country to a place that didn't have... well, that didn't have people like *Finn*.

Usually in moments like this, I'd think of The Surfer, but as my thoughts slid his way, arousal flared through me, hot and searching. The fragments of my dreams paired with Finn's abs—and chest and shoulders and back—had me panting. His body should be illegal, especially for someone as horny and overworked as me.

I walked toward the protest, nerves frayed. *Not good, not good, not good,* I repeated to myself. After the vote, I would go find some CEO and have a night of hot, sweaty, tangled-sheets sex. The kind I'd fantasized about, not the kind I'd had. He'd talk about his ambitions and stock options. I'd tell him about my future penthouse in New York. We'd fuck. He'd leave. And I would have worked whatever *this* was out of my system.

As I reached the courtyard, I passed Marla and Jack, who looked, for a moment, kind of tired.

"Hello," I said, eyes tracking over their faces. I sometimes forgot they were older—older than my parents.

"Hello, Avery," Marla responded, but it lacked her usual enthusiasm. "How are you this morning?"

"Um... fine," I responded. "What do the signs say today?" Jack held his up higher: *The Bella View Hotels: Conservation My Ass.*

I bit back a laugh, surprised at my own response. "Oh, I see you saw my interview last night?"

Marla shook her head. "Yes, and you should be ashamed of yourself." Being lectured by Marla and Jack was like being lectured by your kindly, elderly grandparents. It lacked any heat.

"Okay, well... nice to see you," I said, rolling my eyes. They made me feel like a teenager.

"And drink some water! You look dehydrated!" Jack called after me. I nodded back at them, then vaguely wondered when I'd last had anything to drink except coffee.

I made my way through about fifty protesters, grouped together. They usually ignored me, focused on the bigger picture. It was just Finn who focused all of his ire directly at me.

Two reporters were converged on Finn, about ten feet in front of me. He was wearing his usual uniform, and as he brushed his still-wet hair from his eyes, I heard him say, "Which is why, ultimately, I believe we will win. Because we fight on the side of justice. We're fighting for what's *right*."

And just like that, any residual arousal left in a flash. How this Phish-loving, pot-smoking, barefoot, dirty, naive, beach-bum hippie had invaded *my* dreams was beyond me.

Finn finished speaking and then turned, pinning me with his gaze. I swallowed, then propped a hand on my hip, one eyebrow arched. A lazy, heated grin spread across his face. Knowing. He tipped his head at me, as in *all yours*.

Just like that, the cameras turned, reporters hustling to my side with microphones in my face. I kept my eyes on Finn. He crossed his arms across his chest.

"Ms. Dacosta, any comments from the Bella View? Any changes from yesterday?"

"No," I responded calmly. "We were thankful that the San Diego *Nightly News* took this issue seriously and allowed me to come on and talk to the public about the importance of this kind of development. Other than that, I'd just like to reiterate that we intend to win. Because I'm fighting for what's *best* for Playa Vieja." With that, I strode past them, begging off any other interviews.

I stopped when I came to Finn, who had moved from staring at me to the front door. He was sprawled out, all long legs and long arms, in a beach chair with an umbrella. A fucking umbrella.

"Where do you think you are? An amusement park?" I said before I could stop myself.

"Mornin', Avery," he drawled in response, squinting his

eyes against the sun. I tried not to get distracted by how blue they were. He leaned forward in the chair, and I could feel his body heat against my legs.

"You sure got an eyeful earlier this morning," he said, eyes dancing. There was something else in his gaze—a challenge.

"I did," I said slowly, turning away. "And I was *not* impressed." I walked to the door and yanked it open, harder than I meant to. The sound of his husky laughter followed me all the way down the hallway.

8

FINN

J leaned back in the booth, Sharpie in hand, and held up the poster I was working on. I'd glued a picture of Avery's face next to a cut-out of Satan.

"Too dramatic?" I asked Marla and Jack. They were sitting next to me in what I considered "our booth" in the back of the Paradise Cafe.

"Whatever you want, dear," Marla said, coloring away on her own sign. I thought about what Rico said, the morning he'd told me about the Bella View, begging me not to get his parents involved. And yet, here they were—as dedicated as always. And Rico, who'd postponed flying back to Costa Rica, was out there with me more often than not.

"You can't be too dramatic when it comes to Mother Earth," Jack said, nodding sagely. I smiled, winked at them.

"You're damn right. Drama it is, then."

I waved over Hope and Derek, who both greeted Jake behind the counter, grabbed a giant mug of coffee, and slid next to us in the booth.

Hope gave me a mock salute, and I smiled, reaching over to squeeze her shoulder. "We missed you two this morning."

Hope grabbed a strawberry from the giant, communal plate of food in front of us. "Parent-teacher conferences, you know the drill." She looked over at Derek, who nodded wearily. Hope and Derek were two born and raised Playa Vieja natives who owned the organic produce shop next to the surf shop my dad and I owned. Hope was a Black woman with curly hair, dark eyes and a warm smile. Her partner, Derek, was a tall white man with bright red hair and glasses.

Like Marla and Jack, they were out there with me every day. And Hope and Derek did it on top of parenting their triplets.

"You two are amazing," I said, shaking my head. "This protest has disrupted my entire life, and I don't even have children, let alone three."

They both waved me off, and Hope bit into another strawberry.

"I've never felt more passionately about anything," Derek said, motioning for the server. "Plus, we're near the finish line now."

"That's actually what I wanted to talk about," I started. The size of the protest had swelled up to eight hundred people one time—Avery had been *furious* that day. But then, on some days, it had just been me. On average, though, a fairly steady fifty to a hundred and fifty folks were out there, waving signs, chanting. Taking time off from work. Finding babysitters (or, shit, bringing their kids with them). They were out there no matter what—when they were sick, when they had better things to do, when their personal lives were hectic.

"This morning, I was contacted by UC San Diego. They want Avery and me to debate in front of an audience in two weeks—next Friday. I wanted to talk strategy a little—"

"Hey there, heroes," Libby, our server, interrupted. She smiled broadly, giving me a knowing look. We'd hooked up a couple of times a few years ago, and every time I was in the café, she made it quite clear that she was still interested.

I smiled back at her, let everyone else place their orders. Over the din of the restaurant, my ears picked up the daily surf report on the radio—my body tilted for it, the sound as soothing as a lullaby. The majority of people in here were local surfers, and the air was thick with the combined smells of sunscreen and salt water.

"Just coffee for me," I told Libby. "And thanks for the food." I hadn't paid for a meal here in years.

"It's all on the house, doll," she said. "Always. And how are things going over there? I saw you—" She pointed at me. "—on the news last night."

I shrugged. "Same as always, I guess. I think we're having a good impact, but I haven't seen polling numbers lately."

"Polling numbers are slightly in our favor still," Hope chimed in.

"Good," Libby said, tucking her pad of paper into her apron. "If they build a hotel on that beach, we are *fucked*."

I laughed as my eyes caught on the surf videos they played constantly behind the counter. Most folks wouldn't know it, but from the style of that surfer, I was pretty certain it was an old video of my dad.

"So strategy," I started again, and all four of them turned back to me. "What do you guys think about getting people out to the debate?"

"We could amp up flyering, attending neighborhood meetings," Hope said. "Derek and I could head over to the city tomorrow, get people interested. People would want to see you debate, Finn."

My stomach clenched, just a little. The phone call about the debate this morning had made me incredibly nervous. And I was going toe-to-toe against Avery. When I'd re-watched our interview this morning, I was sure she'd come off better than me.

"Perfect," I managed to say. "Other than that..."

"Just keep doing the damn thing," Marla chimed in happily.

I looked at her and Jack. They looked exhausted.

"Why don't the two of you stay home the next couple of days? It's been hot, and your hands from the drums..."

She snorted. "I wouldn't leave that courtyard if the fucking building was on fire." Jack nodded, smiling at his wife with so much love it hurt to look at it.

"Well, okay then. We've been getting pretty good press, huh?"

"Perfect press." Marla reached over and pressed a hand to my cheek. "You're doing such a good thing. Has your father told you that recently?"

I laughed. "My parents have been telling me that since the day I was born."

She tilted her head. "Good. Where is your dad today, anyway?"

"Surfing. I told him the waves were pretty good this morning, and he thought he'd try some afternoon swells out near the docks. I'm on duty at the shop the rest of the day."

Food came, and while everyone else was distracted, I glanced back at the sign I'd been making. I'd printed out a couple of pictures of Avery but couldn't decide which one to use next. They were attractive, but I was finding that photos didn't really do her justice.

Not that I'd noticed.

Avery was the exact opposite of most of the women—

most of the people—I surrounded myself with every day. Corporate, big money, not at all rooting for the little guy.

My community was comprised almost entirely of easy-going surfers and the radical commune members my parents lived with. And, as for women I dated, well, I usually went for surfers, Roxy models, and the random European tourists I met at bars in San Diego. Fun. Easy. Summer flings.

But today Avery had done something new.

Surprised me.

I'd felt eyes on me when I'd surfed out by the rocks at the end of the beach—the far end, where almost no one goes. I'm used to having an audience—when I surfed in more popular areas, a little following of admirers would come out. And at Titans of Mavericks, a good portion of the world watched.

So, no, it didn't bother me that someone was watching me. But I was curious about this dark-haired woman spying on me. Today was the day I could finally see her, just a little. I kept getting distracted by the graceful tilt of her neck, the way the wind tugged at her hair.

And she had *so much* hair. She kept trying to pull it down across her shoulders. But then the wind would whip it up again.

I had a little kink about hair. Something about the way it brushed against my chest when a woman straddled me. Something about the way it felt in my fingers when I yanked on it.

And... I might have given her a little show. She was watching after all, and the dirty exhibitionist inside of me liked it. Peeling down my wet suit like her own private strip tease.

But when I walked closer and saw it was *Avery*? You could have knocked me over with a feather.

Especially since I was under the impression that she thought I was the worst thing that had ever happened to her.

Especially since I thought Avery Dacosta was a goddamn *nightmare*.

But the worst part about this morning had been the way she tossed a glance at me before getting in her car. That perfect blend of defiance and anger—it had my cock twitching inside my wet suit.

Traitor.

Maybe... just maybe this morning when she'd walked past me, I'd noticed the deep mahogany color of her hair. And every day, it was pinned up high on her head in a tight bun, like Audrey Hepburn.

And maybe... just maybe this morning I'd also noticed how beautiful her big, dark brown eyes were.

I felt my cock twitch again as I pasted a giant devil next to Avery's face on the poster.

Traitor. Jesus.

"That Avery sure is pretty, huh, Finn?" Marla asked kindly, tiny bits of Sharpie marker dotting her arm like constellations.

"What?" I said, startled. "What are you talking about?"

"Avery. The developer. The woman whose photo you've been staring longingly at for the past twenty minutes? She's quite pretty. She's just a little..."

"Has a stick up her ass?" This was Jack.

"Something like that," I murmured, certain I'd only been staring at her photo for *five* minutes. When was the last time I'd gotten laid? Because the only way I could possibly find

A very attractive would be if every other woman in the world had simply vanished.

"You've got an audience over there, Finn." Jack winked, nodding at the bar. A woman was spinning gently on the stool, looking at me coyly.

"You should go and say hello," Hope said, grinning. "Greet your adoring fan." I shook my head, standing. Ever since I'd gotten my first sponsorship at the age of nineteen, being recognized was still a trip. Winning Titans last year had only increased the phenomenon.

I stood. "I'll be right back, promise." What made it worse was the fact she was sitting under a giant photo of me hanging on the wall.

"Hey there," I said, extending out a hand to her. "I'm Finn." She was blonde, tan and pretty.

She smiled softly, shaking my hand. "I'm Julie. And I know who you are," she said. "I'm actually a pretty big fan."

"Oh... thanks," I said. I still didn't know how to respond when people said that. It was too easy to come off as an egotistical asshole.

"I saw you compete at Mavericks. 'You must be totally fearless,'" she said, laughing. I laughed back. I got 'you must be totally fearless' a lot. "I never saw waves as big as that before," she said. "I'm definitely more into the smaller ones."

"Just as challenging," I said. "And often can be just as dangerous."

Julie nodded, shrugging. "I guess. You won Pipeline Masters in Waimea too, right?"

"Not every time. I've been beaten a ton by much better surfers. But once, sure. I won. That was a pretty gnarly wave too."

"Aren't you afraid?" She took a sip of her coffee, blue eyes watching mine.

"Fucking terrified," I said truthfully. I remembered the sound those giant waves made, right before they hit. The silence was its own kind of roar, the calm before a storm of water pounded you beneath the foam. Taming something that wild was its own kind of drug.

"Honestly, though," I continued. "I always listen to the fear, to my gut instinct. I believe it's saved my life hundreds of times over the years."

There was an awkward silence. I thought about Avery, the way I'd responded to her this morning. Lately, I'd been feeling amped up and edgy, the endless, infuriating interactions with her leaving me buzzing with energy. And not in a good way. A date with a cute surfer might be just what I needed.

"Hey, this might seem a little forward, but do you want to come join a protest with me?" I asked, hands in my pockets.

Her smile dazzled. "I'd love to."

Fun. Easy. Flings.

9

AVERY

*J*t had been three days since I saw Finn on the beach—and I'd worked hard to forget about it. Distracted myself with work, media interviews, meetings with architects and PR companies. I had to keep going as if the permits were going to pass. As if I wasn't spending every night suddenly terrified that the Bella View was going to lose.

This morning, Finn was sprawled in that damn beach chair, holding a sign that had my face on it. He was talking to someone else, laughing as usual. He wore a white linen button-up shirt. I watched as he chatted, undoing the buttons at his wrists and rolling up his sleeves—one, two, three rolls until he cinched the fabric at his elbows.

I could see the blond hairs on his forearm. His wrists were broad, and I'd never noticed how long his fingers were. The muscles in his forearms rippled.

All that swimming.

He looked away from his friend and directly at me. I'd snuck into work extra early the past few days, avoiding seeing him. Avoiding his smug look and any residual embarrassment I might feel from having him know I was spying on him.

Although, really, if I'd known The Surfer was Finn, I wouldn't have come within ten miles of that damn beach.

Now, as I neared him, I felt his gaze over every inch of my body. A caress. The corner of his lips tugged up.

"Does that sign indicate I am *Satan*, Mr. Travis?" I asked, pointing my finger. My photo was juxtaposed next to a red, horned devil.

"You know, I asked Marla and Jack if it was too dramatic. They thought otherwise. Oh, and while you're here, can I ask your opinion on a few things?"

"No," I said.

"Great," he continued. "I was going to invite some fire-dancers out. Maybe a jam band? You know, really bring home the whole 'hippie surfer' vibe."

"And I swear to *God,* I will have all of them arrested," I shot back. "Including you, Mr. Travis."

Finn looked suddenly serious—actually, he looked pissed. A small tendril of arousal curled low in my belly. His blue eyes flashed, and his jaw hardened.

But then something happened. He seemed to catch it—or at least repress it. And then he laughed, a low rumble that caught in his chest. The small tendril grew.

"When did you switch back to calling me 'Mr. Travis'?"

"Excuse me?"

"Well, it's just that I'd think, *after* you watched me strip on a beach, you'd feel less formal, not more. Just a thought." He paused. "Avery." He said my name like an insult.

I fought the urge to bend down and get in his face. Instead, I stayed standing over him, enjoying the power. "Oh, please. Are you still hung up on that? Because I've forgotten all about it." I looked him up and down, dismissive. "I mean, really. Not much to remember."

He looked pissed again, but I swept inside before he could say anything.

I HEARD Sal coming down the hallway and prepared myself. He'd been at off-site meetings for three days and hadn't spoken to me yet about my and Finn's interview *or* our upcoming debate.

"Finn's interview on the *Nightly News* was better than yours," Sal bellowed. I looked up, nervous. He was leaning against the doorway, fiddling with his phone. "Also, do you know how to text a photo to someone? My wife doesn't believe me when I tell her I have literally three hundred emails to answer before coming home tonight. I thought if I took a picture of my inbox she might lay off." He tapped his chin. "Although, really, I doubt it."

"Um... well, yes, of course I can text a photo for you." I eyed him warily. "And what did you say about the *Nightly News* interview? I thought I was doing well with the media." All of a sudden, it felt like everything I did for the Bella View was wrong.

Sal sauntered in, sitting on the edge of my desk. "Finn comes off as folksy. You come off as..."

I tilted my head, waiting.

"Robotic," he finished.

"You mean smart," I said, before I could stop myself.

"So tell me about this debate we got offered," he said, changing the subject.

"I think it could be a really good thing, actually," I said. "It's through UC San Diego. They want Finn and me to talk about the pros and cons of construction on Playa Vieja. You know, get the constituents riled up." While local citizens couldn't vote on the permitting process, they could make the lives of the city council members hell if they didn't vote the way the public wanted. Polling numbers were important to the members, especially with an election just four months away. Current polling numbers showed a slight uptick against the construction, so we needed the debate to generate all the goodwill we could get.

"They're holding it in their largest lecture hall. They expect three hundred and fifty people to attend." And I had to win.

"You worried about it?" He shot me one of his good-ole-boys grins, and I smiled back, desperate for his approval.

"Of course not. I'm not worried at all," I answered smoothly. That might have been the biggest lie of my professional life.

"Just... be nicer than Finn. He's got that, you know, charming personality thing."

"I have a charming personality," I said, glaring at the back of Finn's head. I'd forgotten to close my blinds, and I could see him there, sitting in his chair, holding up his *Avery is Satan* sign.

"Mm-hmmm," Sal said, noncommittal. "Plus, regardless of how it really goes, we have the whole 'shit-ton of money' thing in our favor."

"True," I said. "And I really haven't heard Finn, or anyone else, come up with a solid source of revenue for that community yet." I tapped my finger against my desk. "Maybe that's what I really hit them with at the debate? They keep swinging with the environment, but so far they've been pretty quiet on the economic issues. Maybe I need to emphasize the job creation."

It wouldn't be hard to passionately defend it in front of hundreds of people. Because I believed in it.

Sal snapped his fingers at me. "That's good, Avery, really good." I smiled again. "Hey, you want to grab drinks with the guys tonight? We were going to head to Malloy's, drink some whiskey." My pulse sped up, just a bit. Malloy's was where all the Bella View executives went to drink and, I don't know, avoid their husbands and wives. Sal had spoken to me about it before but never invited me.

"I thought you had to answer hundreds of emails?" I asked.

He shrugged, laughing. "I can do that drunk. Plus, I think both the kids have soccer games tonight, so they won't miss me."

Jesus, I thought. We didn't play soccer when I was a kid, but my parents were at least always around. Not in the way I wanted them to be, but still.

"O-okay," I said. "You know I'd actually love to go to Malloy's, but I was also going to stay late, get prepped for that meeting with the council members?" I wasn't sure what was better for my potential, future promotion: get drunk with the executives or prove my work ethic was better than everyone else's.

"Ah, shit," Sal said, his head falling into his hands. "I forgot all about that meeting. When is it again?"

"Two days from now," I said, nodding at the giant stack of papers I'd been carrying around for a week.

"You prepped?"

"Very," I said, feeling the exhaustion of poor sleep and too much stress. But I wanted more time.

"You haven't heard anything else about what this is about, right?"

"You'd be the first person I tell." The meeting was

shrouded in mystery, one of the reasons I'd been working so hard to prepare for it. It could literally be about anything. Our relationship with the city council had always been great —friendly and prosperous. This project, however, was proving everything to be wrong.

Sal knocked his fingers against the desk. "Can you meet later today to review?"

"Sure," I said, somewhat wearily. "Later in the afternoon?"

He nodded, looking at me. For a second, I wanted to bring up the promotion, get some sense of affirmation and relief. Ever since he'd admonished me for being "too slow" on reacting to the protest, he'd been vague about what would happen after the vote, either avoiding the question altogether or giving me some kind of company line.

The problem was that as soon as he'd dangled the opportunity in front of me, I hadn't been able to stop thinking about it. I glanced at the photo of my parents on my desk. I didn't want to go back there or any place like it. San Diego was starting to feel too much like home, and at night I scrolled through apartment listings in New York City... Paris... London. Someplace with a bite in the air and a heavy dose of rationalism and reality.

"Sal—" I started to say, but he glanced at his phone, avoiding me.

"Sorry, Avery. I think the wife is calling." He grimaced, looking a little green around the gills. "I'll see you later in the day to review? You'll have to carry a lot of the meeting since I'll probably start drinking early." He laughed at that, crashing back down the hallway.

I collapsed back into my chair, unsure how I should feel about that entire interaction. Was I doing well? Was I fucking everything up?

I heard voices and looked out the window. Finn was standing up, and my eyes followed the strong lines of his back down to his narrow waist. He reached up to scratch his head, and his biceps bulged.

He was chatting with a pretty blonde woman who looked fun-loving and relaxed. She was like a female version of Finn.

And he was definitely getting her number.

I DIDN'T LEAVE the office until after eight. I was tired, so tired, but the thought of sleeping had my heart racing. Insomnia. I'd had it bad before, so I knew the drill. Just had to wait it out.

But these next weeks would be the most important of my career, and I needed to be giving a hundred and twenty-five percent, if not more.

And when I walked outside into the courtyard, Finn was standing there. Waiting for me.

"Long day, huh?" he asked. I'd never seen him here this late, and it was startlingly quiet as I walked to the car, the sudden absence of the protesters feeling strange. The sun was setting behind him, making his tan skin look even darker. He pushed his hair out of his eyes and smiled.

My knees weakened, just a little.

"Why are you talking to me?" I bit out, moving past him. "Isn't it time for you to go home?"

"I was going to walk you to your car."

"Please don't," I said.

He paused, chuckling. "Um, okay. I'll just walk a few feet behind you until coincidentally we reach your car."

I ignored him, striding through the parking lot. I couldn't remember if these pants made my ass look good.

"You didn't ask me about my day."

"I couldn't care less," I snapped.

"Well, my day was pretty good, I guess. Long. We got some new blood coming through, which is good. I'm a little worried about Marla and Jack."

I reached my car, speaking without thinking. "I am too, actually. They look tired. I noticed that the other day."

Then I stopped. Finn looked delighted at my response. "Yeah, yeah, they do. Thought they could use a break. I told them the same thing."

"Not that I care," I said hurriedly. I clearly needed sleep. As if I cared about the elderly protesters currently ruining my life.

He took a step toward me, and I leaned into my car, trying to put as much space between us as possible. He noticed, and his eyes flared.

"I'm not going to bite, Avery."

"I know. I just... why are you talking to me? We're not friends."

He shrugged, taking another step closer. "I liked talking with you on the couch, before our interview. Why does it always have to be an argument?"

"Right," I said, crossing my arms in front of my chest. "You liked talking to me on the couch, but this morning you chanted 'Avery is Satan' for hours." I tilted my head. "We're not friends," I repeated.

"You're right. Friends don't watch each other strip on the beach," he said, taking another small step closer.

I felt my cheeks flush and was grateful for the dim light. "I have bad insomnia, and I go to those rocks when I can't sleep. You don't own Playa Vieja as much as you think you do."

"I don't think that. Not at all. None of us own any part of the earth. It's why I don't think you should build a hotel there," he responded.

"But the house you live in right on the beach, that was built there, is okay? You get your nice sea view, but others don't?"

He opened his mouth, then closed it. "That's different," he said.

I turned around, unlocking my car. When I turned back, he was even closer. Our feet were *this close* to touching.

"It's not, and you know it. Change is inevitable, Finn. You can't stop it. And you can't blame me. If it wasn't me, you'd be arguing with some other hotel developer in this parking lot."

Something flashed over his face, and some of the irritation melted away. Replaced by flirtation. "Does this other hotel developer also watch me strip on the beach?"

"You're deflecting," I pointed out. "And you're not going to use that Finn Travis charm on me, just so you know."

He stepped one single inch closer, sliding his bare foot between my high heels. I moved back, stopped by the hard body of the car.

"You think I'm charming?" His eyes searched mine. Goddamn, they were blue.

"*I* don't think you're charming. But the media does. And..." I said, tilting my head. "So does my boss. He's instructed me to beat you at the charm game next Friday."

"Oh," he said, a slow grin spreading across his face. "You mean the debate. You ready?"

I turned around, no longer trusting myself around his

body heat. That smile. Those eyes. I grabbed the door handle.

Finn's breath stirred the back of my hair. "You're not going to deign to respond to that, Avery?"

I scoffed, "You know what the word '*deign*' means?"

He paused, long enough that I turned back around before I could stop myself.

"Yes. And you're mean when you're tired," he said simply. I yanked the door open and slid in but then regretted it. It forced me to look up at him, something I didn't want to do.

"What was the point of this conversation again?"

He grabbed the car door with one hand, leaning into it. He was so freaking tall.

"Nothing. Just... I don't know. I wanted to tell you I know about the debate and for you to bring your A-game." His eyes narrowed, and he went back to being serious.

I snorted. "Never stopped bringing it, Finn."

I tried to close the door, but he stopped me, holding tight. Then he crouched down until we were eye-level. His hand moved forward, like he wanted to stroke my hair, but stopped, pulling back. Finn looked mildly embarrassed, which I enjoyed.

But also... *what the fuck?*

"You look really tired, Avery. I don't know why I care, but I do."

"That's stupid," I said.

He *almost* smiled. "You have insomnia?"

"Ye-yeah."

"My mom did too. Bad. She used to drink this tea that helped. I still have some of it. I'll drop it off at your house tonight, but I promise I'll just leave it on your door step. You won't even see me."

"You... you don't know where I live," I said, stunned.

He laughed softly. "Well, why don't you tell me?"

I rattled off my address like a robot, unsure why or how things with Finn had gone from *mildly annoying* to *really annoying... but also sexy* in a matter of days. If only I hadn't seen his body. If only I hadn't admired him in the waves. If only he wasn't torturing me in my dreams.

If only.

He stood, hands in his pockets. For a second, he looked unsure, which was so not like him. Then he grinned, cocky again, and gave a mock salute. "See you on the battlefield tomorrow morning. Same time as today?"

I rolled my eyes and slammed my car door.

And watched him walk away for longer than I wanted to.

10

FINN

$\mathcal{I}$ was standing on Avery's porch, finger hovering over the doorbell.

All night I'd battled a whiplash sensation, playing my conversation with her over and over again.

You know what the word 'deign' means?

Avery Dacosta wasn't the first woman to think I wasn't smart. In fact, that might be the final mistake she made before our debate.

She was fucking infuriating. And *so* not my type. And yet, here I was, bringing her a solution to her insomnia like some kind of... *boyfriend.*

The power I'd had in this situation slipped through my fingers like sand. Because, standing on her porch, I realized I could see her through the gauzy pattern of her curtains. She was curled up on the couch, hair in a messy bun. Her glasses were perched in her hair, pen in her mouth. Her fingers flew over a keyboard.

I ached for her. It was nearing midnight.

I watched as the strap of her tank top slipped down her

shoulder. My eyes traced the soft curve of her skin there, her delicate collarbone. My finger hovered again.

What if I stayed? What if Avery opened the door, sleepy and messy and gorgeous, and I told her the truth?

You make me angrier than anyone I've ever known. And I think I want to kiss you.

More than that, now. I wanted Avery up against her door, every inch of her lean curves pressed against mine. I wanted those legs wrapped around my waist, hair loose around her shoulders.

I wanted to kiss her—*no*... I wanted Avery to kiss *me*. Desperate and frantic, like I was the oxygen she needed to breathe.

Not that I cared or *should* care. I dropped my parcel on Avery's welcome mat, rang the doorbell, and left, just like I'd promised.

My phone vibrated in my pocket. I slipped it out, seeing a text from Julie agreeing to get coffee with me. I really, *really* needed to get laid. And Julie was exactly the fun, easy fling I needed.

11

AVERY

I couldn't sleep. And I blamed Finn.

Because if he hadn't come along, I was pretty goddamn sure I wouldn't be planning for a mystery meeting with the city council.

And our conversation had left me unsettled.

You're mean when you're tired.

I felt bad, a little. We'd been flinging barbs at each other for weeks now, but they were always so outrageous they never seemed to land. Not really.

I shifted on the couch, uncomfortable. I hated thinking about Finn. I hated having him under my skin. I hated wishing he'd reached out those big, strong hands and stroked my hair. I would have leaned into his touch, seeking. I would have loved it.

I heard my doorbell and then the sound of a car driving away.

Finn.

I slipped outside, pulling my robe tighter against the evening breeze. There, in the middle of my welcome mat, was a small box.

I picked it up, sniffing. St. John's wort. Inside, the satchels were nestled together, a slender assortment of ten or so. I smiled. I couldn't help it.

I ran my fingers over them, imagining Finn doing the same thing. And then my eye caught something buried beneath the satchels.

"What the—" I said out loud, tilting the box over into my hand. Satchels fell, some landing on my palm and others scattering around my feet like dead leaves.

And there, in the middle, was a long, white joint.

12

FINN

*T*here is nothing more human than surfing.

The balance. Bare feet on a slippery board. The white crest of the foam. The roar of the waves, as sharp and urgent as a freight train. The sense of flying and falling at the same time.

Or, in my case, actually falling. I'd popped up on a wave, my fingertips just grazing the swell, when I thought I saw a figure on the beach. *Avery.*

So I nose-dived into the water like an amateur. It was always a shock, no matter how many times it happened. I felt the leash tug painfully on my right ankle, the wave pushing me down deeper, forcing water up my nose. I had a brief, panicky moment of disorientation before righting myself.

My head rose out of the water, and I took a huge gulping breath. I found my board, pulled myself onto it, and spit up half a bucket of ocean water. "Shit," I said, glancing at the figure on the beach. Who wasn't Avery at all.

It was my dad. I straddled my board and watched him paddle out to me, all gray hair and long, gray beard. Behind him, Playa Vieja glowed pink with the sunrise. I glanced about a half-mile down the beach, where the Bella View Hotel would begin construction if the permits were approved. The view was idyllic—a long stretch of palm trees and wild bougainvillea, oleander and birds of paradise.

"Mornin'," he called out cheerfully, nearing me. "They were serving grits at the commune this morning, so I came out here instead."

"Breakfast burritos at Maria's after this?"

"Gladly," he said, smiling. He swam over to give me a clumsy hug in the waves.

"Hey, I saw you on TV the other night," he said.

I gave him a mock salute. "Finn Travis, local rabble-rouser, at your service."

"That Avery is something else, huh?"

Tell me about it.

"I don't know," I shrugged. "She's your typical Big Business Bad Guy."

He tilted his head at me. "She's smart as a whip, Finn. You're debating with her next week?"

"Yep."

"It's gonna be a packed house. You've done a good job of getting people angry," he said.

"Which I hate, by the way. I hate being angry."

His board bumped against mine. In the water, I felt a tiny fish nibbling at my suit.

"This is important, though. And she's going to wipe the floor with you."

I laughed out loud. "No confidence, huh?"

"Oh, Finn, usually I have supreme confidence in you. But you just might have met your match with this one." He ran his hand down his beard, thinking. "She's pretty."

"Why does everyone keep telling me that?"

He looked amused. "Who else? Marla and Jack?"

I turned away, glancing at a wave up ahead. "You want this one?"

He slid off his board, paddling quickly. "Totally."

I let him swim past me, watching. It was a good wave, and he caught it easily. I could watch my dad surf all day. He was a local celebrity in his own right.

Suddenly the wind shifted, and the wave shifted, just slightly, and his board skipped. He lost his balance.

My heart stopped for a quick second as he slipped beneath the water. It always did when he fell.

But then he broke the surface, shrugging it off. Laughing as the sun kept rising over Playa Vieja, and for a moment, all was right with the world.

WHEN I WAS four years old, my dad tossed me into the ocean and said, "Swim."

I swam.

We'd surf together—small waves, where I clung to his shoulders, my mother waving at us from the beach.

When I was nine, he gave me my first surfboard. Moments later, I experienced firsthand the power of the ocean. My dad wasn't too far away—every time a good wave came, he'd yell, "Up! Up!" when it was time. I waited until I could feel the wave curling just under me, pushing upwards.

I stood up, free. Gracefully. And nose-dived.

I'd been swimming in that ocean for five years at that point and had been knocked down plenty of times. This time a two-wave set hit me at once, and under the waves, the board got stuck, holding me down. All I remember was the most intense feeling of confusion I'd ever had and a very, very small worry that I was going to drown.

My dad's strong arms lifted me up and out, and for a few days afterward, I wondered if he was God. Later that night, still coughing up a bit of ocean water, my dad and I took a walk on the beach.

"That fall was important today," he told me. "Even though I know you were scared."

"Well, I'll probably never fall again, so..." I'd said, brash with a nine-year-old's sense of confidence.

He smiled, didn't laugh. He never laughed at me. "If it does happen again, you should remember that the ocean always wins, Finn." He squatted down until we were eye-level. "I'm serious," he said. Behind him, the waves of Playa Vieja had crashed against the sand. "She's more powerful than you by a lot, and she doesn't dole out second chances. Don't be foolish when you're on that board."

I smiled at the sudden memory, loving the sun on my skin. The familiar chatter of Maria's Taqueria. The coffee in my hand. Except, for whatever reason, my dad's face was drawn with worry. On the drive over, he seemed to shrink into himself. And now he was quiet—too quiet.

"Is everything okay? You seem a little weird," I said, fiddling with my napkin.

The look on his face worsened. "I have to talk to you about something, Finn. And I should have spoken to you about it sooner." A strange feeling settled in my stomach.

"So talk to me," I said, tilting my head. He'd never looked so serious.

"It's about the shop." He paused, seemed to gather his thoughts. "Sales have been down over the past few years, and really they've never gone up the way they had in the nineties. And the past six months have been particularly bad."

I nodded since we'd spoken about this before. "Sure, but they'll come back up again. Right?"

The ugly truth was that over the past two months, I'd barely given our surf shop a second thought. I was too caught up in the protest. I'd hired a couple guys to fill in for me and, except for using the shop as ground zero for protest meetings, I was hardly there.

He nodded, glancing out at the waves. "True. But this one... Finn, this one is more of a pattern, not a fluke. Surf shops, well, surf shops back in the day in San Diego, were cultural. A place for locals to hang out. Talk about the conditions, the wave size. Where swell was firing. Shoot the shit. Now? Surf shops are about the tourist wanting to get some kind of rad experience. Throw on a pair of board shorts, take one lesson, and buy every single Quiksilver shirt we sell."

"True," I said slowly, although I wasn't sure about the point he was getting to. And I'd always wanted Beyond the Breakers to keep catering to locals, not tourists.

"All of that to say... and I hate to be the one that says it, but either Playa Vieja needs to change, or we need to consider closing the shop."

"Wait... *what*?"

My dad sighed—the kind of sigh that told me he had stayed up all night thinking about this. "Your mother is furious with me for even suggesting this, especially since it goes against the entire idea of the commune, but we need some tourism, Finn."

I sagged against my chair. "You want the city council to vote yes," I said, the bigger picture shifting into place. "You want the hotel to be built."

"I... Yes, I think so. Although I wish there was a better way than destroying this place we've loved so much. But surf shops these days thrive in tourism-heavy communities. They want to feel like a surfer for a day and drop a ton of money while doing it. We need that money, Finn, or we'll be out of business by the end of the year. I've run through my line of credit. There's nothing left. And this shop was basically our retirement plan."

My dad reached forward for my coffee mug, lifting it from my fingers, stealing a sip. "This is hard to say, Finn, but not everyone in Playa Vieja can be a Billabong model."

My face warmed. "I work hard for that money, Dad."

"I'm not saying you don't. It's just... more members of this community are struggling than I think you realize. It's easy to be a surf celebrity, but where will you be after the contracts stop coming in?"

I was silent, thinking. I didn't really think Playa Vieja was struggling, although Avery certainly did.

And the future, to me, had never been something to worry about.

"So if Bella View moves in, and all the other business it promises to bring, you think you'll see an uptick in sales?"

"We're the only surf shop in Playa Vieja. We've got the market cornered on that, Finn. You could give lessons even."

I'd always hated giving surf lessons. Surfing was my time —alone with my thoughts.

"We might have to," he said, more firmly, noticing the look on my face.

I ran my hand down my face, exhaled. "If that's what needs to happen, then, yeah—I'll help you do it."

"You think the council will vote yes?"

"Honestly, I have no fucking idea. Every day polls show something different. But, Dad," I said. "Why didn't you and

Mom tell me? I just spent six weeks of my life fighting against something that would benefit our family—and have another month to go of protests. If the city council votes no and we close our shop, it'll be my fault."

I swallowed against a lump in my throat. It was too much, thinking of my parents supporting the protest every day, while at night they were counting their pennies and terrified of their future.

"Oh, Finn... I wish this wasn't happening, I really do. But once I saw the writing on the wall, there was no way I could keep it a secret from you. I know it's terrible timing."

He looked at me for a second and must have seen the turmoil on my face. "To be honest, I would never interfere with something that was so important to you. Your mom and I are so incredibly proud of you. For standing up for what you believe in. For standing up for something your community needs and wants. For... well, for being the David in this David and Goliath scenario. Believe me," he said, staring at the ocean. "David may get all the praise in the end, but it's never easy to be the little guy. Ever."

"I only did what you guys taught me. All the political causes we protested... It was easy to do. It just felt right."

"Don't undermine yourself, Finn. It's hard. And will *continue* to be hard. You're putting yourself out there. Doing interviews. Making mistakes. Winning. Losing. Fighting the good fight. I don't want you feeling that, at any point in time, we felt like you were working against us. You're our son. We'd never feel that way." He paused. "Plus, it's important for kids to fight different causes than their parents sometimes. You need to be your own person. Fight for what you believe in."

I swallowed again, staring at him in disbelief. "But," I

said, choking on the words. "You expect me to keep the protest up? I don't... I can't..."

"I believe in you, Finn. What do you believe in?"

"I believe in Playa Vieja. I believe in the environment," I said, honestly. Earnestly. Hoping that belief would tether me back to something real instead of the confusion I was currently wading in. "But what if the city council votes no? What if I succeed?"

"Then we'll talk. We'll figure something out after we close the shop. Or, hey, maybe you can work your magic on Avery and get her to try and open another hotel for us?" The lines around his mouth told me it'd be worse than that.

"And if they vote yes?"

"A lot of change will be coming our way. A little good. A little bad. Just like life. We'll make it work."

"Why did you tell me if you don't want me to stop what I'm doing?"

He looked away for a second, toward the ocean view of the restaurant. "A few reasons. I didn't want to lie to you. And I wanted you to know some of the other impacts that this fight might have, beyond what you know." He looked at me. "And I've learned a lot over the years as an activist. Most notably? That shit can be *complicated*. If you're going to do this, and I sincerely hope you do, you need to understand the complexities. Carry that weight. Do you understand?"

He stood, crossed over the table, and pulled me up and into a sideways hug, just like when I was a kid and I'd come running—after a nightmare, after a bully at school, after a nasty wave slapped me right out of the air like a fly.

"You going to be okay?" A few people were staring at us, but my dad had never been sparse with his affection.

"I mean... no?" I laughed, the sudden absurdity of this situation too much. "But also, yes?"

He laughed too. "Sounds about right."

An hour later at the protest site, I greeted Marla and Jack with two cups of coffee I'd picked up for them along the way. I was still in shock from the conversation with my dad and unsure what to do about it. But standing here, surrounded by the people I loved, I felt a little better.

But just a little.

"Avery's not here yet, just so you know," Marla said.

"I couldn't care less about that," I replied. She gave me the most knowing look.

I set up my chair and umbrella since it seemed to piss Avery off so much. I chatted with some of the new protesters. My phone buzzed; it was Julie, sending me something cute.

Fun and easy. And maybe the perfect person to take my mind off recent... *complexities*. And Avery.

Speaking of. I glanced at my watch and noticed it was past 8:00 a.m. She was usually here by now.

A lone reporter hung by the sides. The media attention seemed to ebb and flow based on what else was going on, but the local papers were always down for a quote.

"Can I help you?" I asked. He didn't look familiar.

"Oh, um... yeah. I'm Tim?"

"Is that a question?"

He blushed. "Oh, no, I mean that's my name."

"I'm Finn," I said, extending my hand. "It's nice to meet you."

"Oh, I know who you are," he said, shaking it. "I work for UCSD's campus newspaper. I'm a surfer. All the reporters there are, and, um, you're our hero?"

"Is that another question, Tim?" I asked, noticing Avery's car pulling up in the background.

He laughed nervously. "Sorry, I just never met you in person. But I saw you at Mavericks. You are *wild*."

I laughed with him. "Not the first person to say that. But if you want to see wild, you should see my dad. He doesn't do competitions anymore, but he used to surf waves that made Mavericks look like child's play."

He shook his head in disbelief. "But you've got such a distinct style, man. You're so amazing to watch." He looked down at his pad of paper for a moment and seemed to mull something over. "I guess, well, they sent me here to write about the protests. But if you wanted to give an interview..."

I looked past him, distracted by Avery's car door opening. The first thing I noticed was her legs, the actual skin of her legs. Usually every inch of her skin was covered. But today, I could see her calves. Her delicate ankles. The curve of her feet in her high heels.

When she stood and closed the door, I could see why. She was wearing a goddamn dress. Long-sleeved, but still. Those legs.

"Finn?"

"Yeah, Tim," I said, eyes never leaving Avery. She glanced up and saw me, held my gaze for a moment before glancing away.

I was making her nervous. I liked that.

"So about that interview?"

I reluctantly dragged my eyes back. "Listen, this isn't about me."

"But you're the star."

"The star is the *issue*. So if it's cool with you, I think just a story about Playa Vieja and why it's important to maintain its natural beauty."

Avery stalked up to the courtyard. Her hair was pulled up high onto her head. I wanted to lick her neck.

"And why building a hotel is the worst possible idea," I finished, just as she reached us.

"Avery," I said, extending my hand. "Have you met Tim? He works for the UCSD newspaper. Tim, meet Avery. She's a monster who is trying to destroy the last piece of untouched beauty in all of San Diego. And whose company hasn't had to answer to any of the claims by environmentalists about the havoc this would wreak on local wildlife."

Avery arched an eyebrow at me. She looked well-rested. She looked gorgeous. I'd never noticed before how full her lips were.

"Nice to meet you, Tim," she said warmly, shaking his hand. Tim looked like he was about to ejaculate on the spot. "In case he hasn't mentioned this yet, Finn's the egomaniac who'd rather keep his private beach to himself for surfing instead of adding five hundred jobs to the local economy."

Tim looked back and forth at us for a second before excusing himself, leaving us to our face-off.

"You've got a smart mouth, you know that?" I asked.

"Wouldn't you like to know?" she asked, with just the smallest hint of flirtation. Was Avery flirting with me? Was that what the tight dress and bare skin were all about?

She moved past me into her building. "And that's just a preview of what you can expect on debate night, Finn," she called back before the door shut.

13

AVERY

I tugged the hem of my dress down as I walked into the coffee shop that night. It was near the beach and had more of a bar vibe. I briefly wanted to be young and careless and sipping too much wine on a date with someone.

Except I *was* young. I kept having to remind myself of that lately.

But still. The breeze from the ocean felt wonderful on the bare skin of my legs. I wondered why I didn't wear dresses more often. Today, I'd worn the dress because I thought Finn would like it. And the look he gave me as I walked to him in that courtyard would have melted the underwear off a lesser woman. I'd kept him distracted and horny—and that was how I was going to beat him on Friday night.

And when I walked into the coffee shop, the first person I saw was—fucking of *course*—Finn Travis himself.

"Goddammit," I said under my breath. He was seated in a corner with the lovely blonde woman from the other day.

Clearly on a date. They were sitting on the same side of the table, and she was practically in his lap.

He was making her laugh. *He* was laughing. He was always laughing, like life was one big joke and he was the only one in on it. His curly blond hair was a little more under control, swept off of his forehead, and all you could see were those eyes.

And, okay, if you wanted to, you could also see that he had what some people would call "kissable lips."

With his right hand, he trapped a strand of her hair, rubbing it between his fingers. The woman giggled again. He dropped it, sweeping the strands off her shoulder, exposing her neck. A shiver went up my spine. Finn leaned in and kissed the sensitive skin there. The woman's eyes fluttered closed.

"Ma'am? Ma'am?"

I spun toward the register. "What?" I asked, flushing. I was breathing slightly heavily.

The cashier looked like he wanted to spit in my face. "Do. You. Want. A. Coffee?"

I looked around. I guessed I had been staring at Finn for an inordinate amount of time, and now five people stood behind me.

"Oh... um, sorry," I mumbled, digging for my wallet. This night was getting worse by the minute. I handed the guy my card, ordering something small but strong. Might as well just not sleep at this point.

"Can you add soy—" I started but was interrupted when someone yelled out "Hey, Avery!" from across the coffee shop.

I groaned, turning slowly, to see Finn. Waving at me.

I smiled at him but glared with my eyes. He grinned

back at me, motioning me over. I grabbed my coffee, grateful again for the dress. The dress was giving me power.

"Finn. Good evening," I said through gritted teeth. I *just* wanted to go home.

"Avery. Good evening," he mimicked. "This is Julie, by the way." Julie waved at me, her leg still over Finn's lap.

"Hey, Avery," she said. "How do you two know each other?"

"I'm a hotel developer with a chain called Bella View. Finn is currently spending his days making my life a living hell."

Her eyes widened a little.

"Oh. You're *that* Avery. Finn's told me all about you." She giggled and curled into his side. Her phone buzzed, and she glanced at it, distracted.

I arched an eyebrow at Finn. *Really?*

He just shrugged and stroked his thumb down her arm. I ignored it.

"Whatcha got there?" he asked, indicating my Everest-sized stack of papers.

"Research."

"On me?"

I rolled my eyes. "I already did my research on you. Took five minutes."

His eyes danced a little. I was starting to think Finn was turned on by arguing.

I was starting to get turned on by arguing.

"Listen, I know about your meeting tomorrow."

"What meeting?"

"Avery," he said, leaning closer to me. Julie was still distracted by her phone. "We've got guys on the inside too. I know you're meeting with Jacobs and Lewis tomorrow."

They were the two city council members that had always been friendly with property developers.

"I don't know what you're talking about," I said breezily, glancing at my watch.

Finn reached out and grabbed my wrist. I think the skin-on-skin contact shocked us both. He looked up at me, then dropped it. "Just... just don't discount us, okay? We've got as much in our arsenal as you."

"I seriously doubt that." I glanced at my watch again. "And I have about six hours of reading ahead of me. So... have a good evening," I said, with all the sarcasm I could muster.

I turned and walked out to the parking lot behind the shop.

"You know you're constantly walking away before the fight gets good?" The sound of Finn's footsteps were right behind me.

"Finn, I have watched you outside my office for two months now. The fight has already gotten good. There isn't anything left to do except put *your* opinions and *our* facts to the public and let them decide."

I reached my car, yanking the door open and tossing the papers inside. I spun around to find Finn less than a foot from me.

"My opinions?" he asked. He was grinning, but he also looked pissed.

"There is a clear, empirically proven connection between property development and economic growth. Beauty is subjective. The role that nature should play in our communities is subjective. No one has ever shown me statistics that prove leaving a beach untouched does anything, especially one where its residents scoff at tourists who want to visit it and give you money for the privilege."

He placed one hand next to my head, leaning closer to me. "And the environment doesn't play into this at all, Avery? The fact that the construction planned for the Bella View Hotel is going to dramatically alter the environmental landscape? The fact that increased erosion is going to cause more mudslides? Or that the birds—"

"God help me with the birds, Finn," I said, finally laughing a little. "As soon as humans evolved, the environment was fucked. Humans are greedy. We want more, more, more. And we're going to take until there's nothing left. I'm just an agent of that." I leaned closer, poking my finger into his chest. "I didn't invent human nature."

He glanced at my finger but didn't move it. Instead he stepped closer, causing me to flatten my palm. I could feel his heart beating.

"Is it wrong that I want to change human nature? Is it wrong to try and keep paradise a paradise for just a while longer?"

His face was open and honest—no sly grin or hidden irritation. I yearned to be like that again—in love with the world around me and its seemingly endless possibilities. That was Finn, through and through.

But I wasn't like that. Not anymore.

"Finn—" I started, then stopped when I realized I was fisting his shirt in my hand, pulling him closer.

He glanced down, then back up at me. Amused. His hand left the side of my head and traveled down my arm, resting at my elbow. Squeezing gently. This was the most physical contact I'd had in two years, and every nerve ending in my body flared to attention.

He grabbed my other elbow, boxing me in. "Avery," he said, eyes darkening. And then he lowered his mouth an inch from mine.

14

FINN

"What are you doing..." Avery whispered, but it wasn't a question. This close, she was so beautiful—all big eyes and long lashes, that full mouth.

"You really piss me off, you know that?" I said, mouth hovering over her lips. "I'm not that guy."

"What guy?" she said, hand twisting the fabric of my shirt a little tighter. I wanted her to rip it.

"The pissed-off guy."

She leaned in a half-centimeter and I pulled away. Teasing.

What the fuck was I doing?

"No, you're the guy that leaves joints on a girl's doorstep. Are you high right now?"

I smiled, just brushing my lips against hers. She tasted sweet. "You'd know if I was high. I get really horny when I'm high."

"This isn't horny?" she asked. My thumbs traced circles up and down her arms. I nuzzled along her jawline. A small, barely decipherable moan escaped. I wanted to hear it again, but she clamped her mouth shut.

"No, love, this isn't horny. You'd have come by now." She shivered. "But people can see us, and I'm technically on a date so..." Another brush against her mouth. I wanted to kiss her more than anything in the world.

Her eyes narrowed, irritated. And God, that made me *harder*. "What are you doing?" she said again.

I leaned in closer. I could feel the heat emanating from her skin. "I don't... I don't know," I finally said, aching. I cupped the side of her face. Her eyelids fluttered closed in pleasure.

"You just... you drive me fucking wild," I finally said against her lips, and a burst of laughter to my left broke the moment. I glanced over, saw a huge group of teenagers pointing at us, and sighed.

I stepped back, letting Avery go. I bit back a groan. For a second, she was still holding my shirt in her hand, but then she released it. Dazed.

I brushed a lock of hair behind her ear. "I'm—"

"Don't," she said, leaning away. She gave me a push, and I took a step back, letting her get into her car. "And for the record, I don't know what that was or why we did that, but it was an incredibly stupid idea."

I was looking down at her again as she slid her keys into the ignition. I didn't like this view, gave me too many temptations. I wanted to look down at Avery as she slid to her knees, taking the length of my cock into that irritating mouth of hers.

Something told me Avery didn't submit for just anyone.

I crouched down again, like the other night, putting us on the same level. "It wasn't that stupid of an idea. You're attracted to me."

"I think you're a dirty hippie who refuses to live in reality."

I laughed. "And I think you're a money-grubbing capitalist who only cares about the bottom line." She looked a little hurt for a second, then shook it off.

"See? Stereotypes hurt, Avery."

"I don't just care about the bottom line, so you know. I wouldn't be doing this if I didn't see Playa Vieja's need for an economic boost."

I looked at her warily. "What do you mean?"

"Finn," she said, looking exasperated. "Tourism is the lifeblood of any coastal community. For all of its values, Playa Vieja is really struggling. I'm not lying when I tell people this will bring local jobs. That you all need these jobs. It will change lives."

I felt my nostrils flare. "Don't tell us what we need. You live in the city. You don't know."

She nodded her head at the stack of papers in the car. "Research tells me that, Finn. I don't need to have lived there."

"And the opinions and ideas of the residents don't matter to you at all? Numbers can't tell a complete story. Our ideas have merit too."

"You think the residents of Playa Vieja want to keep living paycheck to paycheck? They're not all Billabong models."

I stood up, swearing under my breath. My dad had said the same thing. "Why are you the most goddamn irritating woman alive?" I said, more harshly than I intended.

"Because I'm right, and you know it."

Jesus. "Good night, Avery," I said, turning away. But she reached out and grabbed my arm, stopping me.

"I meant what I said, Finn. I'm tired, I'm overworked, and the whole—" She made a kind of spirit-finger gesture, then slammed her palms together.

"Is that us kissing? Is that your version of that?" I asked, laughing again. She made me feel so out of whack. Aroused one second. Angry the next.

"Oh, fuck you, yes. You know what I mean." Her face was serious. Too serious. Which made me think she was lying when she said, "It cannot happen again. Everything is too important right now." She paused. "And we didn't technically kiss."

I nodded, knowing she was right but still wanting to play with fire. I couldn't seem to help myself. I was hooked now.

"You're right," I said slowly. "So I'll get back to my date. And you'll go home and research. And later, after I've kissed her goodnight and promised to call her, I'm going to take a long, hot shower, and I'm going to touch myself."

I watched her breathing hitch. "I'm going to think of you, just like this, looking up at me with those beautiful eyes. Making you put that mouth of yours to work."

"You wouldn't," she murmured, but it lacked her usual heat.

"I suggest you do the same, love. Because the only thing in this world right now that would be better than your mouth on my cock? Is my mouth all over your beautiful body."

JULIE DIDN'T REALLY NOTICE that I was gone and also didn't notice that my interest in her dropped to basically zero. That fifteen-minute interaction with Avery—a total and complete mind-fuck—had ruined me, at least for the night.

I drove Julie to her apartment, which was close to the beach in downtown San Diego. Which meant she was rich.

As she was getting out of the car, I turned to the waves, a

natural inclination. I closed my eyes, savoring that sound. Of water on sand, the endless, beautiful cycle. I loved it so much.

"Finn?" I heard Julie say, touching my shoulder. "Do you want to come up?" She looked flirtatious and cute, her blonde hair blowing in the breeze. I wanted to have sex, badly, but I wanted to do it with Avery. Couldn't hide from that now.

"What do you think about the situation with the Bella View?"

She shrugged. She was pretty smart, but she was just not interested. "I don't know. You told me it will destroy the beach, make people's lives harder. I believe you."

"Hotels bring jobs though. Recognition. Might be nice for Playa Vieja to have some of that." *Who was I, Avery?*

"Okay, that sounds good too," she agreed. I looked at her, realized I wanted her to fight back a little.

So I leaned forward, kissed her cheek. "I get up at 5:00 a.m. every morning to surf, so... I have to pass."

She looked disappointed, but not terribly so. Actually, she looked like she thought I was really weird. Most people did when they found out my schedule.

"You don't ever take a day off?"

I looked back at the ocean. "No. I don't. I wouldn't ever. It's everything to me."

15

AVERY

*I*t was the sound of her voice that nearly did me in —tinny and tired through my cell phone's small speakers. An odd number I hadn't recognized.

"Mom?" I asked. I hadn't heard her voice in more than two years. "Why are you calling? Did something happen?" I tried to keep the alarm out of my voice but failed.

"No, no," she said. "And did I wake you?"

It was the morning of my meeting with the city council members. I'd barely slept. I was curled on the couch around a pile of notes, dreaming of New York City. Not dreaming of Finn. Or his hands on my skin. The way his lips felt, barely tracing mine. Teasing.

"Not at all," I said. "What, uh... what's up?" We'd only communicated in writing for so long. I wasn't used to hearing her voice.

She sighed. There were voices in the background—even, if I focused, the crash of waves. It brought me back sharply, and I closed my eyes against the onslaught of unwanted memories.

My family and I had grown up in an honest-to-god

commune on the island of Kauai in Hawaii. Our commune generally went nameless, although locals in the area called us Pono, a Hawaiian word they felt spoke to the commune's love of the environment and our giving spirit. The other commune members liked that it also meant "righteousness." We weren't religious, but they worshipped the earth with a religious fervor, and they loved the feeling of being warriors for the planet, of fighting for something others had turned their backs on.

I heard something odd in the background and knew it was the dry, crinkling sound of the beads separating their part of the yurt.

Growing up, our family of five had our own yurt, although part of communal living meant that kids, adults, dogs, chickens, and goats routinely crashed there. Once I'd left at eighteen (my older brothers had already moved out), my parents decided to share their yurt with two other families. It was crowded—it had to be.

"Sorry, just trying to find someplace private," she whispered into the phone. She must be on a cell phone, which was odd. As was the concept of privacy in a communal yurt.

"Mom, you're making me nervous."

"I know, pumpkin. Just a minute. I hadn't expected you to pick up." The endearment hurt a little. We weren't afforded open affection or traditional love growing up, but my mom had always used that pet name for me when others couldn't hear.

I heard her settling and breathing just a little heavy. "How are your knees?" I asked.

"Fine and dandy, for a sixty-year-old." She chuckled. My parents hadn't slowed down, still working in the gardens and on the small farm.

"There, now I'm settled."

"What's wrong? Why are you calling?"

"Well, first, before I say anything, we did get your letter —the last one."

"And?" I sighed since I knew what was coming.

"You know your father and I never liked that job you have. Property development." She said the term like it was a piece of roadkill left on the street for days.

"It's a good job. A steady job," I reminded her. "And I... well, I like it." A foreign concept for commune-dwellers. Individual happiness is lowest on the rung.

"The earth is not property, and it cannot be developed," she intoned, but I'd heard it a million times before.

"Let's not... Listen, what is going on?"

"The commune is failing, Coral." My brothers and I all shared earth names—Coral, Redwood, and Wave. Avery, the name I'd used for years, was technically my middle name. She only called me Coral when something was wrong, though.

I bit back a hundred sarcastic replies. Even as a ten-year-old, I could look around and see it wasn't going to work. Growing older on the commune was somehow worse—in between patches of adventure and wonder and exploring a giant island was this sick, sinking feeling I always had that the adults around me weren't making the right choices. That we were doomed.

If anything influenced my generally pessimistic demeanor, it was that.

"Okay," I said slowly. "Why don't you tell me what's going on?"

"It's money. We need money."

Of course they did. "Why?"

"Kauai is struggling through a tough drought, and it has significantly impacted our crops and garden. We sell what we can at the farmer's market, barter too, but our numbers are growing, and we can't seem to feed them all."

"There are new members? How many?"

"Oh, about thirty or so. With children, some of them."

"Why are you taking on more members if you can't feed them?" This always made me upset.

"You know why, Coral. We would never turn away a potential community member."

"Right, and now your community is about to fail. Can any of you get jobs?"

"We have jobs, you know that. Living off the land is a huge job."

"I know, I know," I said quickly since I had done that job. And it was hard. So incredibly hard. "I'm sorry. I just mean —anyone who can make some extra money working a more traditional job?"

She paused for a long time. "We've tried, we certainly have. A couple of the teenagers are working at some fast-food chains." She had as much disregard for that as she did property development. "And that is helping. The rest of us though... well, we've been out of the job market for quite a while."

And Hawaii's economy had always struggled to adequately employ the sheer number of people who lived there.

"What do you think you're going to do? Are you going hungry?" My stomach clenched at the memory. I knew what that felt like—more nights than I cared to remember.

"...no. I mean, we've eaten better in times past, but we have a few reserves saved up, and some of the local food banks have been nice enough to give us what we need. It's not terrible yet, but I've lived on this island long enough to see what's ahead."

"Which is?"

"This town is changing." The closest town to the commune had been developing quite a bit since I'd left—more tourism, especially. "Bartering used to work well, but these new town folks aren't as open to it as they used to be. They want cash."

"Yes, Mom, most people do," I said, dryly.

"And the tourists... the tourists are terrible. A big hotel, huge, went up, and we can hear them all the way at the commune. There's more of them on the beach, and the way they stare at us... like they've never seen simple people living in community before. Red came by the other day and tried to talk your dad and me into allowing tourists into the yurts."

"How so?" This had come up right before I'd left at eighteen. I'd been working our stand at the farmer's market in town—knotted hair, ratty clothes—and this rich-as-fuck woman came up to buy papayas. She seemed fascinated with me, almost reaching out and touching my hair.

"Can I help you?" I'd asked, already perfecting my image as a slightly irritated, overly sarcastic teenager.

"Where is your farm?" she'd asked me, squeezing papayas between her manicured fingers. I wanted to tell her to look up her ass but instead rattled off what we always said to outsiders: *We live in a simple, communal-style community fifteen miles from here. We are farmers and live off the land. Have you ever considered giving up the material burdens of capitalism to live life authentically with Mother Earth?*

This woman was in the middle of a farmer's market in rural Hawaii wearing a dark business suit, her blood-red nails like talons and tortoise-shell glasses perched on her head. Later, as I lay in the yurt, listening to the waves, I thought about being her one day.

"Question," she'd said, laying a hundred-dollar bill on the table between us. "Do you ever let..." She cocked her head, thinking of the word. "...tourists into your commune? Like as an experience?"

I'd narrowed my eyes at her. At this point, I was eighteen —the only community member that biked myself into town to go to school, shirking the weird homeschooling that was provided in favor of a ticket out. The joy and wonder of growing up in basically my own private jungle and beach had faded with my teen years, and the only thing I wanted was to leave. I didn't like the commune, I didn't like living there, I didn't like their values.

But I also didn't like this woman referring to our lives as an experience. I must have mumbled enough to make her concerned because she left. I pocketed that $100 though, showing it to my parents and some of the other members, unsure. They'd laughed heartily at her suggestion. And dismissed it.

"Well, since you've been gone, we've gotten the question a couple of times. Other communes have done it. And it's a quick and easy buck."

"But?" I said.

"We don't want to. I don't want to have to manage the questions and expectations of suburban SUV-driving Starbucks-drinking robots who destroy the earth with one hand and fund the capitalist regime with the other."

I smiled, despite myself. Arguing with Finn had been making me nostalgic. Hearing my mother spout off about "capitalist regimes" made me feel at home. Just a little.

"What are your other options, though? If the drought won't let up and you can't feed yourselves, you're kind of backed into a corner."

"Or... we could get a loan."

"What bank—" I started. "Oh... you mean from me." I was sitting fully upright now on the couch, biting my lip. "You're asking me for the money."

"A substantial amount, yes."

I thought of the promotion Sal had dangled in front of me—for a yes vote. I thought of Finn, pleading with his community, pleading with me. For a world that was better.

"You know where that money would come from, right? If I get this vote to pass, they're going to bulldoze a stretch of beach to put in a lazy river, a tennis court, a golf course, and a new restaurant. A huge parking lot. And three hundred plus hotel rooms. If I get this vote to pass, there's a strong possibility I would be given a promotion—that's where I'd get the money for your loan."

She sighed. "I figured."

"So you won't take tourists in because they're destroying the environment, but you will take money from your daughter who's doing the same thing?"

"Pumpkin," she said. "I'm not asking for this help as a commune member. I'm not asking for this help as part of our plan to bring back what's good and right on this earth." She paused. "I'm asking as your mother. Things are... bad."

I felt something strangely like tears prick the back of my eyes, but I swallowed against them. It was hard for me to admit that, since leaving the commune, since leaving my family behind, this had been my greatest fear. I wasn't thirty yet, but I had a savings account, a retirement account, liquid assets, health insurance. My parents might rail against the system, but in times like this, the system could help.

But this. It was always *this*. A phone call about one of them being sick and refusing "traditional" medical treatment. Or all of the yurts burning down in some freak accident and having no money to start over because they didn't believe in insurance. That was what kept me up at night.

"Okay," I said. "Okay, okay. Can I... can I think about it? I mean, I'm only going to be able to help if I'm successful. And I won't even know that until a month from now." If I wasn't, I couldn't begin to fathom what that would mean for me. For my career. And now, for my parents.

"Of course you can. Take all the time that you need. And I'm... well, Coral, I'm sorry to burden you with this. This isn't what your father and I wanted."

"Me neither," I said, a little more sharply than I intended. I took a long, slow breath. Tried to relax. "What's happening right now?"

I heard muffled sounds, then she said, "I'm just standing up outside of the yurt. Your dad is with some of the other members, cooking over the morning fire." I inhaled, pretending I could smell it. I loved that as a kid—that earthy, almost-sweet smell of food roasting over an open flame. The crack and pop of the fire.

"Most of the kids just went off in the jungle, but we'll call 'em back soon. Um... well, I can see the morning sun and the sky brightening over the ocean." I closed my eyes, picturing. It didn't matter if you grew up there—most of us still stopped to watch the sun rise in the blue sky and the sun set over the living, breathing force of the water. Slipping under the waves so quickly it was like it had never existed at all.

Growing up without electric lights, you worship the sun just a little bit. Now, depending on the season, there are whole days where I wouldn't have even noticed if the sun had ceased to rise.

"We saw some beautiful humpback whales this morning, just peeking up about a hundred yards out from shore.

They were so lovely, dancing in the water. I wish you could have seen it."

I hadn't been home to see them in more than five years, and even when I did visit, I'd stay in a hotel in town, despite the objections of the commune members.

"Me too," I said softly, staring around my apartment. I'd modeled it after the ones I'd seen in magazines I'd stolen from town growing up. All white walls, white couches. Bare and almost cold. As a teenager, I'd resented the number of people who stayed in our yurt. But as a child, I'd loved it— like one long, giant sleep-over. Sometimes, during thunderstorms, I yearned for community.

There was a pause where a traditional parent would say, "I miss you." But my parents were not traditional, and that went against all of their values. So instead, she said, "It's time for me to go—I'll already get in trouble for using the emergency cell phone to call you."

"Okay," I said awkwardly, wondering if I should say it. We didn't say "I love you" either, but faced with the past two years of exhausting work and the confusion of Finn and Sal's disappointment and the vote and persistent insomnia... I wanted my mom.

"So, good night, then. And don't forget the letter I sent you about the harmful chemicals in your toothpaste. You know they just want to make money off of distorted American beauty ideals. White teeth aren't natural."

I rolled my eyes, sinking back into the couch. "Right. I'll do that. Say hi to dad for me."

"I will." And then she clicked off, quickly, as if we'd never even been speaking.

"You're ready, right?" Sal said, holding open the door to the office building where we were meeting Councilmembers Jacobs and Lewis for a not-so-secret but kind-of-secret meeting.

Ferris and Lopez were the two members who were always pro-development and anti-environment. Harsh, but needed. Neither of them represented Playa Vieja's district. That was Susan McAffee, and she was strongly against this hotel.

No, Jacobs and Lewis were money-grubbing capitalists.

Just like Finn said. And my mother.

I brushed past Sal, adjusting my jacket, trying to focus.

You drive me wild, Finn had said. I hadn't really slept in weeks, and I'd been dreaming of an anonymous surfer who happened to be the person I hated most in this world.

So I fucking knew the feeling Finn was referring to. Last night, I couldn't stop thinking about what Finn had taunted me with—him in the shower, water pouring over his naked muscles and his cock in his hand. His eyes would be closed, dreaming of me. Totally vulnerable. The only sounds would be these tiny, harsh groans and the slick sound of skin squeezing skin.

But I couldn't go there with Finn. The call from my mom, if anything, cemented two things: I had to win. *Had* to. And that meant that kissing Finn again would be a giant mistake. He would love the commune and everything it represented. If they asked him to live there, he'd probably jump at the chance. He would never be the type A-lawyer flirting with me at a mahogany bar.

No. Finn was my past. I needed a different future.

"Avery," Sal said, and I yelped. "Is your head in the game or what?"

No. No. "Ye-es. Why do you ask? Am I not exuding confidence as we speak?"

He looked at me. Really looked at me. Then he said, "All right, let's go."

I stepped into the office where Anthony Jacobs and Bridget Lewis were waiting.

"Councilmember Jacobs, Councilmember Lewis, so happy to see you again," I said warmly, shaking their hands. Sal followed.

"Avery, Sal," Bridget said, nodding before she sat down. Jacobs did the same. These two were nothing but business.

"How's that surfer treating you?" Bridget asked, and I almost fainted.

"What?" I asked, not picturing the way Finn teased his lips over mine again and again. "What do you mean?"

"Finn Travis," Anthony said. "The ringleader or whatever. You know he's been meeting with McAffee for a few weeks now."

I swallowed, re-focusing. "That doesn't surprise me. He's smarter than he looks."

All three laughed, and I joined in but a few seconds too late.

"He's not smart. He's just good-looking and well-known. Unfortunately, in politics, that will take you far," Bridget said. Sal and I looked at each other, unsure if we were supposed to laugh or not. "And the debate on Friday?" she asked.

"At UC San Diego, in the auditorium. Should be a packed house," Sal said. "We're feeling good about it. Right, Avery?" He gave me the kind of look the wolf gave Little Red Riding Hood.

"Of course," I said smoothly, as my stomach began dutifully tying itself in one million knots. "I mean, Finn is smarter than he looks, but he's not *that* smart."

Although he'd said a few things yesterday that had me almost tripping up. I needed to learn everything about those fucking birds.

"So," I said, bringing my palms together. "Let's get to business. You two said you only had a few minutes to spare?"

"Yes, and we'll be brief," Bridget said. "We've had some unexpected developments this past week that the two of you need to know about. We all know the PR for this has been bad from the start. It could have killed us. Although, Avery, I will say you've been doing a great job with those interviews. Great job firing back."

I nudged Sal smugly, warm with the unexpected praise.

"And once the environmental activists get a hold of something, you better believe it's going to be a knock-down, drag-out fight. They're like a dog on a bone," she said.

"Well, but we've got the backing of most of the city council, the tourism board, and the redevelopment agencies," I said. "Plus, we've got facts on our side."

"Two of the members who had originally given us their vote are now wavering," Bridget warned.

"Wavering?" I asked.

She nodded. "It's not certain but... they're reconsidering their positions."

Sal looked like he wanted to reconsider *my* position.

"Anything we can do?" he asked. I felt like I might vomit all over the council members' laps.

There were nine members total, and a vote needed five. Two of the members, Susan McAffee being one of them, were sure votes against it. Now these other two.

"Don't lose the debate," Anthony said. "Not to put you

on the spot, but Finn is going to hit the environment hard in the debate. What's your answer right now?"

"Playa Vieja has been a struggling community for a while. It has not bounced back from the recession. It's admirable that it's held strong to its values, but because of that, very little money flows in. The Bella View Hotel would bring visibility, tax credits, and most importantly, jobs— things the community needs. Things that will help it thrive."

And how on earth this small band of surfer-hippies had dredged up enough support to cause the city council members to look past how much *money* this would bring was beyond me.

"Well done," Bridget said smoothly. "I want your answers to the debate on my desk by tomorrow morning. I'll provide feedback. Is a few days enough time to re-memorize my changes?"

Fuck no.

"Of course," I said, with forced cheerfulness. "I'm happy to honor that request. And what is the second thing we can do to mitigate these changes?"

"Meet with those other two members," Anthony began. "And change their goddamn minds."

Sal's silence as we walked back to the car stung worse than if he'd yelled at me. He'd always been this outwardly gruff but secretly teddy-bear kind of guy, but his quiet disappointment burned.

"Well, that fucking sucked," I said, tossing my bags in the car. I needed to immediately forget that meeting and immediately forget the giant debate I had on Friday. Finn's joint popped into mind.

Sal looked at his feet for a second, then back up at me.

"Avery, one of the hotels on the East Coast is closing.

Poor performance, and the neighborhood didn't like it anyway."

"Oh," I said. As in, *"Oh, shit."*

"Right now, we've been trying to push another location in Monterey, and the permits are being held up because of the bad PR from the East Coast." He paused. "And the bad PR here. No one likes a Goliath."

"But someone has to be the Goliath," I shot back, almost desperately. It wasn't like I grew up dreaming of being Goliath. I'd just grown up with mostly Davids, and after a while, you got tired of always being the victim.

"We need a win, Avery. So go win."

He left me there in the parking lot, stomach in knots and *this close* to heaving into the bushes. I'd always been a winner. Having grown up "off the grid," I was a sole witness to how hard it was (not that my parents would ever admit to that). After I left the commune and put myself through college and graduate school in San Diego, my only concerns were working hard (*within* the system) and moving up. Fuck, after leaving my parents, just having a birth certificate, a driver's license, and paying taxes felt good.

But "moving up" for me also meant a corner office with a view of the New York City skyline. I was edging closer to thirty, and the way I was going to get there would be pushing through a controversial hotel. Dammit.

Because the other option was *not* getting the promotion. Staying stagnant. Staying still. Even, possibly, going backward. And that, well, that was just not possible.

And I knew what I *should* have done that night. I should have gone home, taken out my notes on the debate, and practiced until I fell asleep somewhere around dawn.

Instead I found myself wearing my favorite sundress in

the back corner of my favorite reggae bar, trying desperately to light the joint Finn had left me on my porch.

At my lowest moments, at my most overwhelmed, some part of me would crave pieces of my childhood—the ease. Loud music and bare skin, and, yeah, pot melting through my veins, making even my bones feel loose. This reggae bar was my secret shame—that when my corporate-self needed a few hours of my previous life, I'd come here to bask in its heady warmth.

The music was loud, and it was darker in the back. I liked it. I needed it. It felt good to expose my skin to the warm night air. To sip a glass of wine and pretend my entire career wasn't going to turn on a one-hour debate in a matter of days.

The lighter flicked out again.

And I just really, *really* wanted to get high.

Out of nowhere, a hand cupped around my own. Warm, a little rough. I looked up.

"Need some help?"

It was Finn. And not boyish *"everything's chill, man"* Finn.

This was intense Finn. *"Have you ever fucked in the ocean?"* Finn.

He kept his hand on mine and pulled a chair over, so close his leg slid between my knees.

"I uh... I mean, I guess," I stammered out, still surprised that he was there, like a fantasy come to life. He was wearing board shorts, flip-flops, and a white button-up shirt.

Except all the buttons were unbuttoned, exposing a six-inch strip of his chest and a stomach that made my mouth water.

He took the joint from my hand, winking at me. We had a secret. He lit it easily and inhaled, keeping his eyes on mine. I watched the smoke linger, escaping from the edges of his lips.

He passed it. I took the deepest, longest hit I could manage. He arched an eyebrow, impressed.

"What's a money-grubbing capitalist doing in a reggae bar with a bunch of surfers?" he asked.

I exhaled, feeling the pot working its way into my limbs. Sweet relief.

Finn's knee pressed against mine. "You may not know this—" I began.

"I actually don't know anything about you, Avery," he said. It was loud, and he leaned in close to say it. Too close.

"Well," I said, fighting a smile. "You may not know this, but I was raised by hippies too. In Hawaii." The reggae band came on, and the beat kicked in. Now I smiled easily. "And I grew up listening exclusively to reggae. I don't make time for it anymore. But once in a while... I just *need* it."

He looked delighted. "Really?" He took another hit and passed it back. Our fingertips just grazed each other.

I had a brief feeling of total disorientation and then embraced it.

"Really and truly," I said. "Actually, my parents raised me in a commune in Kauai."

"My parents live in a commune now," he said, smiling. "What was it like?"

"Being raised by thirty different people?"

"Yeah."

I inhaled, the smoke clinging to my lungs. "Fucking terrible."

He laughed, rich and low. "So you were raised by thirty people who loved you on an island most people consider a paradise, listening to reggae every day?"

I grimaced. "We're hedging into personal territory I'm

not overly fond of sharing." I took a second hit.

He squeezed my knee. "Don't bogart it, capitalist."

I laughed and blew smoke in his face. He took the joint back and slipped it between his lips but kept his fingers on my knee. After exhaling, he said, "But you've already shared more than I knew before, so who the fuck cares?" He passed it back again. "Spill."

The weed and the heat and the dark sensuality of the bar made me feel like we were the only two people in the entire world.

Or that was my excuse. "There were about fifty members in the entire commune at any given time, usually fifteen or so couples. I also have two older brothers—they're out of the commune but live in Hawaii still. The most beautiful part was growing up with so many other kids—the constant community." The happiness, full-tilt, of knowing you were never alone. Not like my life now. "And yes, the island, especially from a child's point of view, was like living in a goddamn storybook."

"Adventure stories every day," he added.

"Totally. It was all ocean and palm trees and jungle and strange sounds at night." I inhaled, and the smoke burned this time. Tears pricked my eyes. I missed those strange night sounds.

"It was gorgeous, actually. I did love that part of it. But the commune had two values that made it hard to grow up there."

Finn's fingers flexed on my knee, then crept an inch higher. His hair was wild and shaggy, and I wanted to brush it out of his eyes. That was probably—hopefully—the pot talking.

"They didn't... they don't... believe in money, not in the traditional sense. They're barter-based."

"Cool," he said with genuine enthusiasm.

I rolled my eyes. "I'll admit the concept is interesting, but tell that to a five-year-old who goes to bed hungry because no one in town would barter for food."

I said it quickly, like ripping off a bandage. These memories seemed to hurt more and more the older I got.

His eyes narrowed. "They let that happen?" His thumb traced soothing circles on the inside of my thigh.

I shook my head. "I don't know if they *let* it happen. I can't imagine that's what my parents wanted to happen. But it did. A lot. Sometimes it was a real feast. We had crops, we worked the land, we grew things, and there were more people interested in bartering on the island than you might think."

I shuddered at the memory, the weed painting it in brighter-than-normal colors. "The famine times were just hard. And—" I said, palms out as I passed the joint back to Finn. He took it between his lips but didn't inhale, listening. "—the second value was about child-rearing. The commune felt that society coddled children, had too much control over them."

"Don't treat children like children" was the refrain heard the most. It belittles them. It folded nicely into their non-conformist rhetoric.

"It's why you're so independent," he said, the flame at the end of the joint glowing. There was a slight breeze, and one section of his shirt lifted up, exposing his nipple. He didn't notice.

"I guess," I said, uneasy with the compliment. "When I got out of there, I put myself through school and haven't looked back. I worked at nights, went to school during the day..."

"No time for fun," he finished, his hand moving just a

fraction of an inch higher. I found myself widening my legs, just a bit. Encouraging.

I shook my head. "I had fun on the island. I really did. Being an adult, for me, means working hard. And I'm fine with that. I just wish..." I paused. I was definitely a little high now, and between the muggy air, the sultry reggae, and Finn's fingers, I was oversharing.

He leaned in closer, brushed a lock of hair off my shoulder. I shivered. "I just wish they were more like parents, you know? I liked being independent, but it also meant that when I fell down and skinned my knee, no one came over to hug me. There was no cuddling. No affection." I stopped because a lump the size of Mexico had formed in my throat. I looked away.

I didn't think about those things a lot, and here I was in Finn's company for five minutes, opening wide as a clamshell.

"You have a beautiful laugh," he said finally. I looked back at him.

"What?" I asked.

"Your laugh," he said, and this time he leaned in even closer. His right knee squeezed against my inner thigh, his left arm pressing against mine on the table. "You don't laugh very much. But it's beautiful." He paused. "You should laugh more often."

"I should do a lot of things more often," I admitted and felt a little sad. "You're always laughing. Why is that?"

He grinned, broad like a sunset. "A lot of things are funny. Plus, I don't know, my dad and mom laughed a lot when I was growing up. I'm a lot like them."

He took one last pull from the joint, then offered me the final hit. I pinched it between my fingers, tugged out the last tiny bit, and then burned myself.

"Ouch," I said, shaking out my hand. He grabbed my finger, pulling it closer to his face, examining.

"You've probably burned yourself on joints a lot, huh?" I said.

He pressed a soft kiss against my index finger.

"I don't get high as much as you think, Avery," he said. "My parents did a lot—"

"Along with the laughing—"

"Yeah, along with the laughing, so it took the forbiddenness out of things."

I bit my lip. "You like things to be forbidden," I said. A statement, not a question.

His hand slid up a full two inches, gripping my inner thigh. "I do," he said, eyes on mine.

"Finn fucking Travis. What is up, man?" A large man stepped next to Finn, and his hand slid away.

"Joshua," Finn said. He half-smiled, half-laughed as they executed a complicated hand gesture. "Haven't seen you on the waves recently. Everything okay?"

Joshua shrugged. "Shoulder's bothering me, man. Just trying to rest it." He nudged Finn. "There's a lot of groupies here tonight. Big fans of the big wave surfers. Wanna join?"

Finn nodded at me, the dull bulb next to his bright, blazing one. Joshua looked, grinned at me. "Oh, I'm sorry. I didn't see you there. You are?"

"Avery," I said politely, shaking his hand.

"Right on, right on," he replied. "You ever been to San Diego before?"

I grimaced. "I, uh, I live here, actually. Have for a decade now." It wasn't the first time I'd been mistaken for a tourist. Kind of sucked.

Joshua turned back to the groupies, clearly distracted.

"Cool, cool," he said, glancing at Finn. "So it seems you're, uh, otherwise occupied."

"Very," Finn responded, his voice firmer than I'd ever heard before. His hand found my thigh again, squeezing gently. Joshua laughed, patting Finn on the back, and made his way back into the crowd.

"Everyone loves you," I said. "You should be cockier."

His eyes danced. "Cocky surfers drown. I'd very, *very* much like to live."

I tilted my head. "Okay, then. Before I let you get to your groupies—" He smirked at me. "What's the most embarrassing thing that's ever happened to you?"

He tapped his fingers against his lips. "Nothing."

I laughed, shoving his legs. "Spill," I said, echoing his earlier command. The band was playing an old Peter Tosh song, and I sighed in gratitude, running my fingers through my hair. His eyes tracked the movement.

"Do you know who Eddie Aikau is?"

"Of course. Hawaii's most famous surfer."

"Big waves, specifically. At Waimea Bay," Finn said. "After I'd won a handful of surf competitions in my teens, I watched a documentary on Eddie that changed my entire life. I became obsessed with surfing those waves. The biggest waves."

"How big are the waves at Waimea?"

"Average? You're talking thirty, sometimes forty, feet."

I shivered, even though, in doing my research on Finn, I'd watched him surf waves that high. It was like watching someone fly.

"So I graduated from high school and moved to Hawaii for a year, before college."

"Wait," I said, grabbing his hand. "When?"

"I don't know. Fifteen years ago? Summer is when I

moved there, to train before the winter waves."

My body felt light, airy. "We just missed each other."

"What do you mean?"

"Fifteen years ago, during the summer, I flew from Hawaii to move to San Diego. To make money before college."

He squeezed my thigh again. "Oh, I see," he said, stroking a strand of my hair between his fingers. "We were meant to meet, you and I."

"No way. In fact, I think that shows we were meant *not* to meet."

"You believe in fate, Avery Dacosta?"

"Fuck no," I said, sipping from my wine.

He gave me that smile again, fingers in my hair. Palm sliding up my thigh. I felt like I was melting. "We'll have to argue about that another day, love."

"And you still haven't told me your embarrassing story."

"Well, I guess I was a little cocky when I was younger. I trained on those waves for months, building up strength. Learning to hold my breath for minutes at a time. Welcoming the fear. Worshipping it."

"Why?"

"Keeps you alive," he said. "But I was watching surfers younger than me ride those waves, so one day, when I was stupid, I went out there. Swam past the breakers and waited for the smoothest thirty-foot wave to come and find me."

"Jesus," I said, stomach in knots.

"I was lucky," he said. "It was only a fifteen-foot wave, so when I fell, feet-first, down the face, I didn't die. I was only under for about a minute."

Being held down underwater for a full minute didn't sound lucky to me.

"And I'd charged the wave, taking it from another surfer

who'd been waiting a couple of sets. So in an instant, I was embarrassed and generally considered a total dick."

I winced. "Not good."

"No," he said, and he was laughing now. Hard. "And the final worst part? It was high season, tons of tourists there to watch the surfing. I swam all the way to shore, totally shaken up. Stood up, and in front of literally hundreds of people, including children, I discovered I was bare-ass naked."

"You surf naked?" I was hazily spinning around on that image, my skin hot under his touch.

"Lost my trunks in the waves. It was glorious. I was almost arrested."

I couldn't stop thinking about Finn naked. Which I guessed was the point. Cheeky.

"The audience is going to love you at the debate," I blurted out because it was the truth. I was a robot. Especially in the face of this giant, lovable, naked surfer.

"Don't bring that up," he said. "Can't we just enjoy this?"

"No, I mean, my boss told me I come off as robotic. Unlikeable. People like you. They're going to like you even more on Friday." I guess this was a night for sharing my most intimate secrets and *all* of my insecurities.

"I'm the face of surfing in San Diego, love. People like me mostly just for that. Nothing more."

"You're charming," I insisted.

"You're brilliant," he shot back.

I looked away, blushing. He pinched my chin with his thumb and forefinger, tilting me back. "I mean it."

"You think I'm a monster. And you made a sign that called me *Satan*."

He paused at that, looking down for a moment. "I think you and I have very different ideas of what's right for this community. And, yes," he said, that grin sliding up his face again. "I do think you are a bit of a monster. And a touch like Satan. A very *pretty* Satan, though."

I bit my lip, fighting a smile.

"But I also see that you're passionate, just like me. Just fighting for a different side. You say you're a robot, but I think you burn white-hot."

I let my smile break loose.

"And I think your boss is an asshole."

The chords of a familiar song started up and my eyes closed in happiness. At the same time, Finn and I both said, "I love this song."

I looked at him, then laughed.

"There goes that laugh again. Twice in one night."

"You like Bob Marley deep cuts?" I asked. It was "Turn Your Lights Down Low," and I'd loved it since I was a kid.

He stood, pulling me up. I was wearing tall platform sandals that put me closer to his eye-line. "I like everything Bob Marley."

"Such a stereotype."

"We dirty hippies usually are. Dance with me," he said, pulling me toward the floor. I knew I should say no, turn around, head back to my house. But his skillful fingers had every nerve ending in my body singing. My high was curling around my spine, liquid and sinful.

We reached the dance floor, and I turned, slipping his other hand through mine. I only got a flash of his face before he turned me around so I was facing the stage.

And then he pulled me tightly against him. His hands on my hips, swaying gently back and forth.

His erection, pushing against my ass.

Two years. *Two years.*

Finn pulled my hair over my shoulder, exposing my ear

to his mouth. "There, now you can see the band." His breath was hot against the shell of my ear. "And the lead singer, who thinks you're hot," he said, chuckling a little.

I looked at the lead singer, who had long dark hair and a bright white smile. He winked at me as he sang the famous lyrics.

"He's cute," I agreed.

"And now I want to punch his face in," Finn said, and my heart tripped over itself. He was jealous.

We swayed for a moment, his thumbs digging into the skin of my hips, holding me in place. I felt his lips circling my ear, the skin of my neck, and I arched myself back, right into his cock.

He stopped. I'd gone too far.

Then he pulled tighter, shifting lower so he could rub himself against me. I sighed and let my eyes close.

"You came here on purpose," he whispered. I shook my head.

"Coincidence," I replied.

"You heard me tell Marla I was going here tonight, didn't you?"

I had a vague memory of it. Not that I would admit that to Finn.

"I have no idea what you're talking about." He pressed an open-mouthed kiss against my neck, and I moaned.

The train had officially left the station.

He ground against me, and I placed my hands against his, tightening. He kissed my neck again.

"Who knew you had miles of this gorgeous skin underneath those power suits? I can't get enough of it."

I don't know if it was the weed or the wine or the heat of his bare chest against my back, but I turned my head and said, "I haven't been with someone in two years."

I heard a gentle curse at my ear. I felt us suspended, trapped really, between two inevitable conclusions, and it all rested on what Finn said next.

"Is that what you need, love?" He rubbed against me, harder this time. "I mean, I think you're a monster," he began, with a low, sexy rumble. "But I can give you what you need, Avery." He scraped his teeth against my earlobe. "Just ask."

There was no debate. No development. No career. There was only the fact that if I didn't let Finn give me an orgasm —right this second—I was going to ignite on the dance floor.

I turned my head again, and he grabbed my chin, tilting up. Our eyes met. His were dark with hunger. He hovered his lips over mine, just like the other night. Teasing.

"Please," I finally said, and he slanted his mouth over mine tenderly. I tasted pot and chocolate and the ocean. Finally.

Finn kissed like a dream come true. Firm lips and the slightest scruff shattering my willpower. His tongue met mine—gentle, curious, tracing soft circles. I moaned against his lips, and he deepened the kiss. Greedy. Thorough. One finger traced up my throat. We swayed, back and forth, as he kissed me, slow and lazy. Like he had all the time in the world to taste me.

I turned around and looped my arms around his neck, kissing him for all I was worth. Pressing every inch of my body against his hard one. Next to me, I heard a guy say, "Damn, dude," but I didn't give a *fuck* who was watching.

He pulled away, a fraction of an inch. "Do you need me?"

It wasn't even a question I had to answer. I just yanked his arm as hard as I could and pulled him down the long, dark hallway that led outside the bar.

16

FINN

*W*hen I walked into that bar and saw Avery, I was a goner.

She was sitting in the corner, trying to light a joint. She was wearing some kind of long, floaty white dress—so unlike her. Her hair was finally loose, pulled over her shoulder.

She was toned and smooth-looking, the white of her dress practically glowing against her tan skin.

It was too much. Talking to her was the easiest thing I'd ever done. Her laughter. Her openness. The way her lips tilted up as she smiled at me.

Her quiet, urgent need.

And now she was pulling me outside the bar, and I had no clue what was going to happen next. Except that she was clearly in charge and wanted it that way. Which was fine by me... for a little bit.

We were suddenly outside, in a patio area where employees of the bar clearly came to smoke. It was small, and an open grate let out the sound of the band inside. Tall walls shielded us from the street. A broken chair was against the back wall. Avery yanked me, hard, then tossed me into it.

She stood in front of me like some kind of gorgeous vision. Her eyes. Those lips. I wanted to tear that dress in half. I reached for her, but she stepped back.

"What—" I started to say, but she shook her head.

"Don't touch me," she said, then slowly undid the straps of her dress.

"Avery," I said with as much warning as I could. I reached out again. She stepped back farther, lightly swatting at my hand.

"I'm in control," she said simply. "Hands on your head."

I arched an eyebrow at her. When she peeled her dress down to the tops of her nipples, my mouth watered.

"Hands on your head, Finn, or I swear to God, I will bulldoze your precious beach tomorrow."

My cock was harder than it'd ever been. "You fight dirty, you know that?" I threaded my fingers into my hair.

She exposed her breasts to me, a small smile on her face. "I'm well aware."

They were gorgeous, bigger than a handful, plump and begging to be touched. Her nipples were hard.

"You're goddamn perfect," I growled.

Avery dropped to her knees in front of me, and I lost my mind.

She reached her hands out, touching the ridges of my stomach.

"You're so hard here," she said, eyes mesmerized.

"I'm hard everywhere," I said, teeth gritted. Her fingers danced over me, light as a feather, trailing up to my chest, my nipples, my neck. She leaned forward and pressed her tongue right above my belly button, then dragged it up.

My head hit the back of the wall, hands tightening in my hair.

"Goddammit," I cursed. I wasn't sure if this was pleasure or torture. She leaned forward, licking up my body, fingernails scratching. Soft moans. Her hard nipples against my skin.

"You taste good," she said. My cock twitched, and I know she felt it. With just one finger, she traced the length, over and over.

"You're so big here," she said.

"Use me," I choked out, and I knew I was begging.

She answered by straddling me. It took every ounce of strength I had in my body not to grab her hips.

She kissed me, hands on both sides of my face. I groaned as she wrapped her long legs around my waist, her lips hot and greedy. Avery kissed like she was born to do it, like we were the last two people on Earth. I fell into her, totally and completely. I fucked her mouth with my tongue, loving the desperate little sounds I was wrenching from the back of her throat. I bit her lower lip, and she dug her nails into my chest.

"Fuck," I said, pulling away. She looked at me, all big eyes and raw lips. Panting. I didn't want her to stop, to regret anything, so I thrust up with my hips and her eyes rolled back.

"Oh my God," she moaned, rubbing her clit against my erection. I leaned forward and captured her nipple in my mouth, rolling it against my tongue. She ground harder, and the sound she made was almost guttural.

Two years. This woman hadn't been pleasured in two years, and I was the one who was breaking her dry spell. It made me want to possess her, like take-you-back-to-my-cave possession. The kind I wasn't always proud of, but *fuck* if Avery wasn't bringing it out in me.

I bit her nipple, not gently, and she cursed. I moved to the other one, wishing I could use my hands. She kept working herself against my cock as I licked my way up her neck. "Let me touch you," I whispered against her ear.

"No," she moaned, a wicked smile on her face.

"Let me," I said again, and I was begging this time. She kissed me, practically swallowing me whole, fingernails digging into my arms, pushing them up. She laced her hands into mine, gripping my hair. She dry-fucked me faster, and even through the fabric of my board shorts, I could feel how wet she was.

She groaned in frustration, her legs shaking. She was close but couldn't get there.

Before she could do anything about it, I let go of my hair, grabbed her hips, and stood up.

Then I slammed us against the wall.

Avery cried out, pulling away from my mouth. She looked furious.

"You're hot when you're mad," I said, lowering her just an inch so I could get the angle right. I rocked against her, and she bit her lip.

"And now I have to bulldoze your... bulldoze your..." she started to say, but I'd already begun to grind against her the way she needed it, and her head fell back against the wall.

"What the fuck," she moaned. I yanked her arms up over her head and bit her neck, marking her. I moved my mouth to her ear, one hand holding her up, the other pinning her wrists.

"You can boss me around all you like, love." I thrust hard, finding the rhythm she liked. Her legs were shaking again, but not from effort. She was close. "I like it. But if you think I'm going to sit here and not give you the mind-blowing, earth-shattering orgasm you deserve..."

I pinched her nipple between my fingers, fucking her even faster.

"Yes, yes, yes..." She was moaning, over and over. I loved her like this. Completely fucking undone.

"Open your eyes, Avery," I commanded, and she did. "Look at me as you come." I spread her as wide as she could go. The band stopped playing, and she came at the same time, screaming. Eyes on me.

"That's right, love. Let everyone hear that gorgeous sound," I whispered. She was trembling everywhere, her cunt throbbing against me as she fell and fell. "I need them to know. Need them to know who made you..." I started to say against her ear. "Who made you... they... oh, *fuck*." My orgasm struck like a lightning bolt, completely out of nowhere, and I groaned into Avery's neck as I thrust against her, riding it out.

Holy. *Shit.*

It took a full minute before either of us could speak. She was still wrapped around me, panting. I was surprised I was still standing. I kissed her slowly, bringing us both back down to Earth, feeling her smile against my lips. Wondering how I'd gotten so lucky.

She sucked my index finger into her mouth. "You came," she said, fire in her eyes.

I slid her gently down my body, sat on the chair, and pulled her into my lap. She was punch-drunk and happy. "Like a teenage boy... in my pants," I said, just slightly embarrassed. She laughed and kissed me, curling up against my chest.

What the fuck just happened?

17

AVERY

"*Y*ou came too," Finn said, tugging on a lock of my hair.

"Came is an understatement," I said, and the smile he gave me was filthy.

He pulled me against him, which felt unbelievably right, his chin resting on the top of my head.

I opened my mouth to say something, then stopped myself. I wanted to tell him I hadn't come like that in a long time. That the way the muscles of his stomach flexed under my tongue was the most erotic thing I'd ever seen. His hands, clutching his hair, exposing his big, lean body to my every advance. The sound he made when I straddled him.

That he kissed like a saint but had the mouth of a sinner.

I wanted to tell Finn I hadn't had that much *fun* in a long time.

"Avery," he said against my ear, and I turned, meeting his gaze. I couldn't read the expression on his face.

"Whoa, sorry, dude!"

I almost fell out of Finn's lap. The bartender and one of the servers were standing in the doorway since we had clearly been dry-humping each other in their outdoor break room.

Finn stood, tucking me behind him as I quickly pulled the straps of my dress up. "Hey, guys, sorry about that," he said, all Finn-Travis-charm. If they were women, they would have obediently handed him their underwear. "We were just getting a little air... if you know what I mean."

He winked, and the guys laughed, mimicking a joint at their lips. "We come out here for air all the time," the bartender said. "And also, I don't mean to sound weird, but you're Finn Travis, right?"

Fuck me, I thought. He really was the unofficial mayor of San Diego.

"The one and only. And you are?" He reached forward and shook their hands.

"Jacob," said one.

"Johnny," said the other. "And yeah, we saw you at Stance in La Jolla last year."

"Let me guess. You won," I grumbled behind Finn's back. They didn't even care that I was there. They were so in awe of him.

"Right on, right on," Finn said, nodding. "That was a tough one. You guys surf?"

"For sure," they both said at the same time.

"Hey, after you smoke you wanna grab a beer with us at the bar?" Jacob asked. "Your, uh... your friend can join us too."

I smiled weakly at them, shaking my head. "Oh, no worries. I was just... heading out."

"I'll walk you to the car," Finn said, his hand heavy and warm at the small of my back. Protective.

We were about to make it through the hallway when one of the guys, Johnny I think, called back to Finn.

"Oh, and hey—you're part of that protest group, right? The one with the hotels?"

Next to me, Finn stiffened. So did I.

"I am," he said slowly. "Why, what's up?"

"I just think it's cool, bro. My grandma used to take me to Playa Vieja all the time as a kid, and I loved that it was just locals. I fucking hate that tourism shit."

The debate. Friday. *Fuck.*

Finn laughed, but I could tell it was forced. "Guys, I'm just going to walk Ave—uh, my lady friend to her car, and I'll be back for that beer, okay?"

We turned around, and he pulled me through the bar. The cute lead singer glanced at me briefly, and I smiled at him. Finn's hand tightened.

I got a couple of other glances, a few smirks, and one very presumptive wink, which was how I realized everyone in the bar had heard me orgasm.

I briefly remembered the music stopping and Finn urging me on, but at that point, I had been out of my mind with lust. I only remembered coming so hard I felt it in my toes.

"You're popular tonight," Finn whispered in my ear as we moved toward the entrance.

"Fuck, this is embarrassing," I groaned, avoiding everyone's eyes.

"They're just jealous."

We made it to my car, and as I opened the door, the stacks of debate research I'd brought with me tumbled into the parking lot.

"Shit," I said, scooping the pages up. Just looking at them caused a tsunami-sized wave of anxiety to crash over me. I took a deep breath, and I felt his large hand in the middle of my back.

"You okay?"

"Yeah, I just... We have a debate in a couple days, Finn. And if your two friends back there are any indication, I'm going to come off as the Wicked Witch."

I tossed the papers in the back and turned. As usual, he was standing too close to me. I put my hand against his chest, pushing him back gently.

He arched an eyebrow at me. "I can't think when you're that close," I admitted, then immediately wanted to take the words back. Something hungry and primal entered his eyes before he hid it.

"It's just a debate. You'll talk. I'll talk. Then you'll talk again. We do it all the time. In fact, we do it an awful lot standing in front of this car." He smiled and tugged on my hair again. "Are you sensing a theme here?"

I shook his hand away, suddenly and completely overwhelmed. His eyes narrowed.

"I have a lot of things riding on how this debate goes tomorrow, on how this vote goes in four weeks."

"Me too, Avery," he said, crossing his arms over his chest.

"No, like, my career, Finn. If this vote goes poorly for you, it'll suck because you fought a good fight and you'll lose something you feel passionate about." I swallowed, throat dry. "But if I lose this vote..." I wanted to say the words but couldn't push them past my throat. No promotion. No Tribeca penthouse. And maybe, maybe my parents wouldn't get what they needed. Although I still hadn't decided if I would help them or not.

"What?" he asked, looking concerned. "Are you okay? Did I do something wrong?"

"No, no," I shook my head. I'd already shared more with him than I had any other person. I didn't want him to know any more of my vulnerabilities. "It's nothing."

"Are you trying to get me to go easy on you at the debate?" He was teasing, trying for a smile.

"First of all, you're going to need all the help you can get," I said more harshly than I intended. He inhaled and looked aroused again. "So no, I'm not asking for your sympathy. I just... I needed to... I just wanted to..."

I nodded back at the bar, suddenly feeling naked and foolish in this dress. It was *so* not me.

"You wanted to get a little high and fool around with your archnemesis in an alley?" He took a step closer to me again, and I backed up. I gathered my courage.

"I'm not usually that girl."

"I liked that girl."

"Yeah, well, say goodbye to her." I tossed my hair over my neck, wondering how high you could be and still legally drive. The intensity of those moments with Finn had left me starry-eyed and sober, but still, getting arrested would not help matters.

He cupped my face in his hand, and I leaned into it against my better judgment. "I like this girl a lot. This girl's my speed. But I also like the girl you're going to be at the debate too." He caressed my lower lip with my thumb. "Smart. Sarcastic. Rockin' a pantsuit like it's your fucking job."

Oh God. His smile was wide and warm, and I fought the strongest urge to fall right into it. Instead, I stuck to my guns.

"I'm not saying tonight was a mistake," I said flatly.

His hand dropped. "Oh," he said. Hurting Finn's feelings was like stomping on a sexy teddy bear.

"I'm not. I got it out of my system. I got *you* out of my system."

"I was in your system?"

"But now... now I need to focus. *You* need to focus.

Everything can just go back to normal. And we won't be doing that—" I nodded at the bar. "—again." And I couldn't even *begin* to level with him on the sheer number of reasons why we were entirely wrong together. Starting with the fact that we were currently supposed to be *fighting* each other. And ending with the fact that I wasn't attracted to men like him. *Ever.* I couldn't be.

I slid into my car and turned it on. The papers mocked me. *Shut the fuck up*, I wanted to say. To inanimate objects.

I looked, and Finn was crouched down again, eye-level, like the other night.

"Can I say something?"

"No."

"First, I knew you were going to say that, but I'm saying something anyway. Secondly"—he reached forward, threading his fingers through the hair at the nape of my neck—"I can't stop thinking about your hair." He scratched my scalp, lightly, and I almost purred.

"What the fuck does that have to with anything?"

His lips curled, just a fraction. "And that mouth of yours." He shook his head. "You make me angrier than any other person I've ever known."

"Um, ditto," I said. His fingers tugged at my hair, ever-so-gently, the strands pulling at the nape. Dominant. My toes curled in my sandals.

"But now that I've had a taste of you, it's not enough, Avery," he said. His voice had gone rough as sandpaper.

"What would be enough?" I said, even though not moments before I'd sworn off him. *What was happening?* "And let's start by assuming you could handle me."

He pulled, not gently this time. "Cheeky," he said. Right in front of my eyes, easygoing Finn was turning into something darker and possessive.

I liked it. I didn't want to like it.

He draped his other arm over the steering wheel, his big body invading everything.

"A lot of women make this mistake about me, love. You wouldn't be the first. Because, yeah, I'm a pretty mellow guy," he started, his blue eyes stunning. "And if you ordered me on my knees and told me to eat that sweet pussy for hours, I'd do it in a heartbeat."

His eyes traveled down my body, to the junction between my legs. "In fact, I might have been getting myself off on that image for a week now."

I wanted him to kiss me so badly.

"But back there, in the alley?" He leaned in close, lips inches from mine. "I also would have fucked you through that wall."

I whimpered.

He pulled back. "After making you beg for it, that is."

Finn stood up, towering over me. "If you don't want to hook up again, I respect that. You've got a lot on the line right now, and I'd never do anything to jeopardize your happiness. But tonight? You asked me for something you needed, and I gave it to you." He tilted his head. "Ask me again, Avery. I'd fucking *worship* you."

18

AVERY

$\mathcal{I}$ stared into the audience in the auditorium at UC San Diego. The room was packed. Easily two hundred and fifty people had crammed into the space. My heart rate sped up by about a million beats.

People really cared about this fucking hotel.

Next to me, Finn shifted in his seat, his leg brushing against mine. I'd been ignoring him since we were seated ten minutes ago. It wasn't too hard—his fan base kept coming on stage to shake his hand.

If I heard one more person say, "I saw you surf at..." I was going to lose my mind.

Our moderator was a Community Development professor—Dr. Maria Gonsalves. She was supposed to be neutral, but she had to have a favorite side.

"The debate will start in a few minutes, okay?" She came over, laying her hand on the table. I nodded stoically, and Finn said, "Great, thank you." Dr. Gonsalves smiled at him.

"I hope you're ready," he whispered next to me before turning to his next adoring fan. I shivered. As soon as I'd gotten home from the bar, I'd chastised myself pretty brutally, remembering the pact I'd made when I was given this account. *No distractions. No men.*

His words at the end of the night had left me hot and itchy, a steady, irritating pulse between my legs. My insomnia welcomed that with open arms, keeping me up most of the night. And the two nights after that.

In the audience, Sal sat next to Jacobs and Lewis, all three looking grim. The Council members had a lot riding on this debate tonight. The community didn't get to vote on the permits, but depending on how people felt after Finn and I spoke, they could flood their councilmembers with phone calls, emails, and even more protests. And, with an election just two months away, they could lose critical votes.

The city council liked happy, pliable constituents. Not pissed off ones. Lopez and Ferris had both left me voicemails today reminding me of that fact.

"In polling, a slim majority of people in the city of San Diego are in favor of adding the new hotel. Let's keep it that way." I played that message over and over again, like a mantra. *Let's keep it that way.*

I saw two people who could only be Finn's parents in the front row, waving at him enthusiastically. He was the spitting image of his father. They had a cadre of communemembers who had barely taken the time to get dressed, plus Marla and Jack and the other thirty-five protesters I recognized from our morning routine.

Next to me, Finn waved back to his parents. Two of his female fans sighed.

He had a *community*. I looked away for a second, swallowing. The butterflies in my stomach were replaced with something like sadness. It was hard for me to see parents like Finn's—warm, supportive. They might look like my parents, they might live in a commune like my parents, but their relationship to their son was more *Leave It to Beaver* than anything else.

I wanted *Leave It to Beaver*.

I stared at my notes on the table, but all I could really think about was my phone call with my mother. Only my mother would express her complete and utter disgust over my career choice while asking for money at the same time. But I wouldn't—*couldn't*—be ashamed of my job. I liked it. I was good at it. After the total fucking chaos of my childhood, climbing a clear, successful and societally approved career path felt like sinking into a warm bath on a cold day.

But to my parents, I was Big Brother. Big Business. Part of the Corporate Takeover of Mother Earth.

Finn would probably agree.

I had financially supported my parents a few times before, but only in small amounts. Now, some selfish part of me wanted to punish them.

The lights flickering in the audience caught my attention: it was time.

We were seated at a long table with tablecloth, paper and pens, laser pointers for our presentations. Finn was scratching something down. He waved at a few more people in the audience, then slid the paper across the table.

I thought about you all night.

I flushed, reading it. I wasn't sure which version of him had me more flustered. Charming-surfer Finn? Dirty-talking-secret-alpha Finn?

Or this. This... thoughtfulness.

I wrote back: *So you're saying you're not prepared?*

I heard him laugh-cough into his hand.

My grip on that career ladder was slipping every time he seduced me. I wasn't going to lose it because of him. Because of one out-of-this-world orgasm. Or because of his abs. Definitely not because of his abs.

"Let's begin," Dr. Gonsalves said, and the audience quieted. Large white screens were pulled down, and I mentally recited my notes.

"I'd like to introduce Avery Dacosta. Originally from Hawaii, Avery has lived in San Diego for more than a decade. She is a developer for the Bella View Hotel chain and holds an MBA from UC San Diego. Ms. Dacosta has spearheaded the development of a large, resort-style hotel on Playa Vieja, a small beach community just outside the city. Thank you, Ms. Dacosta, for joining us this evening."

I nodded at her as the audience politely applauded.

"I'd like to also introduce our other panelist this evening, Finn Travis. Most of you know Finn as leading the protests outside the downtown San Diego office of the Bella View hotels. He is part-owner of the Beyond the Breakers surf shop in Playa Vieja and is a lifelong resident. Finn holds his master's degree in ecology also from UC San Diego."

My knuckles whitened on the table. Master's degree?

Under the table, I stepped on his foot with the heel of my stiletto.

He didn't bat an eye. "I don't mind a little pain, love. And you never asked," he said, out of the corner of his mouth as he smiled at the audience. A much larger round of applause went up for Finn.

"Ms. Dacosta, why don't you begin by giving us an overview of the Bella View's plans for development on Playa Vieja?"

I nodded, standing. I glanced at Finn and he gave me a small, secret smile.

"Certainly," I said, bringing up an image on the screen. It

was the beach, specifically, the last half-mile. I clicked and a huge, twenty-story hotel appeared, overlaid on the image.

"This is the original design we've been working on for about a year now," I started. High points, high points, I thought. "In designing, you can see that the hotel has the look and feel of some older San Diego properties. That was on purpose," I said, smiling at the audience. "Bella View Hotels wants this property to blend into the background as much as possible."

I heard Finn snort.

"Our goal is to feel like a beloved member of your community. Of the Playa Vieja community. The Bella View has a long history of working with, and improving, the tourism industry in coastal towns across the country. This would be similar," I said, indicating with the pointer. I clicked, and several swimming pools appeared in front of the building.

"The hotel would obviously attract tourists from around the world, who would love to sink into one of our state-of-the-art infinity pools. Play a round of golf on a beautiful golf course. Again, the idea is to provide the customer with full view of the gorgeous Playa Vieja beach."

I smiled again and clicked.

19

FINN

*A*very was doing her song and dance, and the audience was totally falling for it. Shit, *I* was falling for it. I kind of wanted Avery to do better, for the audience to agree with her more.

And I wasn't lying when I told her I hadn't been able to stop thinking about her. A small part of me wanted to see her disarmed by the knowledge, off-balance, before she took the stage.

A larger part of me was just desperate for her to write back, *"me too."*

Because only if she felt the same way would I feel some sense of clarity around this slow-burning obsession. In between my fun, easy summer flings, I'd had only a couple of relationships, although none lasted longer than a few months. All of those women were laidback and soft around the edges. It wasn't that they weren't smart, it was just that the main things we talked about were surfing, the ocean, and also surfing.

Avery was a confusing blur of hard and soft, and every

word out of her mouth challenged me in a way I wasn't used to. I wanted to talk to her just as much as I wanted to kiss her. And I wanted to kiss her very, very badly.

Watching her click through those slides, I wanted to throttle her boss for calling her robotic. She wasn't. She was just... Avery. Smart. To the point. No bullshit. I felt a sense of pride as she made a joke and the audience laughed.

She blushed, just a little. She hadn't expected them to respond like that. After the other night, those hard-yet-soft edges intrigued me even more. I pictured Avery in that commune, needing love, needing affection, always having to comfort herself. It was in such stark contradiction to my childhood, which was one extended moment of happiness.

"Development will be fast-tracked because we want the least amount of effect to be felt by the local residents. I know how important that is to the Playa Vieja community and want this audience to know we take that very seriously."

She clicked, and a pie chart came up. "I want to talk a little bit about jobs." She paused, seeming to gather a bit of courage. "This is not easy to talk about. I know that the recession hit Playa Vieja hard, and it's taken a while to bounce back."

I shifted in my seat, feeling awkward. The year of the recession was when I had my first real break. A Billabong ad rep had seen me at a surf competition in Mexico and wanted me as a model for their upcoming line. It might have been a recession for Playa Vieja, but that was the year I became semi-famous: selling Vans, posing with surfboards, appearing in ad campaigns. Between the sponsorships and the money I made from the surf shop, my income was pretty steady. I wasn't incredibly rich, but I definitely wasn't hurting like the other residents of Playa Vieja.

"The recent Census indicates an unemployment rate of 13 percent in Playa Vieja, which is six points higher than the city of San Diego." She paused again, then said, "Your community is struggling, and the kind of financial incentives that come with tourism can no longer be ignored. In the first year, our experts estimate another five to six hundred jobs would be added, in everything from construction to hospitality."

She clicked again. "And with the impact tourism generally has, those same experts estimate fifteen hundred new jobs over the course of four years."

Fuck me. Why had Avery gone first? Because now I was going to be the guy to talk about the importance of the environment over the needs of people who were out of work. Both Avery and my dad had brought this up beforehand— the larger implications of development beyond the environment. I'd straight-up ignored them.

"I'd like to leave some time for my colleague Finn to speak, so I'm going to end by saying: I know tourism can be controversial, especially in close-knit communities like Playa Vieja. I think the Bella View Hotel is the right thing to do for a number of reasons. I think it will put Playa Vieja on the map as a beach destination. I think it will enhance your community. I think it will strengthen your local economy and provide folks with a decent living. Thank you."

The audience clapped, a little more strongly than before. They liked her.

Avery's face was flushed and glowing. She looked beautiful.

She sat next to me. "Top that, hippie," she said, out of the corner of her mouth.

I grinned broadly at her, then turned to the audience.

"Well, that's hard to beat, everyone. Except that I'd like to talk about something larger than a hotel. Larger than a swimming pool and a tennis court and tiny chocolate mints left on your pillow."

I stood, moving to the center of the stage. "I want to talk about the earth."

20

AVERY

$\mathcal{I}$ might have exceeded the expectations of this audience, but Finn was playing right into their hands. Because it was true, very true, that Playa Vieja needed tourism to jumpstart its dwindling economy. All coastal communities did. It was a harsh reality, but fishing could no longer be their lifeblood.

But the people who needed jobs the most weren't in this room tonight. Tonight, it was filled with higher-income former hippies who still cared about the environment more than anything else.

Finn was relaxed on stage, open and warm and so damn handsome it hurt to look at him.

"One of the things I studied for my master's thesis was the impact of tourism on the environment, especially in coastal communities. As residents living in and around the city of San Diego, we've seen it firsthand."

Finn clicked, and a chart popped up with images of sandy beaches.

"Erosion. San Diego loses valuable, beautiful coastline every year to erosion. Humans cause erosion and coastal loss too. One way?" He looked at me, then clicked. "Property development."

Tiny sea turtles struggled to pull themselves across a sandy expanse. The audience exhaled an audible "awww." I fought rolling my eyes. "Sea turtles, which are currently listed on the Endangered Species List, nest up and down our beaches, especially on Playa Vieja."

He clicked again, to an image of a small child, picking up a baby sea turtle and showing it to his friends. "Increased activity on the beach—especially from tourism—has been shown to dramatically impact the survival rates of nesting and newborn sea turtles."

I suddenly had a memory—of watching a baby sea turtle, no bigger than my palm, struggle across the beach to the pounding ocean waves. Of my mother, lightly touching my shoulder, as the sun rose over the water. "*The earth is bigger than us,*" she'd said.

I fought it back. Finn clicked again. "Generally speaking, hotel development always impacts the local community, and often those impacts are felt immediately." He paused. "And not easily mitigated."

He clicked. "Bella View Hotels plans to install a five-star restaurant on-site, specializing in local seafood."

I wanted to yell out, "*Yeah... that's where the jobs come from,*" but held my tongue.

"The impact of human lives on fish in the Pacific Ocean has been incredibly detrimental. Adding even just one more restaurant contributes to overfishing. Plus, the hotel will bring an increase in the use of water, energy, additional cars and contribute overall to increased pollution. And we could all night talking about the other dirty secret of tourism. Playa Vieja is comprised almost entirely of life-long residents like myself—who choose to stay and raise their children in a place they have come to love over generations. Tourism raises property taxes, raises rents. The Bella View has yet to give a real answer when it comes to environmental impact. And it has yet to fully take responsibility for the families who will have to leave the community they know and love because they can no longer afford to live there."

Finn turned off his presentation and stood, facing the audience with his arms spread.

"I don't want to make it seem as though the economic issues facing our community are something to be scoffed at in the name of an ocean view."

I coughed loudly into my hand.

"And I'm not saying that tourism is always bad. I just..." He seemed to struggle for a minute before finding his words. "I just... Playa Vieja is a unique community. The beach feels like a wild, overgrown paradise. It is a paradise. It's the last, remaining vestige of the San Diego we all know and remember. And I don't think it's wrong for our community to want to keep that. I don't think it's wrong for us to stare in the face of progress and change and wonder if it's the right kind of progress and change. For us."

He paused and then looked at me. "I just think we can all work harder to be a little bit better. To rise above the need for new money, new things, new hotels and enjoy the ocean for a little while longer."

There was a long pause, and he kept his eyes on me, so much so that Dr. Gonsalvez cleared her throat awkwardly. Finn turned, and said, "Thank you," to the audience, who just about lost their damn minds clapping all over each other.

Goddammit.

21

FINN

$\mathscr{T}$he audience was asking us questions now, and Avery and I were fielding them easily. We were thirty-five minutes in and supposed to be ending soon. It wasn't clear to me who the audience favored, but a low level of tension clung to every exchange Avery and I had. Next to me, she simmered with irritation. *You're doing great*, I had scribbled, honestly, on the piece of paper between us at one point. She ignored it.

"Ms. Dacosta," an audience member said, raising his hand. "Can the Bella View Hotels answer to Mr. Travis's allegations that development on Playa Vieja will have long-term environmental impacts?"

I saw her hesitate. Throughout the debate, my master's degree had come in handy, and it was clear to me that environmentalism wasn't Avery's—or the company's—strong suit.

"I can," she began, slowly. "But I want to make sure this is clear to everyone in the audience—all development has an impact on the environment. We're not saying we won't, just that we'll try our best to work within our legal obligations to ensure we're meeting regulations on things like water quality and air pollution. But, yes, it will have an impact, but one we're hoping will be mitigated by the fact that this community will once again be economically thriving."

She paused, then I felt her stiletto press down on my foot again. My fingers curled against the table as I grit my teeth. "And I just think that to deny a community the benefits that tourism can bring out of a desperate desire to preserve an ocean view, well, that..." She pushed, just a little. "That, to me, is just selfish. You can't have it both ways: economic success without property development. It's just not possible."

What the fuck. I yanked my foot away, jostling her a bit.

"I'm sorry," I said, feeling my temper rise. "But did you just insinuate my entire argument this evening has been about my own self-interest?" I saw my dad shake his head softly. *Careful.*

She looked at me in mock outrage. "Well, I'm not the one who has the ocean-view property on the beach in Playa Vieja. Which, coincidentally, will have a giant hotel in front of it if plans go through."

The audience was getting into it a bit, and Dr. Gonsalves pulled the microphone close to her face.

"Well, it seems like this debate just keeps getting hotter and hotter!" she said, laughing awkwardly. I was staring Avery square in the face, but she kept avoiding my eyes.

"Can I say one final thing?" I asked. Dr. Gonsalves looked less-than-confident in me, but I flashed her a slow grin, and she relented, handing me the microphone.

"First, thank you, everyone, again for being here this evening," I said, trying to sound as calm as possible. "Clearly, this issue is very important to the both of us, and we can get a bit... hot under the collar about it," I said, chuckling, and the audience laughed.

"Secondly, most of us here are Playa Vieja residents, and we owe it to ourselves, to our community, to stop this hotel from being built. You and I both know this is more than just about preserving our ocean views," I said, placing my hand under the table—and pretty damn high up on Avery's bare leg. She jumped just a bit. She was making me so fucking angry, and I was getting so fucking turned on.

"And finally, take note. Bella View Hotels do not have a good track record with environmentalism. Tourism, quite frankly, can come and go. Avery can tell you all she wants about jobs. She gets paid either way."

I slid my hand even higher, fighting a groan. I waited for permission, and when she widened her legs for me, I slid my fingers under her skirt, until the tips rested against the fabric of her panties. Which were soaking wet.

I watched Avery's knuckles whiten against the table, heard her sharp intake of breath.

"Okay," Dr. Gonsalves started to say, but Avery bit out. "I have seen coastal communities rise and fall with opportunities like this one. Playa Vieja deserves to thrive. Bet on tourism, and your community will prosper. And I promise... you can count on Bella View to do right by you."

She crossed her legs, crushing my hand between her thighs. Hard. Her hand landed on my cock, squeezing. I held back a curse. Thank *God* there was a tablecloth.

The moderator yanked the mic back and looked at us both like we were children she was admonishing at the playground.

"And that's our program, folks," she finished, staring at us. I could feel the gentle flexing of Avery's thigh muscles under my hand. The audience was silent for a second and then applauded. Heartily, actually.

"I think they liked us," I whispered to Avery. She responded by uncrossing her legs and standing swiftly, smoothing down her skirt.

I shook out my fingers. "Those things are like a fucking vise," I said, gaze traveling up the legs in question.

She narrowed her eyes at me. "In front of this entire audience, in front of my boss, you implied that my employer would screw the *shit* out of an economically struggling town? And that I'd just cackle away with my paycheck because money is all that I care about," she said, voice low and sounding hurt.

My anger abated, just a second, before I said, "Wait a minute. You're pissed at me? You implied in front of my entire community that the only reason I've dedicated my life to this protest the last two months—and gotten all of them involved—is to preserve my ocean view. That I'd let my neighbors go jobless and hungry because I'd hate to be inconvenienced in any little way. Are you *serious*?"

I was standing now, looking down at her, my body warring with the desire to never see her again... and another darker, more primitive desire, to bend her over the table, rip that skirt in half, and fuck her.

"Ms. Dacosta? A few questions...?" We both looked over. It was camera crews from the local media.

I felt a similar tug and turned. It was Julie.

"Heeeey," I said. She kissed me, which was a surprise since we hadn't seen each other since our date.

"You did great up there." She lowered her voice. "You clearly won. She was terrible."

I bristled. "That's not..." I started to say, and then I was mobbed. My entire body was over-stimulated—angry and aroused and now surrounded by people. Councilmember McAffee grabbed me first, pulling me off to the side and away from Julie's wandering hands.

"Finn," she said. "That was absolutely terrific. Many, many happy constituents this evening."

I still got a bit nervous when she spoke to me. "Good," I said as smoothly as I could. "Listen, I'm sorry about what Avery said. I would never want you—or anyone else—to think I was in this for my own personal gain. The environment, and the community, is my main concern. As it is yours, I presume."

She nodded, looking distracted, then said, "Sure. Oh, absolutely," but it lacked conviction.

"What is it?" I asked.

"Oh, nothing. I just... well, I liked how you attacked her at the end."

"She attacked me first," I said, defensively and hated how I sounded. Like a child throwing a tantrum at school.

"Everything you said up there was on point, but I have to say you made me think about some ways we can hit back against the Bella View a little harder. They're a huge hotel chain. They've got thick skins."

I thought about Avery's soft skin under my hands, my fingers gliding up her thighs.

"I think we could demonize her a little more."

"Who, Avery? I literally carry a sign every day that implies she's Satan," I said, feeling oddly protective of her. "Plus, I don't know, you don't think she has some fair points? We do need to improve Playa Vieja's economy. She's not wrong."

McAffee tilted her head at me, an odd smile on her face. "You're not a politician, Finn. It's kind of refreshing. But I'll still have my team dig a little, see if we can't find something to use against her. I loved what you said though. Either way, she still gets paid." She tapped my shoulders gently. "I liked that. You did well."

She spun around and left me before I could even reply, leaving me confused and a little sad. Hearing my words said back to me made me slightly sick.

But I didn't even have a chance to think about it before a local newspaper reporter propped a mic in my face.

"Finn Travis! Great debate. Any other quotes you want to say about Avery Dacosta? Things were getting a bit, uh, tense up there."

I shook my head. "It's not about that; it really isn't. Avery and I, in fact, are good—" Good what? Good at dry-humping each other in the alley of a restaurant? Good at fighting with each other in parking lots? "—are colleagues. Avery and I are colleagues and are just both very passionate. At the end of the day, we just want what's right for Playa Vieja." I smiled. "Same passion, different sides."

The reporter raised his eyebrows and laughed. "Should have heard what she said about you, man."

"What?" I asked, but then my parents and their entire commune swept me off the stage. "Wait, what?" I called back, but my dad had his hand on my back and was pushing me through the audience.

People were calling out to me, thanking me, and for a second, it was just nice to bask in their warm praise. To remember why I had dedicated the last months of my life to something so out of my ordinary life.

And I wasn't just being selfish. Right?

We were outside of the auditorium when my mom turned around and hugged me, hard.

"Hello," I said, laughing, trying to untangle myself. She had always been the World's Longest Hugger. "Thank you for coming. And thank you," I said to the top of her head, nodding at the half-dressed commune members. "It was nice to see some friendly faces in the audience."

Marla and Jack poked their heads around. I winked at them. "And it was nice to have our resident shit-starters, the Bongo Twins."

Next to me, I heard my dad laugh, and my mom squeezed me even tighter. She said something, muffled against my chest.

"What?"

"We're proud of you," she said, beaming up at me. At six foot three, I was officially more than a foot taller than her.

"You're always proud of me."

She shook her head. "This is different. You're finding your voice. Using your celebrity for good."

"Oh... well," I started, thinking about Councilmember McAffee's's odd comments at the end. About how heated everything got. About my beachfront view. "I don't know if we're going to win or anything, but I guess it's still important."

"To educate your community about the harmful effects of big business and capitalism? To stop the impacts of development on the environment? Yes, yes, it is," one of the commune members, Meadow, said brusquely. "And I don't like that Avery. You were right, Finn. She's just out for herself, not for us."

I nodded as my mom finally let go. *You can't stop human progress, Finn. I'm not the enemy here.*

"Yeah..." I said, staring off. I caught a glimpse of Avery's long legs as she exited down the opposite hallway. I swallowed against a wave of yearning and furious anger. I was happy the majority of the audience didn't seem to agree with Avery's accusations, but it still stung.

"How about a beer on the porch before I head back?" my dad asked, distracting me. "You look like you need one."

I INHALED THE OCEAN, exhaled the waves. Inhale. Exhale. I used to do this all the time when I was younger, contemplating surfing a giant wave that could definitely get me killed.

My dad and I were sitting on my front porch, feet propped up on the railing, watching the water. It'd been easy to forget, during the debate, that my parents' future also potentially hung in the balance. That I was fighting *against* something they needed. Now, my mom's praise stung, and I sat uneasily next to my dad. I wasn't sure what to think.

"They're gonna win, right?" I finally asked. *Maybe it'd be easier if they did.*

He shrugged. "I don't know, Finn. You put up a pretty good fight up there." He paused. "Avery did too. She's as smart in person as she is on TV."

"She's really smart, even though I think she doubts herself. But it's pretty obvious to me that she can do anything she puts her mind to." I took a sip. "She's also really independent. Did you know she put herself through college and grad school all by herself?"

Dad looked at me, a bemused grin on his face. "No, son, I didn't know any of those things about Avery. How do *you* know them?"

I took another sip of beer, stalling. "We shared a joint together at that reggae bar off of Collins Drive."

He coughed on his beer. "Well... all right then. Kind of a *Romeo and Juliet* thing you got going on?"

"Hardly," I said. "I also don't... you know, *do* things with women. Avery and I are just good—" I stumbled over that word again. "Good colleagues. To be honest, we see and interact with each other once a day, every day. I know we're supposed to be enemies but..."

"Life's not really like that," he finished. I inhaled the ocean, exhaled the waves. I was feeling amped up and edgy. "You know, and absolutely no pressure here, but you could always *do a thing* with a woman. A partner. If you wanted to. Just because your mom and I live in the commune now doesn't mean we're against that. We're still married."

I smirked. "Marriage is a contract between the patriarchy and the capitalist machine. A business relationship that demeans women." I paused. "That's a direct quote from mom. She told me that when I was sixteen years old."

My dad's laugh echoed across the sand. "Well, your mom is right. Except our marriage isn't like that at all."

"You two have the best marriage." I'd always admired it. Held it on a pedestal that loomed high above other relationships.

My dad shook his head. "We have an honest marriage. Doesn't mean it's not hard. And the women you've dated before, well, they just don't seem to challenge you very much, Finn."

"Or at all," I said. "They're beautiful and fun and... they like surfing, I guess."

"Life is more than surfing."

I pretended to fall out of my chair, making him laugh again. "'There is nothing more important than surfing.' That's a direct quote from *you*."

"Ah, Finn," he said, taking a long swig. "Even parents continue to learn things after they're done raising their children. And please don't take this the wrong way, but Avery... she seems like quite the challenge."

"Like you wouldn't believe. I've never met a woman who —" I stopped myself.

"Go ahead," Dad said.

The wind shifted a little. "You heard the things she said about me tonight. She doesn't share my values or our values. She fights dirty. She's absolutely infuriating to talk to. She's uptight and stressed out and—" Except that every word out of her mouth was both interesting and unexpected. Except when she wraps her long legs around my waist and rides herself to orgasm.

I stopped, lost in my thoughts. My dad was the master of silence. He never felt its awkwardness, instead letting it stretch out, like a long road.

After a while, I finally said, "How do you feel about all this? With the shop and your finances and... I mean, are you still *okay* with the protest? Am I doing the right thing?"

He didn't immediately respond. "These things are complicated. You think I didn't lose friends, shit, even family members, for some of the things I've stood up for over the years? Some of the causes were a clear case of right and wrong. Civil rights, women's rights, fighting for justice and equality. But something like nuclear power?

"You felt *nuclear power* was complicated?" I couldn't begin to count the number of protests I was dragged to as a little kid about that.

"Sure," he said, swigging from his beer. "You know how I feel about both of those things. But you know what war and nuclear power have in common? They create jobs. And your mom and I might feel one way about money. About capitalism. But that's way different for a single mom with three kids just trying to put food on the table every night. If she works in that nuclear power plant and it provides her with some semblance of security..." He trailed off. He looked like he wanted to say something else but stopped himself.

In front of us, a giant wave crashed against the shore. Even now, in the dark, I felt my body responding, my fingers itching for a board to hold on to.

"But yes. You're doing the right thing."

LATER THAT NIGHT, much later, after my dad had left, I dragged out my boxes of books from when I was in the master's program. My thesis. Old papers. I found the notebook I'd kept during that time with ideas I had for improving Playa Vieja. Ideas I'd given up on to get back to surfing. Ideas that felt too... *practical* for my idealistic mind.

I flipped through the pages, seeking, searching. Remembering. Tapping my finger against one word that kept coming up over and over, highlighted and underlined and circled: *ecotourism.*

22

AVERY

I knew where they'd be. I'd seen signs of them last time I'd caught Finn surfing—just behind the last rock, close to the tiny cave. Safer, a little secluded. She'd made the right choice.

She was a good mom.

It was three in the morning. I walked down Playa Vieja, nothing but the full moon lighting my way. Tiny crabs scattered at my footfalls. Inside the houses lining the beach, people slept. I walked past Finn's house—he'd be up soon.

But not yet. It was still just me.

The fact that I'd come at the right time was nothing short of a miracle. The mound was already shaking gently, shuddering with life. I sat, yards away, close enough to see but not close enough to disturb them. My brother Wave had taught me that when we were kids.

"They'll think you're a predator and stop hatching," he'd whispered, pointing at the tiny heads pushing through. I wished he was here.

I sank into the sand with a giant blanket and a thermos of hot chocolate. Just like in my memory, the first tiny head poked through the sand, looking around. Opening its eyes for the first time.

"Good morning," I whispered to the baby sea turtle. As a kid, I'd get too attached to them until I had to stop coming out. About half of them wouldn't even make it to the ocean —just get snapped up by a bird, or a dog, or pass out from exhaustion and die on the sand. Even fewer would make it through the harsh waves.

This one, though, I had a feeling about. He was a fighter. Kind of like Finn.

Oh God, don't name it, I thought. But it was too late. As its tiny front legs pulled out, my heart gave a little leap. A few other heads were starting to make their way out. The ocean was flat this time of night, almost glassy. A good time to take the plunge, so to speak, if you were a newborn turtle.

After the debate, Sal and I had gotten fairly tipsy at the bar next to City Hall. I'd asked him about the environmental impacts of the Bella View. I'd worked on countless hotels; I wasn't naive. But we'd done the absolute bare minimum to prep for it. Enough to get the environmentalists off our backs. Nothing more. And Finn's statements wouldn't stop rattling around in my head.

"Environmentally though... impacts on Playa Vieja will be minimal? Right?" I said, two Long Island Iced Teas deep. The world had taken on a kind of milky color. Underneath the bar, I crossed my fingers.

"Are you fucking kidding me, Avery?" Sal said with an evil grin. "That beach is fucked. Capital F *fucked*. When have we ever cared about the *environment*?" He couldn't even really finish the sentence, he was laughing almost hysterically. He'd also drunk twice as much as me. And his wife wouldn't stop calling his phone. I wondered if he ever missed her. I wondered if he thought fucking over the environment (his words) was the right thing to sacrifice your marriage over. And your kids.

I swallowed, mouth dry. "Oh, okay. It's just that—don't you think Finn brought up some good points? I mean, it's just continuing bad press if we, you know, fucking murder all those snowy plovers or whatever he kept talking about."

He laughed again. "It always got me when he talked about the birds. The birds!" Sal looked me dead in the eye. "Listen to me when I tell you: The Bella View Hotel chain doesn't give a good goddamn about the environment. And neither should you. That's a land mine you don't want to touch. It'll just go off in your face."

The tiny Finn turtle was all the way out now, along with two of his siblings. They started pulling themselves along the sand to the ocean. Toward home. A circle of life so primal I felt it ingrained in my skin. Somewhere deep and private. A sense of something bigger than myself.

The earth is bigger than us, my mother had said that morning. The tiny sea turtles hatched and stretched and tumbled for the sea.

I watched, waiting.

THE NEWSPAPER WAS TAUNTING ME. My assistant, Samantha, had dropped it off with a knowing grin and a swing in her step. "Looks like you won, huh?" she asked, nodding her head at my window. The window that faced the protestors.

"Is Finn out there?" I asked, *so* obviously. He wasn't there when I walked in, like he had been the past morning, every morning.

"Nope, haven't seen him," she said, before closing my office door. Now I was just staring at it. After the debate last night, I felt confused, although I should have felt triumphant. The council members were pleased. Sal had taken me out for congratulatory drinks. I felt proud of myself. The last two years of my life were finally starting to feel like they were worth something. That the sacrifices were warranted.

And don't fuck it up, I reminded myself.

But Sal's dismissal of Finn's claims irked me. And those damn baby sea turtles wouldn't leave me alone.

There was a knock on my door.

"Come in," I said. Samantha had the biggest shit-eating grin on her face. "You have a visitor." She stepped aside to reveal Finn. Dressed in a suit. A dark gray suit. A *power* suit.

And shoes.

I felt my mouth drop open for a second, before recovering.

"Yes?" I asked, irritated.

"Do you have a minute?" he asked. His hair was slicked back, blue eyes blazing. Instead of his usual scruff, he was clean-shaven.

I looked down. There were fucking *cufflinks* at his wrists.

"I'm pretty busy."

"Good," he said, stepping inside. He strode across my office and stood in front of my desk. Towering. He was a glass of cold water on a sweltering day. *This* Finn. Crisp white shirt, open at his throat, dark tie, shoulders like you wouldn't believe. His pants clung to his thighs, thick and muscled. He looked like a power-hungry CEO.

Or a type A lawyer.

"You own a suit?" I asked sarcastically. I fluttered my hand to my mouth in mock surprise.

Finn's eyes narrowed. "For the record, Avery, I'm furious with you."

"Well, I'm pretty pissed at you."

"So I thought, since you clearly don't respect me as a professional, we could meet and have a professional meeting, in your professional office, about the multitude of reasons why building your hotel will have countless harmful impacts on the environment and the community."

He sat down in the chair, leaned back like a king. "And for the other record, I know why you're pissed at me." He reached forward and flipped the newspaper open with one long finger.

"Playa Vieja is a paradise just waiting to be discovered by the world," he read. "The fact that Finn Travis, for his own selfish reasons, in cahoots with Councilmember McAffee, would work to halt the flow of tourism into an economically struggling community to preserve his ocean view is not just wrong. It's immoral, and against the values and goals of the Bella View Hotel chain."

I cringed inwardly, although I'd felt good saying it last night.

"You're pissed I didn't tell you I had a master's degree."

"What?" I asked. "I couldn't care less."

"You assumed I was stupid. That I was a shallow surfer too stoned to actually accomplish anything."

Every muscle of his body seemed coiled to strike. And he was absolutely right.

"I'm not... that's entirely inaccurate," I said, covering. I was ashamed to admit it, but I'd assumed he wasn't formally educated.

He shook his head. "You didn't think I'd bring anything to the table and environmentalism, love, isn't your strong suit. The audience stumped you. I stumped you." He glanced over at my framed MBA. "That won't get you far with the Playa Vieja folks."

"Oh, and a master's degree in ecology will?" I snapped.

"It does when your hotel chain still refuses to answer to the many environmental concerns—legitimate, legal concerns—we've brought to your attention."

"The birds," I gasped, clutching my hands together mockingly. Then realizing I sounded just like Sal last night. Heartless and happy about it.

"Don't be cute," he said. "I'm being serious, Avery. You need to take me seriously."

"Is that why you wore the suit?"

He stared at me, for a long time, until I fidgeted. "You grew up in paradise."

"That paradise wasn't real, Finn. We barely had enough to survive, and at some point, some company, somewhere, is going to bulldoze that beach and build a hotel for rich people. It's just a reality," I said.

"But you liked it there. Loved it there. Right?"

"You don't know how I felt."

He crossed his arms, stern in his suit. It was *so* not like him.

And it was turning me on *so* much.

"Tell me, then. Or here, I'll tell you a little bit about my paradise. Playa Vieja."

I glanced at the wall clock, desperate to stop this conversation. "Finn, I've got—"

"I didn't have a television growing up," he started, talking right over me. I glared at him, leaning back in my seat. "I didn't have a television, so all of my entertainment was outside. And, to be clear—" He cleared his throat awkwardly. "—we didn't have a lot of money growing up either."

"Oh," I said.

"That house was inherited, or we would probably have

lived in a communal yurt, like my parents do now. I support my parents. Financially. Not entirely but quite a bit."

"Your sponsor money?"

"That and any other publicity I can get my hands on." I glanced at the photo of my parents on my desk.

"To make ends meet, my mom would sometimes work as a housekeeper in a hotel. A hotel that treated her like shit, by the way."

I bristled. "That's my fault?"

"No. I'm just saying... you talk a lot about bringing in jobs and not a lot about how folks in those jobs would get treated. Or how little they'd be paid."

I opened my mouth to argue, but he cut me off. "My dad owned the surf shop, which did well sometimes. And not-so-well other times. Also, my parents were not the best at controlling their finances. Every time a friend or family member needed help—or shit, even a stranger—they'd give them all we had." He paused, and I found myself nodding along. *What's best for the community is always best for the individual.* That had been drilled into my head over and over again as a child. I had watched the commune give the last bite of food to a stranger on the beach, even if that last bite was meant for me.

"All of that to say—I didn't have a TV because we couldn't afford it. And—"

"Television is a tool of the government, the sword of the oppressor. It turns the masses into robots that shirk their communal duties in favor of buying dishwashers." I quoted my parents before I could stop myself.

He grinned, slow like molasses. "See? You know what I'm talking about."

"A little," I admitted. He cocked his head. "Okay, a lot."

"So, the beach was my entire entertainment. During the

nesting season, my parents would take me out there in the morning, and we'd watch the baby sea turtles hatch and pull themselves toward the shore."

"Environmentally speaking, that's not a smart idea," I countered.

"From a *safe distance*," he said. "And then add in the fact that I surfed most hours of the day and spent the remainder exploring the beach, and you have one pretty idyllic child-hood." He spread his palms on my desk. "I want that for other children."

"But your family struggled to put food on the table," I pointed out, a little too harshly. "Plus, it's not like we're taking over the whole beach. Not the part where, you know, where you..." I stopped.

"Where you watched me strip off my wet suit off?" His gaze was a mix of playful and predatory. "And it's the prin-ciple of the thing. Tourists will take over every square inch of that beach. It'll be ruined. We'll lose our home."

"I don't operate in principles, remember? I operate in numbers. Money."

He loosened his tie. "So then, money-grubbing capital-ist. Tell me about the paradise you grew up in."

"I already told you. It wasn't a paradise."

He shook his head. "Not the commune part. Not the way they treated you," he said, voice softening. I wanted to melt against his hard chest. "The parts you loved. The parts you cherish."

The blue of his eyes was so dark I was tempted to fall, head-first, into them. "I don't like to think about it anymore. It's too... complicated." There was no better word for a child-hood that was one-half heaven and one-half hell.

Finn swallowed. "You don't want that for other children? Because at the rate we're destroying the environment, they're never going to have what we had. See what we saw, every day."

"I want other children to grow up with parents who love them and show them they love them. I want children to grow up in financially stable households. I don't think turning a beautiful beach into Disney World is really that bad."

"Then I was right then, last night, when I told everyone you just cared about your paycheck. Tell me I'm wrong." He stood up, hands on my desk and leaned forward.

It was hot in the office, hot under my suit. Everything was tinged in red. How this man could arouse me one second and piss me off the next, I'd never understand. I stood up and leaned in, until I was inches from his face.

"I care about *your* neighbors, Finn. And now you're just trying to pick a fight with me."

His eyes were on my lips. Up close, he was almost too handsome, the only defect his crooked nose—broken, I'm sure, by a wave.

"And why do you think that is?" he murmured. He leaned forward, nuzzling his nose under my ear. I suppressed a moan. I felt him shift, then run his tongue up the base of my throat to just under my chin. My eyes fluttered back.

"Can you tell me why every time I talk to you, I'm hard as a fucking rock? Can you tell me why every time I fight with you, I get even harder?"

"N-no," I said, loving the feeling of his lips against my ear, the gravelly vibrations of his voice. I fought for clarity. "Although it could be that you know I'm right?" His tongue traced around my earlobe. "It could be that you know I'm going to win."

My eyes were on my half-open office door, the open

blinds of my window. Finn's hand slid up and under my shirt and splayed across my stomach. He hissed in a breath. "Can you tell me why your skin is so goddamn *soft*?" I didn't know if I wanted those fingers higher or lower, but I wanted.

Oh, how I wanted.

"People could see us," I said, as he traced his mouth down my neck, kissing softly. Those fingers finally made a decision, slipping beneath the top of my skirt. Testing. Teasing.

"Tough shit. I'm an exhibitionist. If I had known it was you at that beach, I would have stroked my cock for you. Let you watch." His mouth was still at my ear, shredding my nervous system and any scrap of willpower I had.

"I wouldn't have watched," I said, taunting now.

His fingers stroked the top of my panties. I leaned forward even more, and before I knew it, I had nearly crawled onto the desk.

"That's right, love," he groaned. "Crawl to me."

I stopped. "I don't like to take orders."

Suddenly his face was in front of mine, his hand removed from my skin. "Mistress of your own destiny, huh?"

"*Always*," I replied. Then I grabbed his tie, yanked him roughly, and kissed him.

I had forgotten what Finn had tasted like, but within seconds his skilled lips had me melted like butter on hot asphalt. I'd never had a man kiss me the way he did. Unhurried like he had all the time in the world. Deliberate like my mouth was something he could devour—slowly and exactly the way he wanted.

Devoted.

He pulled back. "Get on the desk."

I looked again at the office door, the open window, the

blinking lights of my phone. "No way." I was holding onto the world's smallest shred of willpower.

"Avery," he said, pulling at his tie again and shrugging off his jacket. I'd messed up the knot. He walked over, closed the door. Locked it. Shut the window blinds.

He turned back to me, now a man on a mission. Unhurried? Not anymore.

"Get. On. The. Desk." He slapped his hand down on it. I liked control, I really did. But the look in his eyes promised something dark and beautiful for my submission.

I crawled up on it. *Goodbye, willpower, it was nice knowing you.*

He arched an eyebrow at me. "As much as I like you on your hands and knees, love—" He spun his finger in the air. "—I need you sitting on the edge." I turned around, facing my office chair. My legs were trembling.

Finn was suddenly in front of me, the buttons of his white shirt pulling as his chest muscles flexed. I licked my lips. He slid off my high heels, tossing them into a corner. He reached forward, and before I knew it, my pants were unbuttoned and off my body.

He growled and pushed my legs open. His eyes were fixed on the tiny, black lace of my underwear.

"You make me so fucking furious. Why is that?" he asked, pulling my legs up onto his shoulders. He smoothed his hands over the muscles, running his tongue up my calf. I was up on my elbows, watching him, but as soon as his tongue touched my skin, my head fell back.

"I don't know," I said breathlessly. "I already broached the possibility that I'm right all the time. And you're—" He bit me, and I whimpered. "—wrong."

"Loving the environment isn't wrong," he murmured, mouth against my leg as his hands squeezed my thighs roughly. "Wanting to keep things the same isn't wrong." His thumbs moved up to my hip bones and slid under the scrap of fabric there. He lifted, and I watched the lace glide down my legs and off. Finn placed the fabric against his mouth and inhaled. His eyes fluttered closed.

"I've wanted to do that for a long time," he said. He tucked them into the pockets of his pants. "And these are mine now."

"I paid a lot of money for those," I said, too aware that my pussy was bare and glistening and open for Finn. Fucking *Finn*.

"Why do you rely on the capitalist machine to make you happy, Avery?" he said, a smirk tugging at his lips.

"Why do you refuse to believe that big business can be good sometimes?" I sighed. "And don't tell me you didn't spend a lot of money on your surfboard." His hand moved up my leg, halting just an inch from my opening. "Hypocrite," I whispered.

Then he slid two long fingers inside of me.

"Fuck me," I groaned, falling back onto the desk. He hooked them, rubbing the pad of his finger against my G-spot. I briefly saw stars. "How do you know how to do that?" I gasped.

"Practice," he said smugly. "And you didn't really answer my question."

"Which was..." I said, arms over my head now. I wanted to arch my back. I wanted to scream. His fingers just kept stroking. Rubbing.

"Why do you make me so angry? Why can't I stop fucking thinking about you?" His other hand slid under my top and bra, his rough palm scraping against my nipple. I swallowed a cry.

"I don't... I don't..." I couldn't talk. I felt his thumb circle my clit, ever-so-gently. "Why can't I stop dreaming about you," I whispered, then immediately regretted it. He stopped, everything. All his movements. I moaned in frustration.

"You dream about me?" he said softly. I sat back up, woozy at the sight. My bare legs open and spread, Finn standing between them, his fingers inside of me. Thrusting. Thumb hovering over my clit.

I nodded, biting my lip. And then my phone rang. I jumped, but Finn pressed me down, pinning me to the desk. "Answer it," he said. He sat back in my chair, lowered his head and blew a long, hot breath over my clit.

"I can't."

Finn lapped his tongue lightly over the tiny bundle of nerves. "Answer it or I stop."

I picked it up. "Avery Dacosta's office," I managed to say. Between my legs, he gave me a lazy grin, then bent his head back down.

"Avery, it's Sal." *Of course it was.*

Finn resumed flicking his tongue, and I tried to close my legs on his head. He shoved them back open, nipping at the skin of my inner thighs.

"Hi... uh, Sal," I said.

"I want to meet later. About the debate and the vote. And I want to talk promotion. New York City might be in your future after all," he said.

Finn was slowly finger-fucking me, swirling his tongue in big, lazy circles. Up. Then down.

"Oh. Okay then," I said, barely hanging on to my last scrap of lucidity. I didn't give a flying fuck about New York City. The only place I wanted to be here was here with Finn. "Later, definitely. We can meet... we can meet..." Finn's tongue had changed direction.

"We can meet later," I finally managed. "But I have another call coming through, so I'll talk to you then." I hung up the phone and threaded my fingers through Finn's hair, yanking. "That wasn't funny," I moaned, trying to pull him closer, but he pulled away with a dirty smile. Keeping his fingers skillfully moving inside of me, he lifted his other hand and began removing his tie.

"Do you remember the night I left you that joint on your porch?"

I nodded, fascinated. My hips were beginning to match his rhythm.

"I wanted to kiss you," he groaned. "So badly." We both watched his fingers moving in and out of my body. "I wanted to know what your lips tasted like."

He slid the tie from around his neck and down his chest. One-handed, he began rolling it into a tight ball.

"But even then, I knew—" He slid his fingers out of my body. They were slick. "One taste wouldn't be enough for me." He sucked his fingers into his mouth, and a growl escaped his lips.

I moaned.

"You taste better than any fantasy, Avery. All of my fantasies. So sweet." Finn shoved his fingers back in roughly. "So gorgeous." My body gave up the fight, my back bowing, a scream trying to claw its way from my throat.

"Last time you were too loud, and everyone heard us. Not that I mind. In fact, I want everyone to know who's making you come harder than you ever have before." He held the rolled-up tie next to my mouth. "And who is that, love?"

I was on fire. "You," I panted, and then he shoved the tie right into my mouth. I bit down on it, tasting his skin.

"But you're going to be a good girl for me, right?" I

nodded. "Quiet because this entire office can hear you. Quiet because you don't want your boss to know you're getting eaten out on your fucking desk."

I moaned, and the tie muffled it. Pleased with his handiwork, he settled back between my legs and pressed his tongue flat against my clit. My hips jerked, and it seemed to rile him up, the patterns he worked with his tongue beyond anything my mind could comprehend. Pleasure raced up my spine, sharp as a knife. He gripped my hips hard, lifting me closer to his mouth. He was wild, the animalistic sounds he made vibrating against my skin. I wrapped my legs around his neck, holding him in place.

Finn was something else entirely. The dedication I'd noticed when he was surfing? That single-minded devotion? The full force of it was on me, my clit, my breasts, my legs. My pleasure. He watched me with those blue eyes, stealing my breath. Owning it. Pushing me closer to an edge that was approaching rapidly.

His hand slid back up to my nipple, stroking. Pinching. I soaked his tie with my saliva. His fingers found my G-spot again, applying the perfect amount of pressure. It was almost too much. I threaded my fingers into his hair again, pulling him closer. He liked that, almost snarling against my skin, speeding up the movements of his tongue, the wet, slick sounds of his fingers moving inside of me making me heady with bliss.

I looked up at Finn Travis, six foot three surfing sex god, head between my legs like he never wanted to leave, eyes boring into mine and begging me to give him what he wanted. I flew the fuck apart, my orgasm crashing over me like a tidal wave. I screamed into his tie, tried to close my legs, but he was relentless—letting me down gently with steady licks. But the sensations refused to ebb, and he noticed. With a devilish grin, he sucked my clit between his lips, and I climaxed. Again.

I stayed with my eyes closed for a long time. He nuzzled the inside of my legs, stroking. Soothing. His hands gently removed his tie from my mouth. I was in heaven—a floating, warm sea of orgasms.

I felt movement, a shift, and then his big body crawling over mine on the desk.

"Hi," he said, and I opened my eyes.

"We're going to break the desk," I mumbled, still hazy. Finn, hovering over me, was too much to handle. Instinctively, I wrapped my legs around his waist, pressing up. He groaned, running his fingers through my hair.

"Two times, love?" he rumbled at my ear before kissing me deeply. He nipped at my lower lip. "Greedy."

"Deserving," I shot back. "It's been two years." He thrust between my legs, and I arched up. I slid my leg under, wedging it against his chest. He had an amused expression on his face—and then I flexed my foot and pushed hard.

He fell backward, landing in the chair. He arched an eyebrow at me, waiting. I sat up.

"Take out your cock," I said, sliding from the desk. Every muscle in his body tensed as his hands made quick work of his zipper. He twisted his wrist and was suddenly grasping his cock, heavy and long in his hand.

My mouth went dry. "Sweet Jesus Christ," I said.

"Like what you see?" he smirked.

"Shut the fuck up," I said, straddling him. His strong arms embraced me, pulling me snug against him. I reached down, grabbing his shaft, and he let out a string of curse words.

"Now who's in charge?" I bit his neck. Marking him.

"You," he gasped, pumping into my hand. I liked this. I

liked Finn, vulnerable and on edge. Gone were the easy grins, his surfer bravado, replaced with a savage need. I kissed him, teasing the head of his cock against my entrance.

"I need you," he said against my lips. "*Please.*"

"Where's a condom?"

He groaned in frustration. "I don't have one. Do you?" He bruised my hips with his fingers.

"Oh, sure, yeah, I keep a ton of condoms in my drawer for all the guys I fuck on my desk."

He pulled my head back by my hair, scraping his teeth along my jaw. "I have some ideas for that smart little mouth of yours, love."

I sighed happily, rocking against him, keeping him close. Loving it. The head of his cock brushed against my clit, and I moaned.

Knock knock knock.

"Avery, you in there?"

It was Sal, calling through the door. Knocking like a cop about to burst through. "Hey, your door is locked."

A strangled sound escaped Finn's lips. He leaned his forehead against mine. "Avery. I'm not trying to be dramatic. But I might die if I'm not inside of you in the next second."

"We... we..." I started, but it felt so good to be wrapped in his arms, balancing on that sharp, sweet point between tension and release.

"Think of..." I said, desperate. "Think of... um, dirty, gross hippies. Communal bathrooms. Smelly feet that have never been washed. Um... bongos." Finn started laughing, and I did too, unable to keep a straight face. "People who never wear deodorant or brush their teeth. Naive, unrealistic ideals that refuse to accept the complexities of the world we live in," I continued.

He slowly lifted me off his lap, still laughing, and tucked his cock away. His very hard, very large cock. "Naive? Maybe the freaky fucking commune you grew up in was naive, but my parent's commune has been working on the front lines of environmental advocacy for years—"

"Avery. Are you in there? I hear voices."

"That is the most ridiculous thing you've ever said," I glared at him, suddenly pissed again, pulling my pants on and slipping into my heels. I grabbed the door. "Oh, Sal, it seems like the lock is stuck. God, how did *that* happen? Hold on a minute."

I pointed my finger at Finn. "You and I grew up in the same type of environment, and you know the kind of damage that can do, advocacy or no—"

"So your negative experiences growing up in communes equate with not giving a flying fuck about the environment *at all*? I honestly do not understand a single word out of your—"

"Your pants are still undone," I said, yanking at the door-knob. "Sal, I think I've got it. Just one more try—" I wiggled the handle, huffing and puffing and faking it like a Hollywood movie star. I looked over at Finn, who had thrown his jacket back on. He pulled out my underwear and wiped his mouth on it, then slid it into the breast pocket of his suit jacket.

I gaped at him, hot and desperate to come even though I was rounding out the day with two orgasms so intense my legs were still shaking. "You've got a lot of nerve," I said, indicating the scrap of lace peeking from the pocket. He strode back to me with the easy grace of a lion stalking its prey on the savannah.

He looped his arm around my waist, yanked me up, and kissed me for all he was worth.

"Remember when I said that thing about worshiping you, love?"

Remember? I played back that memory a few times an hour, every hour, every day.

"Maybe," I said.

"That back there? Barely getting started."

He dropped me, scanning me quickly to make sure nothing was out of place, and then yanked the door open. Sal fell in, and I prayed to every single god he hadn't been listening.

"Sal! How are you this fine day?"

"Finn? Oh… I—" He was clearly surprised to see our archnemesis standing so nonchalantly in my office. My locked office. "Didn't expect to see you, I guess."

"Didn't expect to be here," he said, grinning. He rubbed his chin. "I just wanted to follow up with Avery on some of the more… distressing points of her presentation last night."

Sal nodded, his face grim. "We're going to have to agree to disagree on a lot of that, I'm afraid."

"Yeah," he said, eyes wandering back to mine. "I'd have to say Avery and I did quite a bit of disagreeing. I may even need to follow up with her later, really get into the issue."

I kept my face neutral.

"How's the, uh… the swell today?" Sal was *so* not a surfer. But he'd recently watched *Endless Summer* and fancied himself an expert.

"Bitchin'," Finn said, laughing. "And that reminds me, I've got some waves to catch."

He faked tipping a hat at me. "Avery."

"Finn." I scowled.

He shook Sal's hand, who leaned in closer to his breast pocket. "That's a nice pocket square you got there. Lace? Haven't seen that before. Where'd you get it?"

I willed a hole to open on the floor beneath me. Just take me away.

"This old thing?" Finn said, eyes full of mischief. "Had it for years. It's my absolute favorite."

SAL and I both watched Finn walk down the hallway, my eyes lingering on his surfer-butt. I don't know what Sal was looking at—just another victim of Finn's aggressive charisma.

I cleared my throat and forced myself to sit in the chair I'd just been straddling Finn on. Miraculously, my desk appeared untouched—although I'd always know.

Finn's tongue, his hands, my spread legs.

"What did you need, Sal?" I asked, praying we wouldn't be addressing the locked door issue.

"The vote's in two weeks."

"Obviously," I said, feeling my heart lurch in my chest.

"You did well last night. The council members were pleased. A few told me this morning they've already seen a small uptick in their internal polling."

"*For* the hotel?"

He nodded. I exhaled a sigh of relief. "Then those celebratory drinks last night weren't premature, then."

"Oh, I just drink constantly," he said, shifting in the chair. "But yeah, they were technically celebratory." He gave me a wolfish grin. "I wanted to talk about what I said on the phone. New York."

That's right. In the middle of Finn licking my pussy, I'd had a short conversation with my boss. And I'd completely forgotten.

"Right," I said slowly, hoping he could finally give me a

firm answer on the promotion. Sal had left me on tenter-hooks—after his initial enthusiasm two months ago, I continued to worry about his vague back-tracking.

"Just that based on last night's performance, and the fact that it now looks even more likely that the permits will be approved, you are officially the candidate we'd choose to move forward. For New York or another large East Coast city. Boston, maybe. Or Chicago. So it's yours, if you want it."

My eyes widened. I couldn't help it. "And, to be clear, a promotion would be a bigger salary?" The commune rattled around my brain. Not that I'd made a decision yet.

"Oh, yeah," Sal said, leaning back. "Big salary. Big office. But, you know, bigger responsibility. You think you can handle it? I want to see you moving up those ranks, Avery."

"Of course. Gladly," I said quickly, trying to ignore the slight discomfort I felt in my stomach. Leading this project had been like a promotion. It had been wonderful and exciting and thrilling.

And it had nearly brought me to my knees on countless occasions—stress, insomnia, constant anxiety gnawing at my bones.

"Can I ask a question?"

"Shoot."

"How do you... how do *you* do it? The added responsibil-ity? Especially with... you know, a family." Finn popped into my head, but I kicked him out. He was the absolute *last* person I'd start a family with.

Sal looked thoughtful for a second—the most thoughtful I'd ever seen him. But instead of some pearl of wisdom, he just spouted, "I like money, I guess. I like the title. I like being in charge. Don't you?"

"Money-grubbing capitalist," I said weakly. "That's me."

But was it? I'd been waiting for a conversation like this my entire professional life. Why wasn't I happier?

"And another thing to discuss would be your year-end bonus. Contingent upon success, of course, but—" Sal said, smiling wildly again. "—you're looking at probably $20,000."

I'd never gotten a bonus that significant before. I fought to keep my jaw closed.

"This is what we live for, Avery. You should look happier."

"I am, yes, of course," I said, light-headed. Between undergrad and graduate school, I had so much debt. *And the commune could use that money,* I thought.

"Do something wild with it. Take your friends to the Bahamas. Or, I don't know, a boyfriend or two. Celebrate."

I nodded along. I wasn't the kind of person to spring for a spontaneous trip to the Bahamas.

And you don't have any friends. Or a boyfriend.

My inner monologue was not helping today.

"So a yes vote means a promotion. And a bonus," I clarified.

Sal nodded. A vote for the hotel, for my business, for a project I had worked on for two years. For something good and right for Playa Vieja. For success. $20,000 for me to win. Against Finn. Who, for all of his infuriating ways and arguments, really, truly cared about what happened. To be honest, cared much more than I did, in some ways.

But in other ways, this hotel was the reason why I got into property development to begin with. Finn might think of me as a corporate drone who hated the environment, but I did believe it was the right thing to do.

"And a no vote means..." I started nervously. In the drawer next to my feet, my phone vibrated.

Sal shrugged. "I don't know, Avery... it wouldn't be a *demotion*, so to speak." I cringed. "But, you know, if the responsibility was, or is, too much for you, then we'd keep you here in San Diego. And we'd evaluate how much you could handle. It happens all the time. Not everyone's ready to run with the big dogs."

My phone kept vibrating.

"I don't want that to happen, Sal," I said earnestly. "I don't want to... go *backward*." I'd promised myself that when I moved out here. Only forward, only away from my past. Toward my future.

"Well, then... Hey, are you going to get that?" The vibrating had started up again.

"Oh, um, yeah," I said, pulling open the drawer and finding my phone. I glanced at the screen—it was my mother again. I was sad, seeing her number. And I didn't know what to do about it, so I silenced it.

"You've gotta win, then. Stay focused. No distractions."

"What?" I called out, since my fingers had snagged on something strange. Soft, a little silky, but slightly damp.

"You know. Keep doing interviews. Keep convincing the people. Don't let the protesters distract you." He'd said that last part oddly. *Did he know?*

My fingers slid the item out, and I swallowed a yelp. Finn had left his tie there, for me.

"Do you think they're distracting you?"

"Who?" I asked, head still down, fingers squeezing the tie. I'd thought the most erotic thing to ever happen to me was licking Finn's rock-hard abs in the back of that bar the other night. But no—it was definitely him yanking off his tie and shoving it in my mouth to keep me quiet.

Sex, relationships, were always hard for me. The commune had some hedonistic tendencies, which made me wary of sex—and when I did have sex, I almost never knew how to ask for what I wanted. Finn made me crave something I'd never had before, some sharp blend of dominance and submission. He made me so angry, I wanted to hold him down and use him like a sex toy. And he was so sexually tempting—so charming and attractive, I wanted to drop before him in complete and total supplication.

My mind fought over the tie, the role of the tie. I pictured myself on my knees in front of him, hands tied behind my back. I pictured him, trussed to a big bed and begging me to ride him. I wanted both. I wanted it all.

But you shouldn't want it.

"Avery, did you hear what I said?"

I sat up so fast I got dizzy. "What? Um, no. Sorry," I said sheepishly.

"Are the protesters distracting you? Because I need you focused these last few days. The last thing we need is some kind of media fuck-up that changes the council member's minds. And what's that in your hand?"

I looked down. I was clenching Finn's tie between my fingers. "Nothing," I said. "And no, I'm not distracted. At all."

"Good. I believe in you. But just get it done, okay?"

I felt a blush creeping up my neck. "Just get it done, I got it." Crisp leaves. Dark suits. Promotions. Dreams come true.

I dropped the tie. No distractions.

23

FINN

I won Titans of Mavericks on a sixty-foot wave—or so they told me. When you're on it, there's no time to stop and think. No time to measure or process. It's just you, your board, and a wall of water rising up in front of you. White spray that stings your face and a wave that curls around you tighter and faster than you can even imagine.

A tunnel that dead-ends before you can get out.

When I decided to become a big wave surfer, Titans was the goal. One of the most prestigious surf competitions in the world, I knew it would put me on the map. And though I'd medaled at Pipeline Masters, a big wave surf competition in Waimea, Hawaii, I hadn't won. I'd come in second place both times.

In my bones, I felt Titans. Waves bigger than Waimea—colder, more ferocious. When a Mavericks wave crashes down, it could be felt on the Richter scale. And there were jagged rocks below the water that you'd be pummeled into if you didn't catch the wave just right.

Whether or not the competition was even called was a magical blend of science, weather, and destiny. For two years, the swell hadn't been high enough—and then, suddenly, it was. Forty-eight hours was all you had to get up there and stand with twenty-three other competitors in the face of waves so tall they blocked the sun.

And no, I didn't know how I did it, which was the first question most people asked me. "You're the Mavericks guy, right? How do you *do* that?"

Practice, was what I wanted to say. Dedication to your craft. They wanted to hear me talk about some crucial piece of my brain that was missing, or that I was an adrenaline junkie, getting high off the fear.

I was a bit of an adrenaline junkie... but just a little. Other than that?

Practice. I memorized the ocean, as much as she'd let me. My master's degree helped with that—the role of the currents, the sweep and set of the waves, the way the wind changed everything.

Although my dad's advice was still what I held true to: The ocean always wins. She always does. You could study currents all you wanted, but one day that wave would crash down on you, and you'd have never seen it coming. That's why it was important that a crucial piece of my brain *wasn't* missing. I needed the fear. It was primal. Biological. It knew the ocean—it came from the ocean.

This, though, I could not deny: The moment, at Mavericks, when I caught that sixty-foot wave perfectly, and I mean perfectly, was the greatest moment of my life. Big wave surfing felt like that—you were taller, faster, more powerful, and you had the weight of the earth shifting and lifting you up. Pushing. Forcing. I could have ridden that wave for days.

I was drinking a cup of coffee, standing in the sand in front of my house and watching the water. I'd been out of the waves for an hour, but I was still chilled. I was thinking about that wave, that wave that could have very easily killed me but instead let me ride straight to victory—to sponsors and commercials and fun, easy, flings.

There was a feeling in the pit of my stomach that day, when I finally pushed up onto the board. That rollercoaster feeling but better—the tension of my body saying, "This is wild," but my brain saying, "I can do this."

It'd been two weeks since I'd had the privilege of pleasuring Avery on that desk. I'd jerked off countless times, but still my desire roared back with a deep need I knew only Avery could fill. Her cunt tasted sweet and musky, and she came like I suspected she would—open, vulnerable, clawing at the desk like she was falling. Moans stifled by my tie in her mouth. That small, secret smile afterward.

I'd given her that.

And yeah—I'd called her. Twice.

Okay, three times, which, it should be noted, I had never done before. Making it worse? The fact that every day I was still showing up with sixty-five other protesters to stand in front of her office with bongos and Frisbees and Phish blaring and signs calling her Satan. And every day, for the past fourteen days, she had walked past me like I didn't exist.

No confrontation, no verbal barbs, no stinging one-liners. Just... nothing, except a cool, "Good morning to you too, Mr. Travis."

Last night, Julie was on my doorstep with a hurt look on her face.

"You didn't call," she said. *Yeah*, I wanted to say to her. *I'm the guy that doesn't call.* But I brought her inside for a beer and a joint and tried desperately to make conversation with her.

But she wasn't Avery.

And before the protest, it really wouldn't have mattered. Julie checked off all my requisite boxes: pretty, sweet, interested in my interests. She was happy and light and freckled in adorable places. That night, we'd had the usual conversation—the swell that day, growing up on the beach, our favorite place to watch surf competitions.

Good stuff. Stuff I like.

I was bored though. The entire time.

I wanted Avery—raven-haired and slightly brooding, sarcastic and filthy-mouthed, brilliant and too serious.

My parents never challenged me. Yeah, we didn't have a lot of money, and yeah, sometimes—just sometimes—I'd feel a small spark of frustration when I bailed my parents out, yet again, because their ideals kept them from managing their money well. But it was so different than Avery's childhood—my parents loved me with their whole hearts. Their support and adoration came as easy as breathing. They were affectionate, warm, and still owned every piece of art I made in school

If I'd told them, "The sky is purple," they would have said, "What an interesting perspective on our sky!" If I'd said, "Today, I've decided to become a graffiti artist," they would have proudly shown off my illegal artwork to all of their friends. (Points deducted, of course, if I had joined the military or become a CEO.)

Last night, as Julie had laughed at my jokes and agreed with every inane thing out of my mouth, I pictured Avery, pointing her finger at me, scowling as she said, "That is the most ridiculous thing you've ever said."

I wanted to fight with Avery. I wanted to disagree with her. I wanted her to disagree with me. I wanted to get angry. I wanted her to challenge me, make me uncomfortable. I wanted to fuck. I wanted that smart mouth of hers doing what I told it to do. I wanted to make her come every day— every *hour* of the day.

I wanted to make her laugh, to help her shake off that coat of armor and embrace the silly, complex, fucking thrilling parts of life. With me.

I pulled out my phone again. Still no call.

THE DAY before the city council vote, the waves were high and perfectly spiraled, practically begging to be surfed. I welcomed it—a way to soothe the constant confusion I found myself in ever since Dad had told me about the shop.

And ever since I'd first laid eyes on Avery.

I spent the day before at Beyond the Breakers, combing through our books. Researching. Trying to find a way to save the shop that *didn't* involve tourism. I re-read my thesis, for the sixth time in the past two weeks, which only contributed to my sense of disorientation. The people of Playa Vieja did deserve a chance to thrive, and maybe development *was* the key to success.

This morning though, staring at the waves, I tried to remind myself that being an environmentalist was about accepting that the earth was bigger than yourself. Accepting that long-term change wouldn't happen in your lifetime, but that didn't mean you shouldn't still fight for it. That every grain of sand on this beach that would be disturbed by Avery's hotel would leave long-lasting, negative effects on future generations—even if, in the moment, it *might* help my parents.

That wanting to worship a woman who was okay with

that level of destruction was not good. In fact, it was pretty stupid.

I shivered against the cold water seeping into my wet suit. I pulled the hood up, protecting my ears, and watched the waves warily. They were rougher than usual. Minutes later, though, I was up on the board, coasting under a gorgeous barrel, and all thoughts of Avery and my dad and protests were gone.

That is, until I noticed Avery watching me.

A second set had rolled in, and I picked a wave that looked promising. I'd pushed up onto the board, looked back for a second, and saw her, perched on that same rock as before.

And fell right in.

Immediately I was under nine feet of heavy surf. Salt water shot up my nose, burning, and my left arm got tangled in the rope tying me to my board. I felt for the surface, right arm hitting air, and kicked my legs up.

I shot out, pulling my board to my side and climbing onto it. I shook my wet hair out of my eyes and saw her, standing. Watching. Maybe worried. I wanted to call out to her, but I was pissed at her for distracting me. Pissed at her for not calling.

But then, almost like an afterthought, she held up her hand and waved at me. The wind was whipping her hair across her face, so I missed her expression. But she looked open. Friendly. And before I could even think, I was swimming to shore.

She tracked my every movement, still standing as I walked through the waves and up the beach toward her. She was wearing some giant sweater that hung off her shoulder, hair wild and free. No makeup, and a thermos of steaming coffee in her hand.

Avery held it out to me, like a peace offering. I took it, the tips of our fingertips brushing.

"You look beautiful," I said, the words tumbling out of my mouth before I could stop them. She blushed, sweeping her hair off her neck. I curled my hands around the steaming warmth. "And you've been ignoring me."

Her big, brown eyes looked tired. She must not have been sleeping again.

"I'm up for a big promotion, Finn. And a bonus. If... if I win tomorrow," she said, a pained look on her face. "But if the council *doesn't* vote for the permits, I get none of that. And I'm stuck here—in fact, I'll be demoted. And I promised myself... I promised..." she trailed off.

My hands tightened on the thermos. "What?"

She looked sad. "I promised myself I never wanted to go back to that commune, home. And *especially* not as a failure. Even though, in their eyes, my job automatically makes me one. And a traitor." She smiled wryly at that. "But *I'd* know. I'd know I had achieved what I'd set out to do ten years ago. Succeed. Within the system. Create something that would survive long after I've lived."

"You love your job," I said, even though it was hard for me to see why.

"I mean... yes. I do. I really believe in the things I help to build. I really believe in economic development. Plus, I have some pretty massive student loan debt, so that bonus would be nice." She looked like she wanted to say something more, then stopped herself.

"If... shit, Avery, if I had known from the beginning, maybe I would have—"

"What—stopped? I'm not telling you this to make you feel guilty," she said, eyes on mine. "This, everything, it's bigger than our jobs now. If our positions were reversed—"

She paused. "I would feel a little bad about it. But I'm not sure if I would have stopped." She shrugged, the sweater revealing even more smooth tan skin.

"I'm not sure if I would have either," I said honestly, because she'd been so honest with me. I took Avery in, all of her. What she was starting to mean to me. What she made me feel, even now, freezing cold in the sand. I wanted us on a level playing field.

I needed both of us to have something to lose.

"A month ago, my dad came to talk to me about the shop," I started. She tilted her head, listening. "Do you ever worry about your parents? Like, financially?"

She swallowed. "Why do you think I have insomnia?"

"I know the feeling," I said. "I don't think it's as bad as it is for you, but my parents haven't always made the smartest financial investments. Not like me. And I've been selfish these past months. Unless it's the protest, shit, or a surf competition, I barely notice it." I paused. "Unless it's you," I said. "I've paid an awful lot of attention to you."

She bit her lip. "Point, Finn," she said.

I smiled despite the serious subject. "Anyway. The shop's in big trouble, and I didn't know. Didn't notice. And my dad's been drinking the Kool-Aid. If the permits don't get passed, he's pretty sure he'll have to close the shop down. They have very little saved for their retirement, and I think the shop was his idea of a safety net. I'm not sure." I took another sip of coffee, needing the break. I couldn't read her expression, soft as it was.

"Oh, Finn," she finally said. Nothing more. She knew.

"Yeah, well," I looked out at the waves. They were even rougher, a storm surely blowing in. "Tomorrow's a big day."

"I'm sorry I haven't called you," she said. She took the thermos back from me, taking her own sip. I liked the idea of her lips touching where mine had been. "Sal told me he needed me focused. No distractions." She sipped again. "And you're the distraction, by the way."

I reached forward, tucking a strand of hair behind her ear.

"How am I distracting you?" I asked, secretly pleased. I thought she didn't want to see me anymore.

"Don't make me say it."

"Avery."

"What?"

"I've heard you say much worse things to Marla and Jack in the morning. For all your fancy degrees, you've got the mouth of a sailor." I paused, catching her gaze.

She chewed on her lip but kept eye contact. "I can't stop thinking about fucking you," she said.

I was hard in an instant, in a way that only Avery seemed to bring out in me.

"What else," I said, and it wasn't a question.

She was toying with me now, one hand on her hip, head tilted. "I can't stop thinking about your cock."

"Did you touch yourself last night?"

She took a step closer to me, reached her hand out, and cupped me through my wet suit. I hissed in a breath. "Yes," she said softly. "Twice, actually."

"What do you need from me?" Two strokes of her hand and I would have been finished.

She squeezed, and I watched her pupils dilate. "This. You. Fuck, Finn, I'd let you take me on the beach right here."

She was going to be the death of me. "That sounds like a great idea," I said, and in two steps I'd grabbed her plump, round ass and hauled her up against my body, claiming her lips with mine.

Immediately her arms came around my neck, fingers

tangling in my hair. I kissed her with every ounce of frustration I'd felt these past weeks, with every ounce of yearning. With one hand, I wrapped that gorgeous hair around my wrist—just like my fantasy—and pulled her head back, taking even more of her mouth. She kept making these breathy little moans that were driving me wild.

When I finally stopped, her eyes were dazed. "But I have an even better idea."

"You tie me to your bed?"

I swallowed a growl. "You'll pay for that later," I said, nipping the side of her neck. "And no."

I dropped her, grabbing her hand and beginning to walk back to my house. "I think we should go on a date."

"You want to take me on a date on your deck?" Avery asked, eyebrow arched. "Fancy."

"You'll get to choose your part of the date, so don't get cute," I said, pulling two large pillows from my living room onto my deck. It was large and faced the entire expanse of Playa Vieja. I'd quickly changed out of my wet suit into board shorts and a sweatshirt. The sun was just rising, and it was still chilly.

"But I have a tradition that I do every time I surf, and since this is part of the *part* of the date that I get to choose, we'll start with that."

"Which is?" she asked with all the enthusiasm of a kid on the first day of school.

"Meditation," I said with a grin, guessing her response.

"*Fuck* no," she said, turning back around. "Do you get Netflix? I'll just be binge-watching..."

I grabbed her hand, pulling her tight against me.

"Hey," I said, tracing my thumb along her jawline. "What's the rush? Sit with me for a few moments and listen to the relaxing sounds of the ocean."

"Oh God, Finn, I think it's so *silly*."

I laughed, so incredibly grateful to have this sass back. "You're telling me that when you were at the commune you didn't do this? I figured you'd be a pro."

She shifted on her feet, uncomfortable. "That's not the point."

"So you did do it," I said, lowering myself cross-legged to the pillow and pulling her down.

She sighed, tossing her hair over her shoulder and dutifully crossing her legs. She was too far away, so I reached over, grabbed the pillow, and pulled her until our knees were touching. She giggled.

"Did I just hear you *giggle*?" I said in mock horror. "I would have thought that represented a bit too much spontaneous fun."

"I can have fun," she said, turning her nose up at me and settling deeper into the pillow. "And for the record, sitting on the ground and thinking about absolutely nothing to achieve some bullshit sense of Zen doesn't exactly make you the King of Fun."

I laughed again. She hid a smile.

"Tell me though," I said, pulling a lock of her hair. "Did you and your commune members do this?"

"Of course we did. Yoga and meditation every morning."

"And you don't still do it?" I asked, genuinely surprised. My parents and I had also done that every morning, and I couldn't imagine abandoning something that made my mind and body feel so good.

"No," she sighed, shaking her head. "It makes me... it takes me back too much. And I never liked it to begin with."

"Why not?"

"I don't know. It didn't feel... productive. We had so much work to do every day on the farm and in the garden. It felt like wasted time."

I nodded. "I get it, I really do. Another day, let's get into a long, drawn-out argument about the negative effects the American way of living has had on mental health and distorted views of accomplishment."

Avery rolled her eyes so hard I thought she'd fall over.

"But for today, on this date—" I reached over and grasped her hand. "—if it's okay with you, I want to meditate for ten minutes. Next to a beautiful woman who makes me laugh."

I squeezed her hand and her eyes met mine.

"Only ten minutes?"

I nodded, then faced the ocean.

Inhaled, closed my eyes. Exhaled.

And kept my hand in Avery's.

24

AVERY

$\mathcal{T}$he only reason I'd driven over this early in the morning was because I was horny.

That's what I kept telling myself—on the long walk between the parking lot and Finn's surf spot on the beach. While watching his body in the waves. While kissing him passionately, his wet suit soaking through to my skin.

I'd woken up this morning with a need so deep I wanted to cry. A need for Finn. Something about stress levels, mixed with insomnia, had me clawing at the walls. Plus, the vote was tomorrow. There was no more work to be done. And, also, *fuck* Sal.

I could distract myself all I wanted.

I wasn't lying when I told Finn I wanted him to take me in the sand. In fact, I'd had a fantasy about it on the walk down—yanking his wet suit open and down his body. Finn, holding my hands down, my pants barely off, panties shoved aside so he could plunge into me over and over again. I wanted dominant Finn. Alpha Finn.

I wanted to submit.

I squirmed on the meditation pillow. Finn squeezed my hand briefly, and I stopped.

Instead of throwing me down in the sand and having his way with me, I got sweet, surfer Finn. Which was dredging up feelings I was desperately trying to ignore. The way my heart skipped—just a little—when I made him laugh. His big hand wrapped around mine, the palms rough from years of holding a surfboard.

That he'd told me I was beautiful.

Next to me, his breaths were slow and even. I tried to match mine to his. I had this memory—had tried to forget this memory—of being shaken awake before the sun rose to sit in communal silence.

I could still do it. Or I thought I could. For the first minute, I sank into my body like I used to, listening. Seeking. All I got was a giant mixture of confusion, loneliness. Horniness. Nostalgia. Stress paired with a slight panicky feeling.

So instead I cheated, opening my eyes to stare into his living room behind us. If there was a house that was the literal opposite of my own, it'd be this one. He had traveled to a lot of surf competitions, and his living room was filled with brightly colored, funky-looking furniture from all over. Posters for his favorite jam-bands hung on the wall along with a shelf that held dozens of bongs.

Throw rugs and surf wax and dog-eared books and flip-flops littered the floor. Lived-in and slightly messy. The feel of it reminded me of parts of the commune, and a small, secret part of me wanted to lay down, right in the middle. Curl up in that feeling of community.

He started tracing light circles on the inside of my wrist. I think he was going for soothing, but all it did was light every nerve ending on fire. Circles... the man was good with circles. His tongue, his fingers. I felt slightly light-headed, staring at our entwined hands.

I tilted my pelvis deeper into the floor, seeking the right amount of pressure. Seeking release. In front of us, the waves grew rougher, crashing against the shore with a vengeance.

"I can see you cheating," Finn whispered, thumb still circling.

"If you can see me cheating, then that means you're cheating," I whispered back.

He opened his eyes. A smile blazed across his face. "Do you feel more centered?"

"Uh... no."

He leaned in and pressed his lips against mine. A soft kiss, but I could feel the hunger beneath it. Restrained. His lips teased over mine, one finger tracing up the column of my throat.

"Do you feel more centered now?"

"Is that what the kids are calling it?"

His grin was wolfish. "Do you want to know my other tradition after I surf?"

"You get really, really high and listen to Phish?"

He stood, pulling me with him.

"We get breakfast burritos."

MY STOMACH GRUMBLED on the drive over. "Breakfast burritos sound amazing right now, actually."

Finn reached over and turned on his CD player. Bob Marley's voice lilted through the car speakers.

"Nice touch," I said, settling back into the seat. He'd

rolled the windows down, and the warm breeze caressed my skin.

"What's your favorite food?" he asked.

I tapped my lip with my finger, thinking. "Mexican. You?"

"Same," he said, excited. "See? We do have things in common."

I laughed. I couldn't help myself. "Okay... so we've got, well, we've got the commune connection."

"Commune Connection sounds like the name of a band I'd be into."

"True," I admitted, smiling. "And Bob Marley. And Mexican food. And... that's about it."

He shook his head. "No way. What's your favorite color?"

"Orange."

There was a pause. "I literally hate the color orange," he said.

"See?"

"Both of us were raised without television. Or shoes. And we were both raised near the ocean."

"But you like being in the ocean. I don't," I said.

Finn pulled into the parking lot of a tiny taqueria. Parked. Undid his seatbelt, then turned to look at me. "What the fuck did you just say?"

I shrugged. "I don't like being in the ocean. It's usually cold, and people pee in it, and there are sharks."

He looked at me like I'd just grown seven heads. "You're joking."

"I'm not."

Finn reached forward, grabbed the neck of my sweater, and pulled me across the car until our lips were almost touching.

"You mean to tell me that later today I'm going to fuck a

woman that doesn't like the *ocean*?" His voice was a dangerous growl.

I whimpered, just a little.

"It's just *being* in the ocean that I don't like, not the ocean itself." I gasped. Then, he crushed his lips to mine. This kiss was possessive. Claiming.

"Can we fuck in the backseat?" I panted. He reached his hand under the neck of my sweater and under my bra. He pinched a nipple between his thumb and forefinger. "Please," I begged.

"Everything about you is infuriating," he said in response, then withdrew his hand and opened the car door. That crooked grin came back—which I now recognized as one meant to torture me. "And no, we can't. We're getting breakfast burritos. And you need to think about what you want to do on *your* part of the date."

I climbed out, legs a little wobbly. "You know what I want to do," I said. "Can that be my part of the date?"

He slung his arm around me and pulled me in so we were almost hugging as we walked into the taqueria. "Patience, love," he said, laughing. I curled into his side, grateful for the affection. I'd always had a hard time expressing that need to other boyfriends, but growing up a child with little physical touch had left me desperate for skin-to-skin contact as an adult.

Affection seemed to come easy for Finn. He was always hugging people, touching their arms, rubbing their backs. Every time I was in his presence, he was constantly touching me, somewhere, like he could read my mind. My need.

The taqueria was small and crowded and bright. Mari-achi music blared from the stereos. I loved it. "Is there a menu?" I asked.

He shook his head. "What do you want? I'll order for you."

"Breakfast burrito. Chorizo. Everything on it."

He kissed my cheek. "A woman after my own heart." Then he turned around and ordered our food in rapid Spanish.

"You speak Spanish?" I asked as he turned around.

"Yeah."

"Fluent Spanish?"

"Uh... yeah. Why?" he asked.

He held out a straw, and I snatched it. "I'm implementing a rule for this date."

"Which is?"

"You have to answer every question the other person asks you," I said.

He thought for a minute. "Deal. Now—"

"Uh-uh," I interrupted. "Your part of the date means I'm asking the questions."

I led him to a quiet, tiny table outside under a long row of palm trees. Finn greeted a few people, still speaking Spanish. We sat, and I cocked my head at him. "Do you know everyone everywhere we go?"

"I know a lot of people here. I come here with my dad all the time, especially if we surf together in the morning."

"And they all know you?"

He grinned and pointed his head behind me. I turned. On the wall, there was a large poster advertising some specific brand of surf wax. Finn was on it. Shirtless.

"Oh, for the love of Christ."

"Someone's gotta sell surf wax."

"Okay first question," I said, pointing my straw at him. "Why do you speak fluent Spanish?"

"I learned it in school," he said. "And lots of surf competitions take place in Spanish-speaking countries, so it makes it easier for me to travel. And most folks in San Diego speak it."

"And?" I asked, sensing more.

"Well... you know Marla and Jack, right?"

"Of course," I said, smiling warmly despite how much they annoyed me.

"Their son, Rico, is my best friend. He's originally from a city in Mexico called Puebla. Marla and Jack adopted him when he was thirteen and while he could speak a little English, he still mostly spoke Spanish. Marla and Jack were over my house constantly, meaning I hung out with Rico all the time. He always seemed so lonely. We'd surf together, but I wanted us to be friends. So I decided I wanted to become fluent so he'd have someone to talk to. Marla and Jack didn't speak Spanish fluently, not at first. And I learned Spanish at the same rate he learned English, so within six months, we were able to speak this weird hybrid together."

There went that heart-squeezing thing again.

"Oh," I said. "That's... that was really nice of you. And you were thirteen?"

"Yeah. We've been best friends ever since. You've probably seen him at the protests sometimes."

"When I was thirteen, the only thought I had was how to get out of the commune and *stop* helping people," I admitted. He brightened, thinking we were moving on to me, but I shook my head. "I've still got questions."

"Ask me anything," he said, spreading his palms. Our food arrived, and I was momentarily distracted. We ate in silence for a minute, and then I launched back in.

"How come you don't do anything with your master's degree?"

He choked a little. "Oh... um, so you're really asking questions."

"I don't know. I feel like you kind of play this shallow surfer role and..."

"Surfers aren't shallow," he cut in.

"I know, but there's a stereotype, and I feel like you play right into it. Running a surf shop, posing for... for calendars or whatever it is you get paid to do."

"Those stereotypes are a result of an overworked society that cannot comprehend a person who'd rather watch the waves all day than kill themselves at a 90-hour-a-week job that doesn't make them happy. They assume we lack ambition because our goals are different."

"Except those 90-hour-a-week jobs are what pay bills and put food on the table," I pointed out. "And you're not going to be good-looking enough forever. Those sponsors will dry up, Finn."

"You think I'm good looking?"

"Answer the question."

He exhaled a long breath. "I don't know." He paused again, rubbing his hand along his jaw. "Remember that argument we had after the *Nightly News* interview?"

I racked my brain. We'd had a lot of arguments. "Was it about the hotel in Cabo San Lucas?"

"That one," he said, looking uneasy. "You were more right than you knew. About the competitions and their environmental impacts. I, um... I did actually have an experience like you described. Where I saw, first-hand, how naive I'd been about my role."

"In—?" I prompted.

"Everything. That loving the beach and the ocean didn't automatically make me an environmentalist. And I felt terrible about that—profiting from something I wasn't directly working to save. So, that's why I got the master's degree."

"Wow," I said, impressed. "It makes sense. You're so passionate about the environment. You could translate that passion, and your degree, into a career."

Finn avoided my gaze, chewing. A little girl waved at him, and he waved back. "Who says I want a career?" He looked back at me. "I know you no longer buy into this, Avery, but I think your upbringing must have stuck with you a little bit, right? Careers are... I mean, the very idea of careers is an invention. There is no ladder; there are no rungs. You work, or you don't. Surfing makes me happy. Running a surf shop makes me happy. I pay my bills. Isn't that enough?"

"I think you're selling yourself short," I said and meant it. I didn't know where I was getting all of these perceptions about Finn all of a sudden, but they tumbled out of my mouth before I could stop them. "I think you're afraid to take anything too seriously because you know if you fail it'll hurt so much more."

He opened his mouth, closed it. Sat back in his chair. "I take surfing incredibly seriously. I'm out there every morning while the rest of the world sleeps. You just don't see it because your idea of a serious job involves a pantsuit, a briefcase, and years and years of unending stress. All to reach some kind of ludicrous career goal that's entirely fake."

I smiled. Goddammit, but I *liked* this back-and-forth. "Even if it's an invention that we all buy into, the fact that millions of people are working toward it every day essentially makes it real and negates your entire concept."

"I'll negate *your* entire concept," he said, and I burst out laughing. Finn tried to hold it in but couldn't, chuckling. "Well... I will."

"The truth is..." It was hard for me to say this. "Your protest *worked*. I know you have this devil-may-care attitude about things, but you were organized. Methodical. Inspirational. Used the media. Built momentum. And it worked. Do you know how many other communities Bella View has bulldozed through with nary a peep? Countless. You—" I said, pointing again. "—did that. You made them sit up straight and listen." Underneath the table, his palm closed around my knee, squeezing. "I just think you could take your master's degree and do real environmental work. Make a difference."

"I thought you hated environmentalists."

"I don't hate them. I just think you have to blend a little reality with idealism, and the environmentalists I grew up around never did that. But you... you could do it."

"Why do you want me to?"

"Because I want you to be happy," I said before I could stop myself. His fingers squeezed again, harder this time. He held my gaze for a long time. I fidgeted.

"I..." He struggled for a minute. "I'll think about it, okay? Next question, please. An easy one."

"Is this your favorite taqueria?"

"Most definitely. My parents took me here all the time as a reward for—" He stopped, and that grin came out again.

"Good grades?"

"No... um, as a reward for catching good waves. And expressing my feelings well."

"Oh, well, that makes a ton of sense," I said sarcastically. He winked at me. "Your parents sound very..."

"Like the exact opposite of your parents?"

"Yeah, but also... the same? I don't know."

"They were very loving. Are very loving. They taught me a lot about what unconditional love looked like." He smiled.

"And it doesn't bother you? Bailing them out when they need money? Technically it's yours. Earned with your success. No one would judge you for withholding it."

He shook his head fiercely. "That's a non-starter, Avery. I'd do anything for them." I thought about my parents, the guilt I felt when they asked for money. How awful I felt giving it. How awful I'd feel if I didn't. There didn't seem to be a right way about it. And I couldn't bear to tell Finn I had a slightly selfish reason for wanting his perspective on this.

"First wave you caught?" I asked, a slightly awkward segue.

He held up nine fingers while swallowing a huge bite of food.

"Impressive," I said. "What did it feel like?"

He thought for a second, and I studied his face. I was becoming a little obsessed with his mouth.

"It felt like my body was doing exactly what it was supposed to be doing. Like pure happiness."

"Do you really wake up at five every morning to surf?"

"I do," he replied with a smile. He was happy even just talking about it.

"Even when you're sick? Even when you're tired?"

He shrugged. "I don't get sick very often, but when I do, I skip a day obviously. But when I'm tired... shit, I'm always tired at five in the morning. It's just worth it, though. To be completely alone for a few hours. The privilege of watching the sun rise behind me. That feeling I get when the sun first reaches my wet suit." He shivered. "The sudden warmth. Fish around my legs. The crashing of waves, over and over and over. When the swell is perfect. To be knocked down and to get back up. Remembering that you're alive. That this, this—" he said, tapping his finger against the table for emphasis. "—is the reason for living. Not material possessions. Not competition. Not commercials or television or radio ads or bigger houses or better things or iPhones or Facebook."

I wanted to kiss him. Desperately. I wanted to point out in a million ways the million reasons why he was wrong. Why things and houses and possessions are good—better, even, than the feel of sand between your toes. But I also wanted to curl up inside his world, just for a moment. And remember.

"Has anything else in your life ever made you feel that way? That perfect?" I asked.

He looked at me so long I felt my cheeks grow hot. I watched him swallow, clear his throat, and look away. "Um... no. Not really."

"And you're not scared of drowning?"

"Fuck *yeah,* I'm scared. That's my greatest fear," he said, suddenly laughing again. Fun-loving Finn was back. "Did you see the wave I rode at Mavericks?"

"I might have downloaded the video." And watched it over and over. I shivered, remembering the wall of water that rose over Finn's head. He may have felt scared, but he was all pure, unadulterated joy on that board.

"Did you see the guys on jet-skis? They wait near the surfers so that, if we fall in, they can try and pull us out more quickly. The waves are so big if you nose-dive you can be under the water for four minutes."

"Shit," I said.

"Shit indeed."

"What did you want to do after winning? What do you like to do?"

"After that much adrenaline?" His gaze darkened.

"Fuck." Underneath the table, his fingers slid up my leg, stroking. "You feel more alive than you ever have before. Aware of everything around you—every smell, the breeze, every grain of sand beneath your feet."

"And... and that makes you..." His fingers were captivating. "Aroused?"

"Yeah, Avery, it does," he said simply. "It makes me want to walk out of the water, tear my wet suit off, and grab the first willing woman I see. Throw her down on the sand and fuck her in front of everyone."

"You *are* an exhibitionist," I said, a little breathless. His fingers slid higher.

"I am. And if we didn't have places to be, I'd finger-fuck you under this table. Make you come right here."

I crossed my legs against an onslaught of sensations. "Who says I could even do that?"

"You can. And one day you will. For me, you will." We must have stared at each other for a full minute, tension strung tight as a bow. I was stumbling over the use of the phrase "one day" as in *the future.*

"You need to finish your burrito," I said.

"Next question," he replied. He attacked his food.

"Um..." My brain was hazy with lust. "Most hippie-ish thing your parents made you do as a kid?"

He thought for a second. "Protests. We did a lot of sit-ins, camping out. Political marches. Before I was born, my parents were involved with every major social movement. After I was born, those were the stories they told me at night. Radical fairy tales," he said. "When I was old enough, it was a lot of environmental protests. One time we straight-up chained ourselves to a mangrove forest they were going to destroy to build a Target."

"Even as a kid?"

"Oh, yeah." He reached into his pocket, pulling out his phone. "Hold on, I found this in an old box of pictures the other day." His thumb scrolled, then he turned the screen around for me to see. It was a photo of Finn, no older than seven, holding a sign almost as big as he was that read, "Trees have feelings too." His hair was huge and shaggy, and he was wearing the tiniest pair of board shorts. His smile was wide and open and so totally Finn.

It was fucking adorable.

"See?" I pointed out. "You've got rabble-rousing in the blood. And just for the record, I believe it's been empirically proven that trees do *not* have feelings."

He grabbed my hand, pulling me up. "Oh my God, you realize that you're saying that to seven-year-old me, right?" We walked back to the car, weaving through tables filled with Finn's adoring fans. He gave a little girl a miniature fist bump as he passed, adding, "And, just for the record, I still believe trees have feelings."

25

AVERY

"*I* don't know about you, but I feel like the car is neutral territory on this date."

"Meaning?" I asked.

"Meaning let's stick to general questions we can both answer. And you need to tell me where we're going for your part of the date."

"I already told you," I said, purring. I pulled my sweater over my head and tossed it in the backseat. I was wearing just a small black camisole, no bra. My finger traced under a strap, and slowly began lowering it.

His hand shot out, grabbing mine. He pulled it to his mouth, pressing a kiss against my palm.

"Don't," he warned. "I'm hanging by a thread here, Ave, and I want to go on your part of the date."

"Why?" I pleaded.

"I want to see a different side of you. Show me what makes you happy. Show me what you think is beautiful."

He turned on the car, started to back out. "Plus, you should know something about me, love. The more you beg for it, the longer I'm going to make you wait."

213

I tilted her chin up, defiant. I liked this game. "Maybe I like waiting."

He gave me a filthy grin, and I flushed. "It doesn't matter to me if you like it or not," he said. I broke his gaze, looking out the window, then quietly rattled off an address.

"Is that where you want to go?"

I nodded, although I was still unsure.

"What is it?"

"You'll just have to wait and see."

He laughed. "Little tease." I flashed him a quick smile, and he rolled down the windows and turned up the music.

"Okay, neutral territory, so we have to talk about things we have in common," he said.

"Which is nothing," I repeated.

He shook his head. "Weirdest thing about your hippie parents."

"Okay, okay," I finally said. "We can do this. *I* can do this."

"So... go."

"Our commune generally espoused peace, love, nonviolence."

"Same as my parents."

"Everything was shared in our commune—money, most importantly. Living arrangements. Property, food, clothing. We were on about twenty-five acres of land, and we collectively owned it. They've been downsizing these past few years, due to some financial troubles."

"Same for my parents' commune. Land is expensive."

"And communes are not money-making or really that sustainable."

Finn grimaced. "That can be true."

"Wait," I said, grabbing his arm across the car. "Are you agreeing with me about something?"

He gave me a side smile. "Just keep talking. And you haven't answered the question yet."

"Well, we had about fifty members total, including children. Some were societal drop-outs."

"Kind of like my parents."

"Totally, or no longer wanted to be in the system. Nonconformist. Others just wanted to raise their children in a simpler environment, you know, living off the grid by living off the land. It was actually my parents who had the most radical ideas in the commune though. You know, like we were talking about the other day."

"The 'no TV' thing."

"My mom would toss around this phrase: Capitalist Barbie."

"Who was that—you?" He grinned.

"Any woman who participated in the system. It went beyond feminism. She thought true feminists, like herself, would overthrow the patriarchy by refusing to work, to pay taxes, to vote. The government was the ultimate tool of men, and you had two options. Turn against it or overthrow it."

He was quiet for a minute. "Wait, are your parents going to..."

"Overthrow the government?" I shook my head. "No, they're too peace-loving. Plus, they're too old now. So the option was turn against it. No participation. One of the hardest things for me when I was applying for colleges was that I didn't have a birth certificate and didn't know my social security number. That was a long process." I shifted in my seat. "Now my mom calls me 'Capitalist Barbie' so much I think of it as an endearment."

"Jesus," he said. "At least my parents believed in social security cards."

"They're actually quite important if you want to get into college. Or have health benefits. What about you?"

Finn turned left down the street that would lead us to my part of the date. Tiny butterflies unleashed hell in my stomach.

"It's hard for me because now the things that made my childhood different—our childhood different—I totally dig. And if I ever had children..." He coughed awkwardly. "I mean, I don't know, but if I did, I'd raise them in a similar way."

I bit down on my thumb. "Ugh, I really want to argue with you right now."

He poked my arm. "Neutral territory. And I'd like to point out that both you and I were raised by varying types of hippies and turned out perfectly fine."

"You did *not* turn out perfectly fine," I said.

He pulled into a parking space, parked, and turned off the car. He turned to face me. "Excuse me. I've graced the cover of not one, not two, but *three* Billabong magazines. I turned out more than fine. Great even." He cupped my face with his palm. "And you? You, Avery Dacosta, grew up to be a spirited, independent, beautiful badass whose only flaw is that she denies herself fun in the pursuit of career success."

I'd been running through a bunch of pithy replies, but I'd snagged on, well, on everything he said about me.

"You didn't answer the question," I pointed out, desperate to veer away from this tender, sweet territory. I didn't want this Finn. "Weirdest thing your parents ever made you do."

"Easy," he said with a melt-your-panties grin. "For a year, my parents were fruitarians. So we just ate fruit. And a handful of seeds if we had 'em."

"What the fucking—"

"You don't even need to say it," he cut in, laughing. "It was terrible and awful and all the usual things an Avery-Dacosta-type person might say. And now," he said, pressing a kiss against the inside of my wrist. "It's time for your part of the date."

26

FINN

$\mathcal{F}$or the first time in the months I'd been around Avery—watching her, studying her, fighting with her—she looked nervous. Which wasn't usually her gig. But now, standing outside the car, I took her hand. Tugged her closer. She was so fucking pretty, hair wind-blown, eyes dark and wide.

"Lead the way, love," I said.

"I've never taken anyone here before," she said. "Just so you know."

"It's a privilege, then."

She led me around the corner through a large gate, up three stairs to an elevator. We got in, the doors sliding shut behind us. In a second, I had her pressed up against the wall, every inch of her luscious, warm body against mine. She sighed, shifting against me. I grabbed her hands, lifted them up over her head. Her back arched.

"Hello," I said against her lips.

"Hello," she said back. "You said we couldn't do this on my part of the date." I could feel the pulse at her wrist under my thumbs. Quick, like a hummingbird's.

"I know what I said, Avery," I growled, nipping at her bottom lip. "And you'd do well not to argue with me right now. But a man can only take so much." I thrust against her, allowing her to feel the rock-hard erection I'd had since this morning.

"You called me beautiful," she whispered, eyes on my lips. I placed mine against hers, gently, even as a hurricane of lust ripped through my body. But I didn't want to take her, not yet. Even though I could have—God help me, I could have, up against this wall in the elevator, just riding up and down the floors until that sweet cunt clenched around me.

"You are beautiful. I tried so hard to ignore it but you—" I kissed her again, a little harder this time. "You're under my skin, Avery. I can feel you there, night and day."

Her eyes widened. "And where are you on the Satan issue?" Her smile was tentative.

"As in, are you Satan? Or are you not Satan?"

She nodded, curling her fingers through mine.

I ran my tongue up the column of her throat to her ear. "To be honest," I said against it, and I heard her breathing hitch. "I'm still on the fence. Fifty-fifty."

"Oh, fuck you," she said, laughing and shoving me away. I laughed too, pulling us through the opening doors of the elevator and onto the largest rooftop community garden I had ever seen.

"Oh," I said, shocked and a little delighted. More than delighted. "Oh, wait... we're at a garden?"

"Yeah," she said, tying her sweater around her waist and picking up two pairs of gardening gloves from the tray at the entrance. "And I'm putting you to work." She tossed them at me, and I caught them, but just barely. She tilted her head at me, looking adorably defiant. "And you'd do well not to argue with me here, Finn. This—" She said, nodding at the rows and rows of dirt. "—is my ocean."

She turned and walked, a little sassy, down a row, and I followed like an obedient dog. Her plot was in the very back and larger than most. "Wow," I said.

"I've had it since I moved here nine years ago," she said, pride in her voice.

"Tell me what's in it." Now that we were on her part of the date, I wanted every secret to spill out, one by one. Pretty as pennies. And we were going to start with her fucking plants.

"Tomatoes. Basil. Mint." Avery pointed with her finger at each small crop. "Marigolds. Star jasmine on the side. Watermelon when it's in season. Bell peppers. Kale. And papayas." She knelt in the dirt, pulling on her gloves, and gestured for me to join her. I settled next to her, shoulder to shoulder.

"Papayas? You mean in that tree right there?"

She nodded. "They grow in Hawaii. They were my favorite food. And they're easy to grow if you have space for a tree. That's why I bought up basically five plots just for myself."

She touched my hand and directed it to a tiny weed, intruding on a small bell pepper plant. "See these? Can you pull them out for me? They're everywhere. I've been busy with, well, you know." We hadn't implicitly banned talk of the city council vote, but we'd nimbly sidestepped it throughout the day.

"And distracted," I said with a goofy grin, winking at her. She smiled back, and goddammit if I still didn't trip over it. Although I'd have been lying if I didn't say that severe, no-bullshit Avery did it for me too.

"And yes, I can help. Anything you need," I said, and she

blushed a little. I remembered the first night she'd let me touch her. As I practically begged her for it on the dance floor.

I can give you what you need. Just ask.

I pinched one of the weeds between my thumb and forefinger and pulled gently. It popped out of the dirt, roots and all, and I showed it to her. "Like this?"

"And you didn't think you'd put your master's degree to good use," she said. I laughed, then pulled another. And another. I'd weed every plant on this rooftop if it made her happy.

"So, and correct me if I'm wrong, but I believe the rules that you set mean I get to ask you all the questions I want. Since we're on your part of the date."

She wiped her hand across her forehead, leaving a smear of dirt. "I do, technically, remember saying that—"

"Why haven't you fucked anyone in two years?"

She let out a long breath. "Jesus."

"This is payback."

She opened her mouth. Closed it. Sighed. "Fine." She shifted on her knees. "I worked the entire time I was getting my MBA. But not at Bella View, at another property developer in town."

"Let me guess—you tore down low-income housing to build luxury condos?"

"*I* didn't. I just worked for the person who did."

"Avery." I reached over and grabbed her by the scruff of her neck, yanking her toward me. "We're going to have to put a pin in that discussion."

"Luxury condos bring revitalization and revenue into low-income communities. Revenue brings jobs. Jobs bring better paychecks. Better paychecks mean no more need for low-income housing."

"You're talking about systemic change within an economy that can take years, if not decades, to exhibit the reforms you're talking about. Yes, better paychecks mean no more poverty, but when, Avery? And how quickly? And where do you think poor folks will live until then?"

She leaned in for a kiss, but I pulled away. "Are you picking fights with me just to turn me on?"

"Maybe," she breathed. The look she gave me was too much—daring and defiant and sexy as sin.

"Smart girl," I said. "And, as you have reminded me oh-so-many-times on this date... you didn't answer my question."

Flushed, she leaned forward, pulling more weeds.

"As I was saying, I worked the whole time I was getting my master's degree. And, actually, the entire time I was getting my undergrad too."

"You paid for it yourself, right?" I wasn't sure I could have done what she had—leave everything I'd known, move to a strange city at eighteen, and never look back. Even when I left for Hawaii, I'd lived with friends and called my parents constantly, their voices on the phone tethering me to Playa Vieja.

"I got a few scholarships, interesting story and all. You know... 'hard-working, ambitious young woman just wants out of weird hippie commune.' At the commune, I did odd jobs in town for a few years, and that at least got me a plane ticket and first month's rent on a shitty apartment. I'd go to classes during the day, work at night—"

"When did you sleep?"

She grimaced, crinkling her nose. "Sleep and I have a very unique relationship."

"The insomnia?"

"Yeah. That and I've always been too busy to sleep. From

the time I was eighteen until... well, until now, it was school-homework-work. And now, work-work-work. I've only ever had a few relationships, none of them serious. I just never had the time. Also, relationships were... different in the commune."

"How so?" Growing up with my parents, I was used to every single permutation.

"My parents were—are—monogamous. They didn't swing or swap partners. But some others did, although they couldn't seem to do it without drama. When it worked, they'd flaunt it in our faces. And then, inevitably, it would fail. And the fallout always led to one or both of the couples leaving. It would take months to find and recruit new members, meaning more hard work for the rest of us." She paused. "Back-breaking work that usually fell on me."

"You don't trust relationships?" I guessed. If that was my only model for love, I wouldn't either.

"I guess that's it," she said. "And the partners I've had weren't..." She paused, wiping her hair from her face again. She was smearing dirt all over her face.

"Funny? Smart?"

"They weren't good at sex. Or we weren't compatible. I don't know."

I battled my body's primal response to that statement. "How so?"

"They weren't giving. My pleasure was secondary. Or non-existent. So when my work life got too intense, it was easy to give it up since I wasn't having that much fun anyway."

Avery had removed her gloves and was digging her fingers into the earth. She sighed, and my jaw clenched.

"Aside from the fact that your previous lovers will never be as good as I am—"

She threw a giant clump of dirt at my face. I continued speaking as if she hadn't. "Can I say something kind of brutally honest here?"

She was cupping small, green tendrils of star jasmine between her fingers. I wished I could paint her, capture the image of her happiness.

"Okay," she said quietly. "Go ahead."

"What's the end goal here? Regardless of how I feel about your chosen profession, is developing hotels what you want to do for your entire life?"

"Now who's undermining professions?"

"I don't mean it like that. I mean... does it make you happy? This all-work-and-no-play lifestyle you've chosen? Avery, you're only twenty-eight. When I first met you, you were stressed out. Exhausted. Overwhelmed. Is that what you want?" I asked.

"Finn," she said, exasperated. She looked at the sky for a moment, like she was gathering courage. Then back at me. "Our childhoods were the same. But also so, so different. Maybe if my parents were more like yours, more... affectionate or comforting, the lean times would have felt different. I wouldn't have been so scared. So anxious. So nervous that we'd completely run out of food, for good. When I worked in town, I saw regular families. Normal families. Staying at hotels. Eating in restaurants. Wearing clothing not made out of hemp. Laughing. Hugging. Smiling at each other. As a child, my parents made it seem as if everyone living outside of our commune was a monster. Trapped and manipulated by greed. Bound to the system. When I learned that wasn't true, I felt totally and completely betrayed."

She stood, brushing dirt off her knees and moved to the other side of her plot. I wanted her closer to me, not farther away.

"When I moved here to San Diego on my own, I purposely chose an education and a career that I thought would bring the most stability. To my parents, getting an MBA felt like a slap in the face." She plucked a few errant leaves from her bell peppers. "And I understand their feelings. I do. But to me, when I thought about my life and what I wanted it to be? I just wanted control. Stability. A fucking retirement account. And yeah—" She looked at me, her dark brown eyes almost pleading. "—a career ladder I could easily climb."

"Avery," I started to say, reaching for her. "I'm sorry. For everything that happened to you."

"Don't apologize. You didn't do anything wrong. And I'm not ashamed of the fact that I want that corner office. I want to be the boss. I want to stay late and earn good money and provide for myself."

"But," I said, wanting more from her. Needing more. "I still didn't hear you talk about what makes you *happy*. If your job makes you happy. I mean, I know about a few things that do."

She sat back on her heels, thoughtful. "Like what?" She looked almost sad.

I held up my fingers, ticking them off. "Oddly enough, reggae music."

"You can take the girl out of the island, but you can't take the island out of the girl."

"Also oddly enough, weed."

She rolled her eyes. "Fuck, Finn, you caught me one time..."

"Breakfast burritos." Another tick. "Control. Stability." I said, as a nod to all that she just shared with me. I wanted to understand, and I thought that I did. But as a person who regularly and routinely stood up on a six-foot board while throwing myself at giant ocean waves, chaos was the name of my game.

"You also like control in bed." I said, based on our two encounters.

"Y-yes," she said, stumbling a bit. She scratched at her shoulder, smearing dirt across her collarbone.

"But you want to submit to me," I said, voice rougher than usual.

"Doubt it," she said quickly, but I could tell she was covering. "And if I remember correctly, you submitted to me that first time." She mimicked my pose that first night— hands tangled in my own hair.

"True," I said with a smirk. Because it was.

"And finally?" I held out my hands, palms up. "Secret... gardening?"

"Why do you sound so surprised?" She tilted her chin up. "I have a lot of interests you don't know about."

"I don't doubt it, love," I said, shaking my hand. "It just surprised me. And now you have to spill. Why the garden on your date?"

She narrowed her eyes at the pile of weeds next to my knees. "I'm weeding more quickly than you," she pointed out. "Work faster." I arched an eyebrow at her. She arched one back, head tilted.

I dove back in.

"It's because of the commune. I miss working the land." She dug her fingers back into the dirt again. "I miss the feel of dirt on my skin. Of actually creating something with my hands." She cupped her palm against the bright orange head of a marigold. "I miss bringing forth something alive."

I stopped what I was doing, totally entranced. "What else?" I asked softly.

"We used to get up at dawn too, just us and the ocean

and wild bird song. Working in quiet community. There was such a sense of accomplishment. Of action and motion. Pulling, uprooting. Yielding, lifting."

I don't think she'd realized she'd closed her eyes. "It was harder during the lean times. I had a natural green thumb, so when food yields were low, I'd blame myself."

"It wasn't your fault, Avery. Crop growth comes in cycles —feast and famine. Trust me. I've got a master's degree in ecology," I said, and she smiled.

"I know, really, I do. But it was also that same sense of betrayal I felt seeing families in town. I put those seeds in the ground myself. Why couldn't they grow for me?"

"That sounds like a lot of pressure for a child," I said. I wanted to throttle her parents.

"I miss ocean waves as a lullaby," she continued. "And... well, it's hard for me to say this, but I even miss sleeping with ten different people at night. Not when I first got here. I just wanted what all teenagers want—to be left alone in my room." She smiled, remembering. "But now? After years on my own, there's something to be said for that kind of community."

"It's why you like building properties," I said. She tilted her head at me. "You like it because it's tangible. Action and motion. Creating something where there was nothing." I paused. "You still haven't convinced me that it actually makes you happy though."

She thought for a bit. "Can I get back to you on that?"

"Of course," I said softly. "And no wonder you were the best in the commune. Look at your plots compared to everyone else's." I indicated behind me. "Your little jungle paradise is thriving." And it was. Bell peppers the size of my head. Papayas dripping from tree branches like emerald jewels.

"Thank you," she said, flushing a little. "I don't really like to share about myself."

"I loved it."

"Stop fucking around," she said, giving me the side-eye.

I laughed, standing. "Where should I go next?"

She looked up at me from her kneeling position, and I tried to keep my gaze neutral. Non-sexual. She'd been open and giving, and I wanted to learn more. But standing over Avery on her knees was an image that had stalked my fantasies for weeks now.

"You are totally covered in dirt," she said.

I crossed my arms over my chest, and I saw her gaze flick to my biceps. "So are you, love. All over your face."

She gasped, bringing her hands to her cheeks. "Oh my God," she said.

"It looks good on you. I like it. You look wild and... undone. It's kind of sexy," I said. She responded by throwing another large clump of dirt at me. It hit my chest, kind of hard.

"*He*-ey," I said, laughing. "I say you look sexy, and you respond with an attack? And, for the record," I said, staring at the giant brown stain on my new white shirt. "I prefer your attacks to be verbal." And then I tossed a handful of dirt back at her. She yelped, half-falling on her side. Laughing. I knew I'd do anything to inspire that sound.

Her second attack hit me square in the face. "I think some dirt actually got in my mouth," I said, spitting. Avery was wiping tears from her eyes, still laughing.

"I'm sorry, I'm sorry," she said. "It's just the look on your face when it hit you."

"This?" I said, pointing at my head, "This is the money-maker, Ave." I was fighting back laughter.

"Oh God," she said, wiping one last tear. "And we haven't

even gotten a chance to point out how hypocritical it is for you to deplore the effects of capitalism on our society when you use your abs to sell an unhealthy body image that also sells material possessions."

My cock twitched as I picked up a handful of dirt. "You're fighting dirty again, love." I tossed the dirt and hit her square between her breasts. "And don't tell me you don't fantasize about my abs."

"You're avoiding the argument, Finn," she said, launching a handful of dirt and one very sharp rock at my stomach. She was leaning forward, almost on her hands and knees. I wanted her. So badly I could feel it in my teeth.

"Is this garden usually very crowded?" I asked, glancing around. We'd been up here for close to an hour and hadn't seen a single soul.

She shrugged. "Not usually. Plus, we'd hear the door open. Why?"

I nodded, leaning back against the wall closing in her plot. "Because I don't want anyone else to see you sucking my cock."

The expression on her face was a dangerous blend of anger and arousal. "Excuse me?"

"Enough lip, Avery." I snapped my fingers. "Crawl to me."

"Through the fucking dirt?" she asked, but there was a slight purr this time.

"Yes. Through the fucking dirt. And you should have been here by now." We had a short stare-down as I began pulling my belt off. I tossed it in the garden. I unsnapped the button of my shorts. I watched her swallow. I watched her lean forward, on her hands and knees, and crawl through the dirt to me. Slowly. Lithe as a cat, hair in her face.

I dragged the zipper down, and the sound seemed to

echo across the rooftop. She made a small noise in the back of her throat. She sat on her knees, directly in front of me. Obedient. I pulled out my cock, and her eyes widened.

"This is what you want," I said, no more questions.

"More than anything," she moaned, and I almost came right there. I was covered in dirt. She was covered in dirt. And then she took the entire length of me in her mouth to the back of her throat.

"Holy *fuck*," I bit out, grabbing onto the wall. The shock of her mouth wrapped around my cock was almost too much. She held me there, humming softly, eyes closed in pleasure.

"You want to see me lose it, isn't that right, love?" I pushed my fingers through her long, dirt-filled hair. Her hands came around to squeeze my ass, pushing me harder into her mouth.

I felt her tongue flick against the head as her cheeks hollowed. I really was going to lose it. "Avery, maybe this was a bad idea." She moaned again, a soft shake of her head. No, it isn't, she was saying, but couldn't, because I had finally filled up that smart-ass mouth with every inch of my cock.

"You're gonna kill me, love," I groaned. "I've thought about this every fucking hour since I kissed you in that parking lot." She sped up her rhythm, one hand coming around to cup my balls.

"I used to..." I swallowed, struggling with the words. Struggling with breathing. Christ, Avery gave head like she was born to do it. "I used to think about this when you walked into work each morning."

I grabbed her hair a little harder, pulling. I could see flecks of dirt in the strands. "Every time you fought with me. Every look you gave me. Every snarky little... *shit*." I could feel everything inside of me tightening. Clenching. I was so close I could taste it. Wanted to drench her throat.

"I'd think about taking you behind the building. Putting you on your knees like the good girl you'd be for me." She was moaning louder than I was, the vibrations sending every sensation into overdrive. "And then... this. This," I groaned loudly, my climax hitting me like a pile of bricks. I felt my hips thrusting out of control between the wet paradise of her lips, my orgasm lingering for longer than it usually did.

She licked up the side of my cock, catching the last few drops, before swallowing. She wiped her hand over her mouth and gave me the filthiest grin I'd ever seen.

I had her flipped over on her hands and knees in no time. With one hand, I hiked up her skirt. With the other, I pressed her face into the dirt.

I pulled the minuscule fabric of her thong aside. "You're soaking wet for me, love?"

"Yes," she moaned. "Yes, yes, *yes*."

I stared at her pussy, enchanted. "This is how I'm going to take you, Avery."

"Unless I'm on top," she groaned. "Taking you."

"No fucking way," I said, even though the thought of her riding me, wild and relentless, had me hard and aching again in seconds.

"I need to taste you," I said, voice strangled. I got on my knees behind her. She wiggled her ass at me, expectant. I gave her a teasing smack, and she stilled. Slowly, ever so fucking slowly, I traced my tongue around her opening. The sound she made wasn't human.

And then the garden door creaked open.

27

AVERY

*F*inn had me standing up, my skirt down, his cock in his pants, and his belt back on in a matter of moments. I could only watch, stunned, since half of me was still in the dirt, face pressed into the soil by his large hand as he prepared to fuck me with his tongue. I licked my lips, tasting the salt of his cum.

"Afternoon," one of the other gardeners said. "We have a group of school children on their way up. Field trip. Is that okay with you?"

"Holy shit, we almost got caught by a group of kids," I whispered at Finn. "Can you say registered sex offenders?" I watched his mouth quirk up.

"Sure thing!" Finn said, grabbing our gardening gloves. "We were just leaving. Avery here has a great plot if your students want to check out some world-class papayas."

He grabbed my hand and pulled me to the door. As usual, his Finn-charm put the man at ease immediately. He didn't even bat an eye at us, even though we were covered in dirt and I had a serious case of sex-hair.

The elevator doors opened, and a whole slew of kids was

standing there, staring. About half of them got out, but the rest stayed. Finn squeezed my fingers as we stepped inside, a subtle gesture that he'd been planning on having his way with me in this elevator.

"*Hey,* guys," he said slowly. There was a teacher in the middle, looking frazzled and tired. "You're not going to the garden?"

"No," one of them answered. "We all forgot our lunches on the bus, so we have to go back."

"Bummer," Finn said, nodding along. The kids looked at him like he was a superhero.

"I know who you are," a tiny girl with dark braids called out. "My dad loves you."

Finn pointed at himself and made a goofy face. "Me? Wait... who am I?" The kids giggled.

"You're a surfer," the girl said, like he was stupid. Finn shook his head, gave me a mock-incredulous look.

"What? Me? A surfer?"

"You ride huge waves, my dad told me," she said. "He said it's 'cause you have giant balls."

"Abigail," the teacher shushed her. "How many times do we need to talk about this, guys? 'Balls' is not an acceptable classroom word." She raised her voice just a little. "Right?"

The kids all nodded in unison, although some were fighting laughter. Finn too.

I nudged his shoulder. "Be an adult," I whispered, and he coughed into his hand, muffling a snort.

"Do any of you guys surf?" he asked. "Let's see a show of hands."

They all giggled, but some of them raised their hands. The elevator landed on the first floor, and the doors flew open. I was holding Finn's hand like an adoring girlfriend.

Watching him entertain school children had a strange, warm sensation squeezing around my heart.

"Maybe I can come talk to you guys about surfing some time?" he asked with a look at the teacher, who just about unbuttoned her shirt and tossed it to him. Honestly, her eyes couldn't have been wider.

"Oh, that... that would be lovely," she breathed, reaching out to touch his arm. I yanked him, just a little, toward the parking lot and away from her lingering fingers. He grinned, waving to the kids, and I swear I heard one of them ask, "What are big balls?"

With his hand on my lower back, he guided me into the car quickly.

"Listen," he said, pulling out of the parking lot as fast as he could. "I know that you and I have a tendency to... disagree."

"Agree," I said.

"But, especially since we're in neutral territory, can we *agree* on me breaking the speed limit to get you home, naked and in my bed?"

"Please," I murmured. "And agree. Again."

"Good." His jaw was set in a hard line, as serious as I'd ever seen him.

"So... you really are an exhibitionist, aren't you?"

He glanced at me quickly before turning back to the road. "The thrill of getting caught with you? Of other people seeing us? Yes."

His words were burning me up. "You really like it?"

"I love it. I think it has something to do with my natural thrill-seeking tendencies. And... and I guess I like the idea that I can't keep my hands off of you." He reached over and grabbed my knee. "That, I don't know, the President of the United States could be giving us a personal tour of the

White House, and right in the middle of a speech about some piece of art from the Civil War, I'd push you into a broom closet."

"A fucking White House broom closet?"

"Yes. Lift you up onto a shelf, knock over all the cleaning supplies. Spread your legs so wide you wouldn't be able to walk the next day. Fuck you so hard you can't see straight. My hand over your mouth as you screamed."

"Because we don't want the President to hear us," I said, voice shaky. Knees shaky. Goddamn every cell in my body shaky.

"That's right, love. Because I have to have you." He looked at me again, and there was something in his eyes I couldn't quite place. "Because we have to have each other."

"Ahh," I said, shaking my head, trying to push us back to silly territory. "Got it. But can I just say that, as thrilling as it has been to dry fuck in that alley—" I ticked off my fingers. "—get eaten out in my office, and blow you in that community garden, I really, really want to fuck you in a locked, private room where we can't be interrupted? Agree?"

Finn grabbed my fingers and placed them against his mouth, sucking one between his teeth. I sighed. Then he bit down.

"Are you going to submit?" he asked, beginning to turn down roads that I recognized. Along our left, Playa Vieja shone like a paradise.

"Disagree," I said, shaking my head. Even though I was lying to myself. We pulled up into his driveway, and just as suddenly he had me out, inside his house, and yanked into his bathroom.

"What are we doing here?" I asked breathlessly as he leaned me against the sink. Finn kept his gaze on me as he reached into his shower and turned the water on. In seconds it was hot and steaming.

"You're very dirty."

"*You're* very dirty," I shot back.

He shook his head. "You have no idea, Avery. Take off your shirt."

I shook my head, biting my lip. I didn't know why, but I wanted to push him to his breaking point, to truly give in to his hidden alpha tendencies, the tendencies that had shocked me to my core the first time his lips had touched mine.

Finn crossed his arms over his head. "Take it off. Or I do it for you. And I'm not going to be nice about it." There was a growl in his voice now.

I liked it.

I tugged my shirt up, past my belly button, just to the bottom of my breasts. And stopped.

"Avery," he warned. I could see the outline of his cock against his shorts.

"What?" I asked, all innocence.

He was across the bathroom and on me so fast it made my head spin. I had forgotten how big he was, how tall he was, how rough and large his hands would feel as he ripped my shirt up and over my head, down my arms. He twisted it, tight, capturing my wrists behind me. My back bowed, like an instrument begging to be played.

"Are you going to be a brat?" Before I could even open my mouth, he had crushed his lips to mine. A heated, hungry kiss that told me how frustrated he'd felt all day. How turned on. His yearning, hot and tight and there. A moment later, those lips were on my nipples, and my knees buckled.

"You have the most gorgeous breasts I've ever seen, love,"

he groaned, biting gently. I yelped. "Gorgeous. I want to fucking live here." His tongue was working some kind of complicated pattern over my nipples, down the sides of my breasts. I was pinned, trapped between the bathroom sink and Finn's hard body.

"More," I moaned, and he stopped. Stepped away.

"Do not test me, Avery. I can see what you're doing." He started to slowly unbutton his shirt, and my entire world came to a halting stop. I'd seen snatches of his body, but not the whole masterpiece.

One by one... hard, toned chest. A dusting of blond chest hair. Shoulders that went on for days. And then... and then... a six-pack carved by Michelangelo.

"What am I doing?" I asked, hands still trapped. Mouth dry. I squeezed my legs together, trying to dull the ache. My need to touch him was all-consuming.

"Pissing me off. Because you want to see me break." He was so, so right. It was so, *so* wrong. But I kept pushing.

His shirt slid off. "Take off your skirt."

"I can't. My hands are tied." His nostrils flared. I shrugged my shoulders. "You only have yourself to blame." How I was still producing words in the English language, I had no idea.

I could see him fighting a smile. Instead, he grabbed a pair of scissors from the cabinet next to him, stalked back to me, and cut the shirt in half. It floated down to the floor, like confetti at a birthday party. "You shredded it."

"You're damn right I shredded it." He pressed his lips to my stomach, licking, kissing, biting. I gripped his hair in my newly freed hands, tugging on the thick locks. He reached the top of my skirt, the top of my panties. He took the entire length of fabric between his teeth and yanked it down my legs. Snarling, like some kind of animal in heat.

I was completely and utterly naked in front of Finn. Vulnerable. Moments away from begging. But he was the penitent one, on his knees in front of me.

His thumb came up and circled gently around my clit. I cried out.

"Are you going to let me worship you now?" His voice was strangled with need. He circled a little harder, and his eyes held a complex mix of emotions. Desire. Yearning. Completion.

"Please," I said, and he pushed me into the shower. I groaned at the sensation of water sliding down my skin. It soaked through my hair, washing away tiny rocks, leaves, pieces of my garden. I smiled, thinking of our date. Our day.

And then Finn stepped naked into the shower, and the only thing I could think about was fucking him. His hair, wild and untamed. Those blue eyes. His full lips, quirked up into a filthy grin. Drops of water rolling down the muscles of his upper body. His cock—for the love of God, his cock—long and rock hard. He turned for a second, closing the shower door, and gave me the briefest glimpse of his muscular surfer's ass.

I was suddenly overwhelmed with what was about to happen. But he didn't give me a chance to say anymore. Instead, he covered me with his body, hands on either side of my face, and kissed me with every ounce of passion he had.

Finn was my secret fantasy come to life. And every inch of him was real, real, real. And every inch of him wanted me.

We stood like that under the streaming hot water, just lips and tongues and teeth and the desperate moans coming from both of us. It was probably only minutes, but it felt like hours. I kept clawing at his chest, trying to get closer. Trying to climb him. His back muscles rippled beneath my touch. I dug my nails deep into his shoulder blades, marking him. I reached down and grabbed his ass, and he flexed under my fingers. He shivered.

"This sight," he whispered against my lips. "You, gloriously naked. Water all over you. Your eyes, needing me." He guided my hands to his shaft. "Needing this. I'll be thinking about this moment for the rest of my life, Avery Dacosta."

He flipped me, pushed me against the wall of the shower. He gathered my soaking wet hair in one hand and lifted it, exposing the vulnerable skin of my neck.

His mouth was everywhere. Nibbling on my earlobes. Biting the sensitive skin between my shoulder and my neck. Licking down my spine, fingers tracing around my nipples, almost *almost* touching and then pulling away. The backs of my knees, teeth scraping the insides of my thighs. He ran his tongue up and over the curve of my ass, grabbing the cheeks. Spreading me.

I was nothing but a bunch of nerve endings strung together at this point. He gently turned me, pushing my back against the wall. Wet hair clung to my face, and when I moved it, I saw him drop to his knees. Place my legs over his shoulders. And stand up.

"Finn," I cried, worried my head would hit the ceiling. But he knew what he was doing, because instead the water from the shower arced down my nipples, over and over. And Finn plunged his tongue inside of me.

"Oh my God," I moaned, but this time it was a plea. A prayer. Atonement for my sins. "I'm going to come, Finn, I'm going to..."

"I know, beautiful," he said, tongue circling my clit. Lapping. "And I was *this close* to fucking you." His hands tightened on my ass. Everything else in me tightened too, gathering deep in my core. A pleasure so sharp it stole my breath. "But I can't resist this sweet pussy, Avery. I just can't."

He dipped his head back down, and I climaxed moments later, from his tongue, from his words, from the heady feeling of clutching Finn's face between my thighs. Using a kind of upper body strength most men would never know, he slid my legs down his arms, then around his waist, until we were face to face. I kissed him full on the mouth, tasting myself. Tasting Finn. I heard the water turn off.

"Now," I said. "Please, now." We didn't stop kissing as he walked us through his house and into his bedroom. Two large sliding glass doors revealed the ocean of Playa Vieja. He laid me down, gently, then turned me onto my side.

On the beach, the waves crashed against the shore, relentless. Curled spirals that shone in the sun. Beckoning. I took a deep breath and smelled salt water. Sunscreen. Hemp. I realized I was smelling Finn, all over his sheets.

The bed dipped, and suddenly his hard, hot body was behind me, his erection pushing up between my legs. His arm curled up and under my head. His lips came down to my ear, nuzzling.

"Condom?" I asked, arching back into him.

"It's on, love," he said, and then he brought his palm over my eyes, darkening everything. My heart tripped over itself.

"What are you doing?"

"I want you to remember this moment, Avery." His cock nudged at my entrance. I pushed back, seeking, and he pulled away. "I want you to hear the sound of the ocean. I want you to feel my breath against your ear. My teeth." He scraped them down my neck and I whimpered. I couldn't see a damn thing.

His hand caressed my nipples, lightly pinching. I

groaned. "I want you to remember what it felt like to have every inch of my cock inside of you." He thrust, fulfilling his promise, and I cried out.

He chuckled softly against me, hand still covering my eyes. Everything was darkness. Everything was sensation, sweet, heady sensation. He pulled all the way out, then plunged back in.

"Fuck," he said, hand tightening against my eyes. "You're so fucking tight."

I responded by clenching my muscles and was rewarded with a low, strangled groan.

"For you," I gasped. "Just for you."

"That's right, love," he said, his rhythm still slow. Agonizingly slow. "You kept this pussy tight for me."

I bit my lip, his fingers working magic over my nipples. He was kissing up and down my neck, thrusting like he had all the time in the world. I, on the other hand, was drowning in bliss.

"Now tell me what you feel." As if to drive the point home, he pulled all the way out and stopped.

"You," I panted. "Missing. I want... I want..."

Finn slammed back in, and I cried out again. "Now what," he said against my ear, breathing heavily. "Tell me, Avery."

"Every... every inch of you," I said, as he started to fuck me again with that slow, maddening rhythm. "You're so big I... I can feel you everywhere." He tilted my hips a half-inch, and I saw stars.

"Faster," I whispered, pushing my hips hard against his. Fucking him. He stilled, then gave me a ringing smack on my ass. And then another.

"No," he said calmly, then resumed his methodical fucking. I felt his fingers caress my stomach and land gently against my clit. He rubbed it, motions matching the rhythm of his cock, so deliberately I felt suspended between the lulling waves of desire and the racing relief of orgasm.

And I wanted the orgasm.

I made a decision. Before Finn could say a word, I knocked his hand from my eyes, untangled myself from his body, and had him flipped on his back.

"Who said—" he started to growl out. But I grabbed his hands and held them over his head. Watched his eyelids flutter as I lowered myself—inch by inch—onto his cock. Watched his body war with his need for control... and his need to let me take what I wanted.

I kissed him fiercely, fucking him in short, rapid strokes. "I need this," I said, twisting his chest hair between my fingers and yanking.

"Avery, fuck," he groaned, his forehead pressed against mine. He took my nipple into his mouth, tongue rolling around the tip. I lost my ability to breathe.

"I know, Finn, I know," I said, letting go of his hands and leaning back. His cock nudged my G-spot, and I smiled, rocking back and forth. Grinding myself against him.

"I've never felt anything like this," I gasped. My hands dug into his abs, meeting only hard resistance. He gripped my hips, slowing me down. Dragging my clit against his body. He held my gaze, the fire in those blue eyes blazing through me. Sweat dripped down his chest. He kept making these harsh, low grunts.

Finn was a man undone. And *I* had undone him.

"I need to kiss you," he groaned, and I started to lean down. But instead, he sat up, his legs wrapping behind me, arms around my waist. The position was even more intense than before. I opened my mouth to scream, but he captured it with his lips, drowning me with a kiss so furious it made me lightheaded.

He grabbed my ass, rolling me against him, rocking my clit against the hard ridges of his body. He thrust his hips up, a rhythm that had me clutching at his shoulders, his hands tangled in my hair.

"This is what you wanted, love," he grunted. "You wanted me wild for you." He grabbed my hips even harder and lifted me up and down, arm muscles bulging, wrenching me against his cock. I was so close to coming I could taste it, could see it.

We lost any semblance of control—mine or his—grinding into each other like the world could end any moment. The only sounds in the room Finn's heavy breathing and the slick noise our bodies made as they moved together. I couldn't stop saying his name over and over. An invocation.

"Come for me, Avery. I need you to. I need you. I need..."

My toes curled. My breath stopped. I watched as an orgasm crashed over him, and I fell with him, screaming his name as the sparks of my climax lit every fucking inch of me on fire. Finn wrapped himself around my body, groaning into my neck, as I rode out every last moment of sensation, unwilling to let it go. Wanting it to last forever.

28

FINN

I wrapped Avery in a giant blanket and carried her to the hammock on my deck. I laid her down on it, then curled up beside her. We had a perfect view of the ocean.

I stroked my hands through her hair, watched her eyelids get heavy. I didn't want her to fall asleep, not yet. I wanted to keep talking.

"I can't believe you don't like the ocean." I nuzzled against her neck, smiling. I watched her smile too, all loose-limbed and blissed out.

"I didn't say I didn't like the ocean. I just don't like *being* in the ocean. But I love looking at it. Since we didn't have a TV in the commune, I spent a lot of time watching the waves. Watching the whales. Wondering about life. About everything."

I pressed a kiss against her shoulder blade. "Well, well, who's the dirty hippie now?"

"No way," she said, laughing.

"Yes way," I replied. "'*I liked to watch the waves and think about life. About everything.*' That, love, is a very dirty-hippie thing to say."

She rolled her eyes and hid her face, blushing lightly. "Whatever."

"Ah, that means I won the argument. A first, ladies and gentlemen! Avery Dacosta is backing down from an argument."

"I just had the most incredible orgasm of my life. Let me lie here on this hammock and look at the goddamn ocean."

I snuggled closer to her. "Well, when you say things like 'most incredible orgasm of my life,' who am I to argue?"

She pressed a quick kiss to my palm and then exhaled, long and low. "Okay, one last thing before I take a well-deserved nap on this hammock."

"What is it?"

"We each have to share with the other person one thing they've done that makes them the most like the other person."

"I have no idea what you just said."

"So," she said, tapping my nose with her finger. "I'll go first. Until I moved here on my own, I never once cut my hair. Or shaved my legs or underarms."

"For the record, I like a hairy-legged woman."

"Well, if this was ten years ago, you would have had her." She sat up a little bit and held her hand all the way down her back, indicating. "That's how long my hair was."

I stared at her for a second, then kissed her. "You're very cool. You should grow it long again."

"Never."

"What if I vowed to give you an orgasm like you just had every hour of the day, every day of the year?"

She paused. "Still no." I laughed, pretending to shove

her out of the hammock. She grabbed me tighter, holding on. "Wait, wait... you have to share yours."

"But are there photos of your hair?"

She arched an eyebrow. "Please. Do you think our commune believed in cameras?"

I sighed, laying back down. "Okay, good point." I thought for a second, even though I'd known minutes ago what I would share. But it was embarrassing.

"After college, before I decided to get my master's degree in ecology, I had briefly, ever so briefly, considered becoming a financial advisor."

"What the fucking fuck?" Avery said, sitting up so fast we almost tipped the entire hammock over. I couldn't stop laughing at the look on her face.

"It's true, it's true. God help me, but it is."

"Why? And you think property development is the devil's work? But you were willing to sign up to help rich people get richer?"

"At that point, I was being invited to surf competitions across the world. I just wanted to surf all damn day. Financial advisors get paid a shit-ton of money and have tons of flexibility. I thought, well, I thought it wouldn't be that bad. Make a lot of money. Travel the world with it. Surf."

"You were going to just get paid tons of money to fuel the capitalist machine."

"Ye-yes. Oh God, I'm so *ashamed*."

"Did you tell your parents?" she laughed.

"No, are you kidding me? They'd disown me."

"You are such a hypocrite."

"*You* are such a hypocrite," I replied.

"What are we going to do about that?" she asked, snuggling sleepily against my side.

"I have some ideas for the rest of this date. We still have, like, seven hours until the day is officially done."

"And they are...?"

"For dinner, you pick the taqueria. Your favorite."

"Deal."

"Afterwards? I thought we'd listen to our favorite Bob Marley albums and watch the sunset over the ocean." She looked up at me with those huge brown eyes. "And in between, you can let me act out every single sweet and filthy fantasy I've had about you," I said.

Those eyes heated with desire, and she gave me the kind of kiss I'd be dreaming about for weeks.

"Agree," she whispered.

SEVEN HOURS LATER, and we were back on the hammock.

I'd put an old Bob Marley album on my record player, and his voice sang—scratchy and warm—out the open patio door and into the night. Avery and I were swinging in silence, exhausted from a combination of arguing, laughing, and fucking. It was perfect.

We were sharing a beer back and forth. Avery was curled into my side, head against my shoulder, my hand idly tangling in the strands of her hair. Playa Vieja stretched out in front of us, so beautiful my heart ached. The vote was in twelve hours.

In twelve hours, everything would change.

"I have a confession to make," Avery said softly.

"Yeah?" We hadn't spoken a *single word* about the future, but for a split-second, I desperately hoped she would say, "I want to see you again."

"I read your thesis. After the debate. I searched for it

online, found it, and read it." I turned, facing her. She tilted her head, open and honest. "I did, Finn."

"Did you like it?" I asked.

She shrugged, rolled her eyes a little. I laughed and kissed her. "Yes," she said, against my lips. "Of course I did."

I arched an eyebrow at her. "Of course? That's a little strong for you, Ms. Dacosta. That thesis did not paint hotel chains like the Bella View in a great light."

"Not a lot of people do. I'm used to it."

We were quiet for a moment. "I've been re-reading it too," I admitted. "Ever since my dad came to talk to me. About the shop. I just... I want there to be another *way*. Ecotourism, especially for places like Playa Vieja, where the community is so close-knit and kind of..."

"Insular?" Avery said with a hint of reproach.

I sighed. "Yeah. Insular is a good word for it. But the goal of ecotourism is to strike that balance between what's right for the community—"

"—and the environment—"

"—and brings tourists to that location in a way that is helpful *and* profitable."

Avery was nodding, a gleam in her eye.

I looked at her, smiling. "Why do you look so excited?"

"I don't know. I really liked your thesis, Finn. And I think your ideas were interesting. Taking a broken system and working within it."

"The system isn't just broken, Ave. It's *wrong*. I was... I was younger when I wrote that. Idealistic. Not as militant."

"So?"

"So... what?"

She nudged me with her shoulder. "I happen to like the system."

"I know. And I happen to hate it."

She took the beer from me, swigging. A little dripped down her chin, and I leaned forward, licking it up. She bit her lip, and I was almost done for. We'd fucked on the bed. On the kitchen counter. In the shower. Back on the bed.

She made me *insatiable*.

"I can't stop tasting you," I groaned, tracing her lips with my tongue.

"And you're avoiding this conversation," she said, giving me a hard kiss before gently pushing me back. I grinned at her, stealing the beer.

"You're honestly saying you agree with everything I wrote in my thesis?"

She thought for a second. "No. It *was* too idealistic. And I'm a lot of things, but mostly I'm a pessimistic, capitalism-loving crony for the system."

"True."

"*But*. It was... interesting." Avery looked out at the waves, the sun beginning to sink behind the horizon. Her hair whipped in the wind, bite marks on her neck, wearing my old fleece shirt.

Something was happening to me. And I knew... I knew what this feeling might be. I'd had this feeling before—on top of a twenty-eight-foot wave, that addictive blend of twisted fear and intense adrenaline, the stomach-cramp-before-the-rollercoaster-drop feeling, the pure perfection of the ocean and the knowledge that you're right where you're supposed to be.

Here. Perched between falling and flying.

"Avery—" I started to say, but she turned around suddenly, that gleam back.

"Do you have a pad of paper?"

"Somewhere, in the office, I think." She nodded, walking

past me and inside. I kept drinking, already mourning her brief absence. Thinking about my dad's words.

We have an honest marriage, Finn. Doesn't mean it's not hard.

Avery had been open and honest with me all day. Sometimes it pissed me off. Sometimes it moved me, made me think. Re-examine. Shift my opinion, just a little. She'd bared her body, her beautiful cunt, her pleasure. She'd unraveled for me, left herself raw.

The waves curled against the shore, but instead of turning my body toward them, I turned to the house. Seeking Avery, instead.

"I have an idea," she said, sliding a chair in front of the hammock.

"You're far away." I grimaced and reached for her.

She shook her head. "Touching you is distracting me."

I winked at her. She pointed the pen at my face. "You're one-half of the problem."

"What's your idea, love?"

She tapped the pen against her lip. "Brainstorm with me for a bit, okay?"

"Of course. About what?" I'd give her anything.

"Your perfect hotel. Go."

"Easy: No hotel."

She laughed. "I'm serious."

"So am I, Ave."

"Finn," she said, exasperated. "I'm *serious*. Pretend you're twenty-five again. Working on your thesis, researching eco-hotels. Pretend we were going to do that *here*."

"In Playa Vieja?"

Her smile blossomed like a flower. "In Playa Vieja. Yes. What if we did something totally and completely different?"

29

AVERY

I woke to Finn's tongue on my nipple.

Which means I woke up gasping, back bowing off the mattress.

"Finn," I groaned.

"Avery," he responded, tongue swirling. We'd gone to bed only a few hours earlier, our brainstorming session lasting long into the evening. We'd argued quite a bit. We'd agreed quite a bit. And now the city council vote was in two hours.

"We have... we have to..." I started to say, opening my eyes finally. He was naked, his body hard and hot in the early morning light. I couldn't get enough of his broad chest. Or his abs, rippling like a magazine cover model.

Except he *was* a magazine cover model. And he was worshipping my breasts.

"I know, love," he said, sucking my nipple between his lips. I felt the pull between my legs, and my hand drifted downward. He caught it, holding it to the bed.

"Patience," he whispered. He alternated between tweaking and pinching with his fingers, and licking and biting with his mouth. He traced his tongue down my ribcage, nipped my hipbone. I spread my legs, and he chuckled softly. "I said *patience*, remember?"

Back to my breasts. I could have wept. It was the sweetest torture. Out of my mouth tumbled strangled, desperate moans.

"Please," I finally said.

"Mmmm, that's better," he said, flipping me on my stomach.

"*Please*," I said again. He licked up the backs of my thighs, holding my legs closed even as I tried to push them open.

"I didn't make you beg enough yesterday," he said simply. A fact. "I like you begging. I *need* it," he rasped against my ear, before biting down my spine. I groaned against the pillow.

He hauled me up onto my hands and knees. My hands gripped the headboard. His tongue traced hard, fast circles against my clit, but as soon as I bucked my hips backward he stopped. One long, thick finger slipped inside of me, crooking against my G-spot.

"*Yes*," I begged. And he stopped. "I hate you," I moaned. He laughed softly again, whiskey-tinged. Reached beneath me to palm my breasts again. I bit the pillow.

"No, no, gorgeous," he murmured. "No cheating. Get that pillow out of your mouth." I bit down harder. He gave me a ringing, stinging slap on the ass. And another. My mouth opened in shock.

"And that's better," he said, before fucking me with his tongue.

"No, *that's* better," I groaned, loving the swirl of his tongue deep inside me. I opened my mouth to cry out, and he stopped.

"I hate you *so fucking much,* Finn*.*"

"Oh, gorgeous," he said softly, placing his palm in the middle of my shoulder blades. Pushing me firmly onto the bed. I lowered, ass in the air. Vulnerable to his every advance. "Don't lie. You love it." He pushed two fingers inside. "You love it, or your pussy wouldn't be dripping onto my fingers right now."

I closed my eyes in agony. This Finn was too much for me, this sharp dichotomy. Kind and charming and funny on the outside. Filthy and dominating behind closed doors. I felt his fingers tangle in my hair, and he yanked. Hard. I gasped.

"Beg for what you need, Avery. Or I won't give it to you. I'll send you to the city council soaking wet and desperate to come." His cock—big and demanding—nudged at my entrance, and I held back a scream.

"Avery," he said, his voice a warning. *Slap-slap* went his hand on my ass. "I'm starting to think you like spanking." *Slap.* "Dirty girl." I shook my head, panting. "Say it, dirty girl. Say what you want." He crushed his chest to my back and dropped his mouth to my ear. "Tell me what you want, love. Let me worship you."

"*Please* fuck me. Please, please, please—" The last two syllables ended on a choked sob as he thrust himself in to the hilt. Tears sprang to my eyes as I gripped the headboard. I had pegged Finn for a lazy, easy morning sex kind of guy. But this—this was an assault on my senses. This was being taken, fucked hard and thorough. We could have been two strangers who'd met in a bar and had their way with each other in the bathroom.

And I fucking *loved* it. I lowered my head to the mattress, but he gripped my hair, yanking me back up, curving my spine. Splitting me in two. I loved the sounds our bodies made as they met, Finn's heavy breathing, my screams.

His hand slid down and around my hip, his thumb finding my clit. The world would fucking *end* if I didn't come, so I kept begging. Begged so much he gave in, circling his thumb right where I needed it and sending me off a goddamn cliff. The orgasm started deep in my spine, roaring through every nerve ending, making me clamp down so hard on his cock he shuddered and cried out my name. Licked a path up my back. Massaged my ass, which was sore from his palm. Stroked my hair as I contemplated falling back to sleep.

"You're a fucking vision when you come," he said, mouth against my neck. "And you can't go back to sleep."

"I hate you again," I said. *Very* sleepily.

"You're supposed to meet Sal at City Hall."

"Fuck Sal."

"Please don't. I'd be heartbroken." His laugh vibrated against my skin. I shivered.

I rolled over, taking him in. Naked and sexy and scruffy as hell. His lips curved into a grin.

"Good morning."

"*Good* morning."

I bit my lip. "I guess we... I guess we go to the vote."

His gaze searched mine. "And then what?" he asked softly. He was as open and earnest as the first day I met him —soul bared to everyone he met. I reached out, touching his chest.

"I don't know."

~

"Are you okay?"

Sal met me on the steps of City Hall. I'd barely made it in time, stopping home to throw my hair up in a bun, pull on my least wrinkled pantsuit, and brush my teeth.

"Ye-es," I said, clearing my throat. Awkward.

He stared at me as we walked inside. "You should look happier. We're about to win. *You're* about to win." He rubbed his hands together, mouthing the word *money* at me. I smiled weakly. I wasn't sure what winning meant to me anymore. Not after Finn. Not after last night.

My phone rang, and I glanced at it. It was my mother.

I'm not asking for your help as a commune member. I'm asking as your mother.

I'd successfully blocked out the vote, the promotion, *and* her request yesterday. If I wasn't sure about winning, then it meant I wasn't sure about my parents either.

Sal and I made it through security, and I gave a few last-minute interviews. Although there was nothing new to say. San Diego's City Hall was large, and the council room could easily fit five hundred people.

Every fucking seat was full. Between the local media and the daily, entertaining protests, people in San Diego wanted to see the outcome.

I just wanted to go back to that date with Finn and live it over and over again. I could see him in the front row, shaggy blond hair slightly combed over for this fancier event. He was seated with his parents, Marla and Jack, and a dozen other members from the protests. If I sniffed, I could smell patchouli and sandalwood. It made me feel at home.

I glanced at my watch. "When does everything begin?" After two years, the first twenty minutes of the council meeting were beginning to feel like ten hours.

Sal glanced at his meeting notes. "Soon. In about a

minute actually. They'll be ten minutes for discussion, then they'll call for the vote."

"Cool," I said, as nonchalantly as I could. I wondered if anyone would notice if I just left. I turned behind me. Local news stations were lined up, the lights of their cameras blinking.

They'd notice.

Councilmember McAffee banged the gavel. "Ladies and gentlemen, next on the docket is approval of the required building and hospitality permits for the Bella View's proposed 300-room hotel and mixed-use property along the beach in the community of Playa Vieja. This mixed-use property would involve the completion of a golf course, a seafood restaurant, a large pool, and multiple tennis courts. Conservative estimates equate between five hundred and six hundred and fifty new jobs just through the Bella View Hotel chain, with an additional one thousand jobs expected to come on board in the next three to five years from increased tourist activity in the area. We will now hear remarks from the council members."

They went into it, but it was all a blur to me. *Two years.* Two years for this, this moment. I watched the back of Finn's head, trying to discern how he felt about what was about to happen.

The councilmembers were debating the estimated amounts of potable water usage and the impact on the surrounding community. I watched Finn tip his head back, giving me the side-eye. Every nerve ending in my body flared to attention. Responsive. I crossed my legs and looked away.

They went back and forth—the same old argument Finn and I had been having for months. Snowy plover nesting grounds. Revitalization of coastal communities.

My phone buzzed against my leg. I looked. Finn's name appeared across the screen, with a message: *Hey there money-grubbing capitalist.*

I looked at the screen, looked up at him. He sat still as the stature. The members were discussing building subsidies. Jobs. Tax incentives.

Hey there dirty hippie. I hit send, then fought the urge to stare at my phone until he texted back.

Erosion. Rising housing costs. Pollution levels.

I can still taste you on my lips.

Fuck me.

You should brush your teeth then.

I heard Finn cough-laugh into his fist.

"It's time for the vote," Councilmember McAfee said, silencing any additional protests. There were some mild grumblings from the audience, but she shushed it. Behind me, I heard a reporter quietly say, "It's go time."

"All in favor of approving the necessary permits to build say 'aye.'"

"Aye," they said, like some kind of dystopic shadow government.

"Head count," she said. They raised their hands, and she counted. Eight. We needed five to win.

Holy shit.

"For the record… any nays?"

Councilmember McAffee. She was the only one.

"The ayes have it then," she said wearily. "Permits for the Bella View construction on Playa Vieja are officially approved."

I let out a kind of strangled yelp, feeling off-kilter. Just like that. Two years of no sleep. No sex. High stress. Total body exhaustion. Two years for this moment, which was turning out to be incredibly anti-climactic.

But...

But...

I'd done it. A beautiful hotel that would bring jobs. Improve the economy. Bring Playa Vieja to the world. Save Finn's surf shop. Save the commune. I heard the sounds of reporters making their way over to us.

"Congratulations, kiddo," Sal said, squeezing my arm. He had a flask of whiskey in the other one. "You just got $20,000 richer. Oh, and pack your bags. You're moving. Hope you like the snow." He grinned, handing me the flask. I took a bigger sip than I should have, but with the words "pack your bags," everything in me lurched dangerously toward panic. From the corner of my eye, I watched Finn's mother give him a hug. There was a confused, sad look on his face. My heart stuttered. In my briefcase, I'd stashed the notes from our talk last night, our ideas for something different.

"Sal... I don't... This is going to sound absolutely fucking absurd, but can we talk?"

"Ms. Dacosta, are you prepared to make a statement?" A reporter nosed her way to us. Sal nudged me, wiggling his eyebrows. The whiskey burned a path down my throat.

I had won. I had won. *You won.* I dropped the briefcase. Squared my shoulders. Flashed my most ambitious grin. "Of course," I said smoothly.

And then everything changed.

30

FINN

"So you *do* feel like you failed to protect the one place you love the most?" the reporter asked, shoving her mic in my face. I fought back a dozen replies, refusing to take the bait, and instead said, "This protest wasn't about winning or losing, necessarily. It was about raising awareness of the detrimental effects that tourism has on coastal communities. About protecting the environment, no matter the cost. Do I think we succeeded in doing that? I do." I said as honestly as I could. She crinkled her nose. I think she was looking for something nastier.

"Great," she said, and I knew most of what I said would end up on the cutting room floor unless they could edit it so heavily it sounded like I said something like "Avery Dacosta is history's greatest monster."

She thanked me and left. I let out a long sigh, still a little in shock. It was a lot of hard work to be over in a matter of moments. I had wanted something more from the city council, some acknowledgment that what they had just approved would have an impact. A positive one, sure. But also a really, really negative one.

After the announcement of the vote, the audience erupted a little bit—let's face it, there were very few folks in favor of the hotel in that room. Next to me, Marla and Jack's shoulders slumped, and my heart ached. I saw my mother grip my dad's hand, squeezing, with a small, secret smile.

The world is a complicated place.

What if... what if we did something different? The excitement and idealism of last night faded quickly against this— this obvious display of corporate greed and consumerism. I could see Avery in the corner, practically shimmering with the news. She had won, fair and square. I didn't know what it meant for us. For whatever else we might have become.

For Playa Vieja.

Reporters kept pulling me outside for interviews, but once they saw I wasn't going to fight too hard, they left me alone. It was more fun to smear Avery *before* our date.

Avery was at the far end of the building, heading outside. She'd refused to look at me, instead adjusting her blazer and doing interview after interview. Nailing it, I'm sure. I'd sent my parents home with the rest of the protesters. We were hosting a "well, we tried" party back at the shop, and I promised to join them. But I wanted... I wanted Avery.

Councilmember McAffee waved me over. I joined her, head hung sheepishly. "Oh, stop, Finn," she said, pulling me in for a hug. "You did a beautiful thing."

"Is it naive to say I really thought we were going to win?"

"Honestly? Yes," she said. "The Bella View has money. It'll make money. Money always wins, I'm afraid."

"Not always," I said. I believed that. Still.

She tilted her head at me. "No, you're right. Because if it won every time, I wouldn't be able to get myself out of bed every morning. You should keep it up, by the way."

"Protesting lost causes?" I asked, feeling miserable.

"Keep fighting. Advocating. You're great at it. And people like you. A lot. Plus," she said, waving another reporter over. "They're not always going to win." She gave me a smile so wide, open, and earnest, I knew she really meant it.

"I think you're absolutely right," I said, and *I* really meant it.

"I'm sorry, Finn," I felt a hand clap onto my back, pulling me from McAffee. It was Sal.

"Me too. Since you're going to destroy my home," I said.

He looked taken aback for a minute. "Listen, it's just business. It's not personal." I glanced at Avery again. The camera guy was basically in love with her.

"For some of us, it is," I finally replied.

"I will say this though... I'll miss the food trucks you guys brought out to the protest every morning. I'm also kind of going to miss those bongos."

I sighed, smiling a little. I'd totally forgotten—tomorrow we'd all go back to business as usual. No Avery every morning. No bullhorns or signs or strategy meetings. It had been an exhausting three months, but at least I had spent my days joined together in a fight I truly believed in, connecting with my community. Uplifting our voices. It had made me feel... strong.

"Me too. It was... well, it was our life for the past three months. What's next for you guys? I guess you just start building right away, huh?"

"I will. Not Avery, though. I'm still waiting to hear back on specifics, but she'll be heading off to our East Coast offices before too long."

I looked at him, alarmed. "Wait... *what*?"

"She didn't tell you? I promised her a promotion if the

city council approved. She just has to tidy up a few loose ends, and then she'll be out of here."

A riot of emotions exploded in my chest. "Oh," I said because that's all I could manage. The thought of Avery living 3,000 miles away was too much to bear.

"You two, though... kind of had a Romeo and Juliet thing, right? I mean, everyone in the office was taking bets on it."

I watched Avery over his shoulder. She was standing by herself, smiling softly, fingertips against her lips. Probably dreaming of a bigger, better city. Away from me.

"I hope you bet against us, Sal," I said, clapping his shoulder and turning away.

THE SURF SHOP was lit like a Christmas tree, and I was mobbed with bodies as soon as I walked in. Marla and Jack. My parents. Hope and Jackson and their adorable children. They were holding a sign that said, "Thank you Mr. Finn." They'd drawn a picture of me on a surfboard... and a giant shark, eating my leg.

"Ah... thanks?" I said, kneeling down and taking it from their son, Mason.

"Thank you for being so brave," Mason said, patting me on my shoulder.

I looked up at my dad, who was giving me the kindest, most loving smile. I sighed. "If I'm so brave, why is this shark eating me?"

Mason shook his head. "This is right before you punch it off of you."

"Oh," I said, and I heard Dad laugh. I laughed a little too. Someone had turned on an old Prince album and thrown open the back doors to let the ocean breeze in. From the vibe of the party, you'd think we'd won.

"Why is everyone so happy when I feel so fucking defeated?" My dad handed me a beer. I took a long swig, downing most of it in an instant.

"Well, they're a little drunk."

I shrugged. "That sounds about right." A group of regulars from the Paradise Cafe walked by, patting me on the back and shoulders.

"Blowing off steam. It was a tough few months. They made a lot of sacrifices to join you. Now? They have their lives back, at least for a little bit."

"I guess it's why I feel so terrible," I admitted. "They could have done so much else with their time. Something so much more useful."

Dad shook his head. "No one here would agree with you, Finn. Listen, I've won as many fights as I've lost. Good causes too. Causes I fought fiercely for. That I lived and died for. But I never felt like that time was wasted. These people, here today, are here for you. Here for Playa Vieja. Here because they don't want to give up the fight. And they're not going to. It's too important. This community is too important. In fact, I think this is just the beginning," he said, pulling me into a side hug. We walked to the back, closer to the waves. Half the people at the party were doing the same thing—surfers—naturally drawn to the sound, almost curving into it.

"Things are going to change," I said.

"Yes. They are."

I took another swig, leaning against the comforting warmth of my father. All around me was the scent of surf wax and coconut oil. The sound of surfers, speculating on what the surf report would be the next morning—the gentle hum of wind speeds and wave heights as soothing as a lullaby.

And I'd be out there. Same as always.

"The ocean always wins," Dad said. "This isn't her first setback. You'll find a way to keep fighting."

My phone rang, disturbing our small moment of peace. I glanced at it.

Avery was calling.

31

AVERY

"And, in summation, I honestly believe this is the path forward the Bella View Hotel chain should take. It's smart. It's savvy."

"It's trendy as *fuck*," Sal interrupted.

"Yep," I said, smiling. "Which means…"

"So much *money*," he finished. "Convince those rich people we care about the earth. I'm thinking, like *Madonna*-level rich."

I clicked through a few more slides, trying to ignore him.

"And it is the *right* thing to do by the environment," Finn said quietly. He was sitting next to me and hadn't said much during the presentation, although at least half of the ideas were his.

Sal waved that off. "Whatever, Finn. I see money. Lots of money."

It was a week past the vote, but I hadn't even been able to go two hours without calling Finn and pitching my plan: that we should bring our little brainstorm ideas to Sal. He had agreed, a little reluctantly, but his silence in this meeting couldn't contain the waves of excitement coming off of him. That, and the fact that every time his leg brushed mine, I was tempted to melt.

Sal flipped through a few more of his notes and stepped out to take a quick phone call.

"Hey," I said to Finn, reaching out. Almost touching his hand. I stopped myself.

"Hey," he said. We hadn't spoken about more than the presentation in a week. And all over the phone. I didn't trust myself around him, didn't trust myself not to toss my suitcase away and plead to live with him in his bed, on the beach, forever.

"Sal told me you're probably going to move," he said suddenly.

I bit my lip. In the whirlwind of the past few months, I had never mentioned it to him.

"It's not set in stone. I mean, it kind of is, but..."

"You didn't want to tell me?"

"I didn't... I didn't plan on sleeping with you, Finn."

Not you, I wanted to say. *Not the last possible person I ever wanted to be with.*

"I have a future on the East Coast." I managed to say, swallowing a lump in my throat.

He opened his mouth to respond, but Sal swept back in. "That was corporate," he said. "We've got a shit-ton of things to figure out, but on the surface, they love it." He pointed his finger at me. "And they goddamn love *you,* Avery."

I nodded weakly. "Thanks, Sal. So... what's next?"

"You wanted to get out of San Diego, right? *Too many damn hippies,*" Sal said before glancing at Finn. "No offense."

"None taken," Finn said, but his smile was fake. The excitement I'd felt from him was fading.

Actually, he looked heartbroken.

"This is the kind of thing you could bring to our properties all over the world. Man, *fuck* the East Coast. I'll send you to Bali for six months. Then Italy for four. Singapore. Costa Rica. Paris. You could travel the world with this, Avery. Setting up hotels like Playa Vieja, living the nomadic life." Sal was gathering up his papers, which was our cue to go. His words shook through me—moving across the country was one thing. Seeing the world, and being paid to do it, was another. A small spark of adventure lit deep inside me.

"It would still be a promotion though, right?" I clarified.

"Avery, this would be like ten fucking promotions. Yes," Sal replied. "Think about it. And think about what we need for Playa Vieja to make this happen. Shit, Finn, you could *consult* on this. You want to?"

Finn shook his head. "No thanks. I'm think I'm... well, I'm happy we're doing this, but I think this is as far as I'm able to go. I'm sorry. Avery, thanks for having me today," he said.

I opened my mouth to tell him... something... anything. *Don't go. Please.* Instead, Finn turned and left.

"You're going to run this company one day, Avery, I'm sure of it," Sal said, kicking back and stacking his feet on the desk. I saw Finn through the window, sitting on the ledge of the fountain in the parking lot.

I nodded, thinking. Looked at my feet. "You're happy, Sal?"

"Am I *what?*"

"Happy," I repeated. "Are you happy? Being 'one with the company' or whatever you'd told me. Working long hours. Never... never seeing your family... or having fun?"

"Avery—" he said, eyes widening. "I'm fucking *rich*. And it's because I work long hours and I never see my family, but shit... isn't the money what you want?" Before I could respond, he laughed and said, "Because it's what I want. I live and breathe this company. It's in my blood. And yeah, I spend more time with you than my kids, but I don't know." He winked at me. "I'm pretty sure this is what life is all about."

I thought about Bali. Then jet-setting through Paris, strolling through Egypt—except that I knew it would be like the past two years, only worse. Harder. Less sleep, more stress. But... it was fucking *Bali*.

And I thought about my parents, sitting with me as the sun rose over the palm trees, our gorgeous, wild, unbroken, untouched home stretching in front of us. The waves. My palms on my knees. Dirt in my fingernails. Breathing deeply. As a child, I felt Hawaii *live* in me. I felt it. I knew it. Even hungry. Even tired or overwhelmed or sore from sleeping on the ground, I was tethered to that community—an invisible string tying our bones together.

And here, in San Diego? So beautifully untethered.

Or so alone... I hadn't decided which it was yet.

"I need to... I'll be right back," I said to Sal. I slipped outside to the courtyard. Finn looked up, face drawn.

"It's weird, isn't it?" he said, indicating the empty, quiet space. "I can't believe I spent all this time here and now... nothing. It's just a regular courtyard. In front of a company."

"I miss those fucking bongos," I said, and he laughed. My heart leapt at the sound. "It's hard to admit, but by the end, I was kind of... looking forward to the protest, in a way. It was—"

"Lively?"

"Yeah, and... I don't know. I might have vehemently disagreed with every single person, but at least they were doing something *different* with their lives, you know?"

Finn tilted his head at me. "Are you saying we got to you, Ms. Dacosta?"

You did, and I hate it.

"Do you remember that first day you were here, all by yourself?"

"I thought you were *so* snooty, God," he said, smiling.

"I thought... I thought you'd be like everyone from my past. From the commune. I... was so angry with you."

"Am I like them, though?"

I studied him. "In some ways, yes. In other ways... not at all. Don't you think it's interesting—your parents, living in a yurt thirty miles away. My parents, living in a yurt on a small island in the Pacific Ocean."

"Formed by similar hands," he said, cupping his palms in front of him. "And yet enemies for the past three months."

I felt myself unraveling right in front of him. Too many contradictory desires—too many wants and needs smashing against each other. I didn't know what to do.

"You should go travel, Avery," he said simply, and my heart broke a little.

"Oh," I said.

"Avery... you know it's a once-in-a-lifetime opportunity. You said it, you don't want to be here anymore. And you don't want to go backward, right?"

"Yes," I said, although my idea of "backward" was starting to shift.

"Then don't. You'll have the world at your fingertips. Just like you wanted. More power." He dragged his index finger up and down. "Climb that career ladder." He smiled, but sadly. "You know you want to."

"They're your ideas too, Finn," I said earnestly.

He shook his head. "I don't need the credit. And really, I don't want to build hotels. You know that."

"So you're just going to go back to the shop and surfing

and competitions, and that's it? That's all you're going to do with your life?"

He sighed. "I have no fight left in me, Ave. So yeah... that's what I'm going to do. Because I *want* to. And you should take that promotion. Because you *want* to, don't you?"

I couldn't bring myself to answer. Because I honestly did not know. And hated it—hated that three months ago, even overwhelmed and sleepless, my future was a brightly lit path, laid out easily for me to follow. Just like I'd dreamed about, the moment I'd landed in San Diego. The dream I'd used to motivate myself through all-nighters and shitty tips and past-due gas bills and an aching loneliness that would spring up when I'd least expect it.

And now I had no answer.

Finn stood, grabbed my hand, and pressed a kiss against my palm. I did melt, just a little.

"It's been..." He stopped, voice rough. "It's been a pleasure arguing with you every day, Avery Dacosta," he said, blue eyes searing into mine.

"Agree," I said. I watched the emotions war across his face. I watched him walk away.

And then I sank down onto the hard bricks of the courtyard, and I cried.

32

FINN

*F*our weeks later, and Avery refused to leave my thoughts. I saw her everywhere. Could still smell the scent of her shampoo on my pillow. Prayed, every morning, that'd I turn on my board and see her perched on those rocks, watching. Waiting for me.

I replayed our moment in the courtyard together over and over, but this time I was brave enough to say, "Stay here. Stay with me. Because I'm pretty sure I'm falling in love with you."

Except I couldn't describe how she'd looked when Sal had told her the news—the ten promotions, the endless travel and adventure. She had looked so... *happy.*

So I walked away.

The clock by the bed read 4:45 in the morning, blaring the alarm I'd heard every day at this time for as long as I could remember. I hoped for rough waves. Big, earth-shaking. I mentally made a note to look up the next big wave competition and go for it. I needed some serious fucking fear and adrenaline to drown out all thoughts of her.

And then my doorbell rang. And rang again.

"What the—?" I said, eyes bleary, pulling a shirt over my head. I opened the door and there, looking sleepy and beautiful, was Avery. She held a wet suit in one hand. With the other, she handed me a steaming thermos of coffee.

"Let's go surfing," she said.

THE WAVES WERE SLIGHTLY ROUGHER than I liked, especially since I would be teaching Avery how to surf. A small storm had landed farther up coast, and Playa Vieja was feeling the after-effects. My stomach tightened as I watched a particularly large swell—part fear, part joy.

It was still dark on the beach, the sun just starting to rise behind us. I set the longboard on the sand next to Avery. She'd been totally quiet in the car, just staring out the window and fingering the material of her wet suit. She seemed to be thinking hard about something. I let her since I was still blissed out by her surprise presence.

"I haven't given a lesson in a long time, just so you know," I admitted. "But we really should start you on the board in the sand. Go over paddling, how to pop up—"

She reached down for her board and lifted it up and over her head—no easy feat. The wind caught her ponytail, lifting it, and the wet suit clung to every muscle of her body.

"On an unrelated note, you look like some kind of surf goddess right now."

She smiled—first one of the day, and my heart lifted a little in my chest. I had absolutely no plan and no fucking idea what we were going to do. But this... this felt right.

"It's probably because I know how to surf. Quite well, actually." And then she took off running to the waves.

"Wait... *what*?" I called out, grabbing my board and racing after her. Avery was already paddling up and over the first wave, arms slicing through the water.

This was not good.

I threw myself into the water, paddling quickly to catch up with her. A larger wave had knocked her off her board. She reappeared out of the water, spitting.

"You okay?" I asked, getting closer.

She nodded and gave me a slightly crazed-looking grin. "Meet me out past where they're breaking?"

"Yeah..." I called out, still completely startled. "Yeah, okay." We paddled silently for a bit, going up and over a particularly rough set. It didn't seem to slow her down though. After the sixth or seventh wave, we reached a glassy section. I straddled my board. She did too, facing me.

"So... a couple of questions," I said.

She arched an eyebrow at me. "Go on."

"First... what the *hell*? This entire time we've been together, slept together, and you just forgot to tell me you *also surf*?"

Her smile was small and secretive. "Finn, I was raised in a commune on a beach in Hawaii. I learned to surf when I was nine years old too. I was never a big wave surfer like you, but... I can handle myself in the water."

I gaped at her. "But... but you hate being in the ocean. Sharks and pee and..." I paddled closer to her, reaching out and grabbing her board. I needed to touch her.

"I don't know." Avery shrugged, glancing at a breaking wave. I think she wanted to ride it. "My entire life as a child revolved around the ocean and working the land. For some reason, I still enjoy gardening—crave it, actually. It doesn't make me sad or angry or anxious. The ocean, though...

being in it brings a lot of those bad memories back. Makes me confused."

She yelped and yanked her foot out of the water. "What was that?"

I laughed. "So the shark thing was real?"

She looked at me warily. "Honestly, though, are there sharks in Playa Vieja?"

I shook my head. "I've been coming out here for twenty-six years. Never seen one." Which was a total fucking lie. I saw them all the time.

I changed the subject. "Where did you guys get your boards from? They're expensive."

"Barter," she said. "Local folks usually have extra boards. We'd give them crafts or some of our produce. Trade eggs, that kind of thing."

"And you just... surfed for fun?"

"Just like you."

"When was the last time you did it?"

"I was eighteen, right before I moved here on my own."

"You moved to one of the surfing capitals of the world. You never wanted to try it out here?"

She shook her head. "I avoided it. Had too much to do." She dipped her hands in the water and sighed a little.

"I've never met a person who surfed their entire life and then gave it up before. It's too addictive." I nudged her board with mine. "You know that."

She bit her lip and gave me a complex look. "I do," she said softly. "I just cut it off cold turkey." Just like she'd cut off her access to fun and happiness and sex and love. Like a light switch, flicking on and off.

We sat quietly for a minute, watching a set roll in. "How do you feel about the ocean now?"

Her lips quirked up, just a bit. "I might be changing my mind. Just a little."

"You know what I've been thinking about?"

She shook her head.

"Why, if the ocean and surfing and overall beach-bum atmosphere make you so uncomfortable, did you move to San Diego? Why not... I don't know, Ohio?"

Her eyes widened, just a little. "It's close to Hawaii, if I ever had to fly home. It was... it was cheap to fly here, and I didn't have a lot of money at the time. Plus, Ohio is freezing."

I laughed at her song-and-dance. "Here's what I think. Well, two things actually. First, I think, deep down, you miss the commune. Just enough to make you naturally drawn to this similar environment." She scowled at me. I grinned at her.

After a while, she looked away from me. "I'll consider your thesis at a later date. Because I don't want to argue with you today."

"I'll take it," I said. "And the second reason goes back to my very original theory—we were meant to meet each other."

She splashed me in the face. "No way."

"Fate," I said, wiping salt water from my eyes. "And ouch." I heard her paddling over to me, board gliding next to mine. I was still wiping my eyes when I felt her lips on my cheek. Soft.

"I don't agree with your theory," she whispered. "But I appreciate it."

I watched her for a while, loving her straddling a board. She looked comfortable. Happy. "What was your biggest wipeout?"

She shivered at the memory. "Ugh, it was terrible. I was out with Wave and Redwood—"

"Wait, who?"

"My brothers."

"How did you end up with the normal name?"

"My given name is actually Coral. Avery is my middle name."

"Oh, I'm *so* only going to call you Coral now."

"Anyway," she said, talking over me. "We were out pretty far that day, and the swell was coming in at eight and nine feet—big waves for our section of Hawaii. Not, as you know, for the rest of the islands."

"Sure, I surfed Waimea and Pipeline Masters."

She cocked her head at me. "Did you win?"

"Second place, both times. The wave at Waimea was clocked at forty-five feet." I was bragging now. Avery waved her index finger around, as in *big fucking deal*.

I splashed her. "Go ahead... *Coral*."

"Anyway, we were out there riding our dinky nine-foot waves, and I got caught late inside a barrel."

I knew the feeling. It was not a good one.

"I remember everything just crashing around me. The wave ripped me up and out of the water like—like a washing machine or something. The worst part was my leash got caught on some reef, and I couldn't get my head out of the water. I had to dive down, untangle it, and swim back up."

"Avery... that's like a serious wipeout." My stomach clenched at the thought of a young Avery, caught beneath the surf, trapped between the reef and the air she needed.

"I was a pretty serious surfer," she said quietly. She looked pensive, then turned back to me. "Okay, Mr. Big Wave. Give me your worst."

I shook my head. "I still get a little nauseous thinking about it. But it was practicing for Mavericks. I took a bad drop down a huge wave—twenty-five feet at least. I'll never forget those seconds, when you have to admit to yourself that you might die. That you're about to be crushed under a thousand tons of furious water. The sound of it..." I trailed off.

Avery grabbed her chest like she was in physical pain. "Sorry, just the thought..."

"No, I know," I said. "I actually wake up thinking about it sometimes. I just remember it was dark and terrible, and I had no idea where I was. But I fought, pretty hard."

"And you still do it?"

"I mean, I did. I won Mavericks on a wave that easily topped out at forty feet."

"And why?"

A fucking beautiful swell was coming up right behind us. I grabbed her board, turning her. "You know why. And this one's all yours, love."

"Wait, I'm scared now."

I shook my head, the wave beginning to crest. "You'll remember what to do." I shoved her, then dove under the wave. When I came back out, I was treated to a heart-stopping sight. Avery was up on her board, riding a pretty gnarly wave like a fucking dream. Crouched low, fingertips in the swell, biggest smile I'd ever seen on her face.

If I had to go nine years without surfing, this would be some kind of hallelujah moment.

Based on the sight in front of me, she felt the exact same way.

After another twenty seconds or so, she jumped off, then came out of the surf whooping. I slapped the water in front of me, echoing her joy. My heart tripped over itself, almost painfully, and whatever walls I thought I could keep up between us came tumbling down.

"How was it?" I called out to her. She was paddling back toward me. She didn't speak, just beamed and laughed—that joyous, uncontrolled sound I'd come to associate with kids jumping in the waves. Just the pure enjoyment of the water knocking me down, the sun in my face, the floating-falling feeling of the ocean.

Avery was gesturing behind me, and I looked—a perfect swell headed my way.

"Here we go," I said. Everything felt like home.

WE SPENT the next hour like that, catching every damn wave we could. I was nervous, being around her, and fell more than usual. So did she. Half the time it was from laughing too hard.

She was so effervescent—ready to float away. I'd never seen her like this. In between sets, I got her to spill more about her childhood, about herself. She even got me to share a few of my secrets. And we only got into two arguments—both of which ended by one of us tipping the other over their board and into the ocean.

It was effective.

At the one-hour mark, Avery looked exhausted.

"Noodle arms," I said, indicating her very tired-looking shoulders.

"Like you wouldn't believe," she said. "I'm going to head in and pass out on the beach for a while."

"You're not going to watch me?" I asked, incredulous. It was hard to imagine a month ago, catching her at this same spot. An exhausted, overburdened Avery watching me from the shore. My striptease.

She blushed a little, and I knew she was thinking about it too.

"Maybe a little," she conceded and winked at me. I almost fell off my board again. *Get it together, Finn.* She turned and paddled away, and I tried to keep my jaw closed as I stared at her perfectly round ass. I'd always been a sucker for a woman in a wet suit. And Avery in a wet suit might have been my new favorite fantasy of all time.

I laid on my board for a bit, listening to the sounds of the water. Listening to my body. Something was happening. I heard that soft rumble, like the growl of a lion. A warning, but quiet. I looked up—the bigger waves were coming.

I felt the joy-fear mixture again, and I breathed deeply into it. From the beach, I saw Avery, perched on her board and watching.

As a surfer, I had to read the set. Understand the language of the ocean. The intricate patchwork of tides coursing beneath the waves—a pattern as ancient as anything on this earth. When to take it. When to dive beneath. When to risk.

The first wave in the set was mine—I felt it. It was rising up larger than usual for this part of San Diego. I hadn't brought the right board for a bigger wave, but this one would have to do.

I thought I heard Avery's voice over the sound of the wave rushing toward me. I turned on the board and paddled hard, feeling the crest under my feet, under my knees, under my thighs, in the middle of my board... and then I was up.

I dropped a foot down the front of the wave and swallowed a fit of laughter. *Goddammit* if I didn't love that feeling. My fingertips curved into the barrel of the wave, opening up nicely in front of me. Spray against my neck. A roar like a freight train in my ears. I pivoted left and took a sharp turn. Another foot. And then another, the wave still pushing me forward, legs low.

I hadn't done this in a long time, but I'd just spent an hour in the waves with a beautiful woman and her dazzling laughter. If I could just arc the board up right...

I took a jump off the top of that wave, grabbed my board, pushed, and executed a perfect flip-then-dive into the water.

Beneath the surf, everything was quiet and still and dreamy. I stayed for a moment, enjoying the peace.

Then I shot up, every nerve ending alive. Heart racing. Avery, clapping on the shore.

And just as suddenly, I needed her beneath me. I thought about my fantasy after Mavericks, of riding that adrenaline high between the thighs of a woman. Specifically the sweet thighs of a raven-haired, smart-mouthed hotel developer.

Every ounce of blood in my body surged to my cock. I hopped on my board and paddled as fast as I could manage. On the beach, Avery's body language changed, ever-so-subtly. She must have known. Or felt it too. Because when I finally dragged myself from that water, I watched her lips part. Her breathing hitch.

Without saying a word, I reached behind for the zipper of my wet suit and pulled, pulled, pulled. My arms slipped out, then my chest. I pulled it all the way down my body, stepping out, wearing nothing but board shorts.

Her fingers flew to her mouth, her eyes raking up and down my body. I needed skin-to-skin. I needed Avery—with a force that stole every bit of breath in my lungs.

"Off," was all I could manage to say. She complied, unzipping her wet suit and peeling it down her luscious body. She was wearing a tiny bikini that barely covered her full breasts. That collarbone, delicate as a poem. The inch-long scar above her hip from a fight with her brothers. Down and down her long legs.

I was on her in an instant, cupping her face and kissing her with all the ferocity of the wave I'd just ridden. She clutched at my shoulders, matching the kiss breath for breath. Her nails raked down my back. My fingers tangled in the strands of her hair. Every inch of her body pressed against mine.

I pulled her toward the rock outcropping—where everything had started. Where we started, in all of our complicated glory. I grabbed the towel from my bag and tossed it in the sand. She was on it in a second, and just as quickly, I was on top of her. I couldn't seem to stop kissing her. I had been dreaming of her constantly, and the reality was almost too good, too sweet.

I moved down her neck, hands sliding under her bikini to tease her nipples. Avery's back arched, and I grinned against her collarbone. I loved her responsiveness, her body's total willingness to let go. To be free. Her skin felt so right against my palm, tightening. I swirled my tongue around each nipple, lingering there. Scraping lightly with my teeth. Her fingers threaded through my hair, holding me forcefully.

I couldn't get enough. The crash of the waves. Her soft, beguiling moans, the sand shifting beneath our bodies. I licked down her stomach, closed my teeth on her hip bones.

I slid her bathing suit bottoms down her legs, paused. Admired her beautiful cunt, wet for me, ready for me. Held her legs open as I plunged my tongue deep inside her. She cried out, pulling me deeper. Greedy. I complied, wanting to give her everything. I slid up to her clit, teasing. Playing.

Fast, tiny circles that had me holding her hips down to keep her still. I slid two fingers, then a third, inside of her. I was like a man possessed, grinding my cock against the towel. And when she came on my face, I swallowed every drop.

But I wanted more. She needed more. I climbed back up her body and grabbed her hands. Held them over her head, our fingers entwined, digging into the sand. Kissed her like my life depended on it. She was limp, glowing.

"Finn," she said. "That was... that was..." I ground my cock against her clit, still sensitive from my advances. She exposed her throat to me, crying out even louder. I kissed every inch of her gorgeous neck. Her ears. Her jawline. Avery was panting now, clawing the skin of my back. "Magic," she moaned. Her legs hooked around my waist.

"Avery," I finally said. My cock nudged at her entrance. "I want you to know. I'm clean."

"Me too," she said. "And on the pill." I nudged again, tempting her. I bent my head and took her nipple between her teeth. A strangled moan wrenched from her throat. "And I want... Finn, I want..."

I thrust into her, bare and completely vulnerable. My world briefly went black, but when I came to, I was alight in the most intense sensation of my life. I held her gaze, our fingers still entwined, as I fucked her. Not slow. Not fast. Just intense and real and honest. No words between us this time —no pushing. No fighting. No challenging.

I watched every emotion cross her beautiful face. I watched the sensations become too much. I watched her desperate to come, matching my thrusts with her hips. I watched her smile, delighted, as her climax beckoned.

I let go of one hand and reached down, circling her clit with my thumb. Every light in her body turned on—sharp and lovely. Her orgasm rushed through her, and as she clenched around my cock, I came too. So strong I had to bury my face in her neck and cry out.

We lay together for a long time afterward. Still no words. I stroked my fingers through her long hair, quickly drying in the sun.

I thought about Mavericks, dropping down the face of a forty-foot wave. The risk. But also the reward.

"Don't take the promotion, Avery," I said, pressing her fingertips against my lips. "Stay. With me. I know it sounds incredibly selfish, and I can't believe I'm asking the woman I love to give up her hopes and dreams to be with me, but I am. I can't help it. Not saying it would be... it would be a total and complete lie."

She stared at me for a full minute, but the smile she unleashed was like nothing I'd ever seen before. "What did you say?" she asked.

"Stay with me."

"No. The other part."

I swallowed, trying to be brave. "I'm in love with you, Avery Dacosta. And I want you to be with me. I don't have any ideas after that, just... us. Here. Together. Like this. I'll play all the Bob Marley you want." I said, kissing her. "And I'll cook you breakfast burritos every morning." I kissed her again. "I'll leave you joints on your doorstep every night, like some kind of Joint Fairy."

She laughed. "But I'm Satan," she said softly.

"You're Avery," I said. "And everything about you is gorgeous."

Her smile was brighter than any sun and twice as warm. And then she whispered the words I realize I'd been desperate to hear since the first day I met her, challenging me in that parking lot: "I love you, Finn."

I kissed her fiercely. For a long, long time. When I pulled back, I could feel her trembling.

"What are you going to tell Sal?"

"I actually have some ideas about that," she said, eyes searching my face. "I have some ideas. About happiness. And compromise."

"That's funny. I was about to say the same thing."

EPILOGUE

Eighteen months later...

"*A*nd remember, kids: Capitalism is evil. Now, let's get started on the meat industry."

"Oh, for the love of—" I groaned. Finn grabbed my arm. I was having a hard time reining in my curse words in front of the kids. "Um... *pizza*. For the love of pizza, which we have today for lunch! Isn't that right, Finn?"

"Nicely done, Ave. Now we'll never get to capitalism," Finn whispered out of the side of his mouth.

"What's capitalism?" One of the girls, Layla, shouted out. Her parents were staying in Bungalow #7.

"Great question, Layla," I said, crossing my arms. Next to me, I could feel Finn buzzing with energy. "It's the system by which our world operates. Good or bad," I said, raising my voice over Finn's fake coughing fit. "Good or bad, we are all participants in it, whether we like to or not, even Mr. Finn. Because he sells things. With his body."

Finn laughed heartily, and I winked at him. The kids

looked back, nodding like tiny adults. Pretending to understand.

"Are turtles a part of capitalism?" Layla asked.

"No," Finn said. "Which is what makes them so wonderful." I gave a serious eye roll, glanced at my watch, and gave Finn a nudge. "You know what else is wonderful? Pizza!" he said. The kids all cheered, heading over to the outdoor kitchen. The kids would be breaking for a few hours, then joining up with Finn later in the day.

"So, uh... what are you doing right now?" Finn asked. He looped an arm around my shoulder, dragging me to his house—our house—next to the Bella View properties.

"Emails, meetings. Sal wants me to look at a potential property in La Jolla."

"Mmmm," he said, nuzzling his mouth against my ear. "That sounds very stressful." We kept walking, away from my car. "I have some better ideas, by the way. Are you willing to listen to them? Or are we going to keep arguing?"

This was the idea we pitched to Sal: Turn the proposed design for the Bella View Hotel on Playa Vieja into San Diego's first environmentally conscious eco-hotel. The ideas were one-half mine, one-half Finn's. And, to be honest, so fucking brilliant it was why Sal wanted me to travel the world, planning eco-hotels in the name of the Bella View.

Instead, I took some time off to think about happiness, my happiness. My future and what it could mean.

Our proposed changes took a *lot* of time, and a lot of effort, especially since the city council had to approve a few more permits and we had to re-design and re-finance everything. But when they did, Finn and I had successfully transitioned a 300-unit hotel into twenty-five luxury bungalows.

There are days where I don't know how we did it. But

then Finn turns that mega-watt smile on me, and I remember.

Working with other developers, environmentalists, and even some of my former commune members, we'd designed San Diego's first eco-friendly coastal hotel.

Instead of a giant, hulking hotel that took up two-thirds of the beach, we built twenty-five bungalows, scattered across the beach property, modeled after Playa Vieja homes. Gave tourists a real-life "beach bum" experience. And we charged an arm and a leg for each bungalow, meaning our profit margins stayed about the same. The restaurant we opened was farm-to-fork and served only seasonal, sustainable food.

Everything was powered by solar panels, and a certain percentage of the profit made from the Playa Vieja bungalows was invested in local conservation efforts. The beach—and the wildlife—was mostly untouched. The best part was that Playa Vieja had gained a reputation for being one of San Diego's most "eco-friendly" communities, and new businesses still came in. Job growth increased. I was finally, *finally* able to prove to Finn that my greedy, capitalist ways could have a positive impact.

Finn's surf shop was able to stay open.

Although, half of his time was now spent doing something he loved—running Bella View's nature camp. Every week, he took the kids staying at the hotel on daily adventures—surfing (of course), nature hikes, exploring tide pools. He gave kid-sized talks on ecology and taught them about recycling, ways to help the planet. And of course, when the timing was right, watched the baby turtles hatch —always a favorite.

I volunteered once a week to help out, mostly to see Finn

in action with a bunch of adorable kids. And mostly to be the voice of reason from time to time.

Or, *really*, all the time.

After the vote, Sal still gave me the bonus—a cool $20,000. After many, many talks with Finn, I decided to give some of it to my parents, but not all of it. (And the commune was back up and thriving—and adding a few tourist components themselves. Finn, to my great surprise, actually talked them into it. Said he was learning the beauty of *compromise*.)

The remainder of the bonus I used to create Playa Vieja's first community garden. On Saturdays, I took the kids to the community garden. I told them about growing up in Hawaii. What I learned there. Why learning how to grow our own food was important. Our responsibility to the earth. I always came home dirty and tired and happy—until Finn would pull me into the bedroom to give me a different kind of bliss.

And me? Well, I told Sal to give those ten promotions to someone else. I wanted something just a little slower and a little less stressful.

I wanted my life to be filled with more daily joy. And so I signed on to manage the Bella View property—consulting occasionally on other eco-hotels when they needed me—but my days were definitely slower. Less stressful.

Every morning as I sipped coffee on our porch and watched the waves, Finn meditating next to me, I was so fucking happy my heart could burst.

"I'm always willing to listen to your ideas. You're just not willing to back them up with actual facts." I strode down our hallway, pulling Finn by the belt loops.

"I think someone—" His breath was hot against my neck. "—is trying to get me angry. Because she knows when I get angry I like to fuck."

"I don't know what you're talking about," I said,

pushing open the door to our bedroom. He slid his large, rough hands under my shirt and lifted it over my head. I laughed as he smoothed my hair out of my face. Pulled me in for a kiss. I sighed against his body. Skin hot and warm from the sun. Smelling like the ocean. Smelling like home.

"Here's what I do know, love," he said, backing me up against the wall. Our picture frames rattled. I loved when he needed me like this—his desire bright as flames.

"What's that?" I moaned, his mouth moving over my neck.

"That you have the most beautiful smile," he said, running his tongue over my nipples. My back arched off the wall. "And your nipples are perfect."

I laughed, my hands weaving through his hair. It had never tamed itself.

He nuzzled along my ribcage, giving me goosebumps. "And I could live off your laugh, Avery. No food. No water. Just that sweet sound."

I heard the sound of his zipper, and then he had me lifted off the ground, my legs wrapped around his waist. We were suddenly face-to-face.

"Hey there, money-grubbing capitalist," he whispered against my mouth. Kissing me deeply. My head spun.

"Hey there, dirty hippie," I said. I trailed my fingers across his lips. He took my ring finger into his mouth, sucking. Nipping with his teeth. He kissed the thin band of silver wrapped around it.

"I know I'm counting down the days until I get to be your husband."

"It's fifty-two," I said. "But who's counting?" His grin was slow and sexy as he thrust inside me.

"I know I love you," I moaned, legs wrapping tighter.

"I know I love you," he repeated, capturing my lips in a kiss that seared.

Outside the windows, the waves of Playa Vieja crashed against the shore, moving in endless, ancient motion. The sun rose. The sun set. The sand shifted with the wind, swirling patterns more intricate than any language.

Inside, Finn and I crashed together, bound by our shared love of breakfast burritos and Bob Marley albums. Of fighting for what we believed in, even if we disagreed. Of challenging the other person to be their best, truly. Of lazy, Sunday afternoon fucking. Of watching the sun set over the waves. The feel of sand between our toes.

Connection.

ACKNOWLEDGMENTS

For Faith, who is essentially Wonder Woman, and is still the best beta reader, copy editor (and best friend) a girl could ask for.

For Kelly, my author-mentor: you teach me something new every day.

For Cait, Erin, Jess (my beautiful wife), McCarthy, and Faith: our group texts (and life-long friendship) give me life, especially when I want to give up. You have my heart. Always.

A HUGE thank you to Tina Smith for her thoughtful beta-reading, guidance, and advice. *Riptide* became so much stronger with your edits.

For Mila, Joyce, Maren, Jess, Kate, Jodi, Tara, Julia, Kiera, Mary C. Jodi, Stacey, Lisa, Nancy, Lindsay, Phala, Imani, Smut Your Mouth, Melanie, Laura, Nicole, Maïwenn, Susann, Laura, Jackiee, Julie, Karen, and everyone else on Facebook and Instagram (because I'm definitely forgetting some people) who have quietly cheered this book into existence. I can't tell you what it means to have that kind of support.

For my parents and my brother, who will never read this book (too much sex) but whose absolute support and excitement over everything I do make my life infinitely awesome.

To Jena at Indie Girl Promotions, thank you for promoting my first full-length book and getting it into the hands of readers!

As always, for my husband, Rob, whose love (and jokes and handsome face) brightens every minute of my day: thank you for marrying me.

HANG OUT WITH KATHRYN!

Sign up for my newsletter and receive exclusive content, bonus scenes and more!
I've got a reader group on Facebook called **Kathryn Nolan's Hippie Chicks**. We're all about motivation, girl power, sexy short stories and empowerment! Come join us.

Let's be friends on
Website: authorkathrynnolan.com
Instagram at: kathrynnolanromance
Facebook at: KatNolanRomance
Follow me on BookBub
Follow me on Amazon

ABOUT KATHRYN

I'm an adventurous hippie chick that loves to write steamy romance. My specialty is slow-burn sexual tension with plenty of witty dialogue and tons of heart.

I started my writing career in elementary school, writing about *Star Wars* and *Harry Potter* and inventing love stories in my journals. And I blame my obsession with slow-burn on my similar obsession for The *X-Files*.

I'm a born-and-raised Philly girl, but left for Northern California right after college, where I met my adorably-bearded husband. After living there for eight years, we decided to embark on an epic, six-month road trip, traveling across the country with our little van, Van Morrison. Eighteen states and 17,000 miles later, we're back in my hometown of Philadelphia for a bit... but I know the next adventure is just around the corner.

When I'm not spending the (early) mornings writing steamy love scenes with a strong cup of coffee, you can find me outdoors -- hiking, camping, traveling, yoga-ing.

BOOKS BY KATHRYN

BOHEMIAN

LANDSLIDE

RIPTIDE

STRICTLY PROFESSIONAL

NOT THE MARRYING KIND

SEXY SHORTS

BEHIND THE VEIL

UNDER THE ROSE

IN THE CLEAR

WILD OPEN HEARTS

OUT OF THE BLUE